Acclaim for the authors of
A SEASO...

JI...
"Finely drawn charac...
with poignancy draw ... a familiar story that
beautifully captures the feel of an Americana romance."
—*Romantic Times* on *High Plains Wife*

KATE BRIDGES
"Bridges recreates a time and place to perfection
and then adds an American touch with
warmhearted characters and tender love."
—*Romantic Times* on *The Surgeon*

MARY BURTON
"This talented writer is a virtuoso, who strums the hearts
of readers and composes an emotional tale."
—*Rendezvous*

JILLIAN HART

grew up on her family's homestead, where she raised cattle, rode horses and scribbled stories in her spare time. After earning an English degree from Whitman College, she worked in advertising before selling her first novel to Harlequin Historical. When she's not hard at work on her next story, Jillian can be found chatting with a friend, stopping for a café mocha with a book in hand and spending quiet evenings at home with her family.

KATE BRIDGES

is fascinated by the romantic tales of the spirited men and women who tamed the West. Growing up in rural Canada, Kate developed a love of people-watching and reading all types of fiction, although romance was her favorite. She embarked on a career as a neonatal intensive-care nurse, then moved on to architecture and television production before crafting novels of her own. Currently living in the bustling city of Toronto, she and her husband love to go to movies and travel.

MARY BURTON

sold her first novel, *A Bride for McCain,* in January 1999. A graduate of Hollins University, Burton enjoys a variety of hobbies, including scuba diving, yoga and hiking. She is based in Richmond, Virginia, where she lives with her husband and two children.

A Season of the Heart

JILLIAN HART

KATE BRIDGES

MARY BURTON

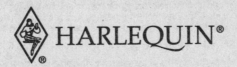

HARLEQUIN®

TORONTO • NEW YORK • LONDON
AMSTERDAM • PARIS • SYDNEY • HAMBURG
STOCKHOLM • ATHENS • TOKYO • MILAN • MADRID
PRAGUE • WARSAW • BUDAPEST • AUCKLAND

ISBN 0-373-29371-2

A SEASON OF THE HEART
Copyright © 2005 by Harlequin Books S.A.

The publisher acknowledges the copyright holders of the individual works as follows:

ROCKY MOUNTAIN CHRISTMAS
Copyright © 2005 by Jill Strickler

THE CHRISTMAS GIFTS
Copyright © 2005 by Katherine Haupt

THE CHRISTMAS CHARM
Copyright © 2005 by Mary T. Burton

This edition published by arrangement with Harlequin Books S.A.

® and TM are trademarks of the publisher. Trademarks indicated with ® are registered in the United States Patent and Trademark Office, the Canadian Trade Marks Office and in other countries.

www.eHarlequin.com

Printed in U.S.A.

CONTENTS

ROCKY MOUNTAIN CHRISTMAS

Jillian Hart

Chapter One

The gunfire pounded relentlessly. Locked in a dream, Mac McKaslin wrestled down the screaming urgency to run. Not to run away from the gunfight on this holiest of nights, but rather to charge straight into the flying volley of bullets where she was waiting for him. Trapped. Held hostage.

As pumped full of murderous rage as he was, he wasn't made of steel, so that meant he was cornered. The second he popped out from behind the boulders he and his team were using as cover, he would catch a bullet. But he had to get out from behind this rock and save her.

Eliminate the first threat. It's what they'd taught him on the first day in training as a Montana Range Rider.

Bam! Bam! The pounding continued, or maybe it was the pulse surging through his veins. Her scream cut through the night as he picked off another outlaw and saw him fall lifeless to the ground.

It wasn't enough. Amelia's scream ripped apart the night and he heard nothing else, not the popping gunfire and the screaming agony of the dying. Nothing, not even the pounding of his heart, because he had no heart anymore, not if she died—

The hammering tore him awake, jerked him too fast and

fierce out of the dream. Mac bolted up, the revolver on his bedside table already in his hand. He'd thumbed the hammer and taken two steps before he'd come fully awake. Before the ribbons of the nightmare fluttered away and he realized he wasn't standing knee-deep in snow in the belly of the Badlands.

"Sheriff, are you in there?" It sounded like Jed from the train station. "We got a problem."

With the ravages of a shattered life around him fading away on the shreds of the dream, Mac lowered his weapon, rubbed his free hand over his face and opened the door. The white starlight drifting over the snowy outside world looked so much like the one in his dreams.

There, on the porch, anchoring him to the present, was the shadow of a man who brought with him the scents of cigar smoke and a hint of Jack Daniel's.

"What kind of problem?" Mac demanded.

"Pull on your trousers and a coat, and I'll show ya."

Long ago were the days of riding the wildlands in the territory, a Ranger looking for wrongs to right. Tonight he was irritated, mostly because he wasn't the calm, controlled lawman he liked to pretend he was.

But also because it was damn cold outside. The crisp clear of it scudded across the floor and caught hold of his ankles, and he gritted his teeth. Cold enough to freeze the meat on his bones. What brand of fool would be out causing trouble on a night like this?

"If this is about kids turning over the outhouse, I'm gonna be mad." Mac emerged from his bedroom into the dark space of the front room, buttoning the last fastener on his trousers. "This better be worth my trouble."

"Hey, don't get all het up at me. The engineer sent me to fetch you. It wasn't my idea to leave my nice warm office." Jed's teeth chattered as he hiked down the front steps. "While I've got your attention, how's it comin' along with my last break-in?"

Not again. Mac jammed his arms into his jacket and launched out the door. It wasn't the easiest thing to keep his cool well after midnight, when the echoes of Amelia's screams were still ringing in his ears.

He had to remember, where once he'd tried to right wrongs and stop bad men before they could do more harm, he was now a small-town sheriff in a little mountain town in the Rockies. Smaller problems, but those matters were important to the people who lived and worked in this town.

So, he shoved aside his frustration and opted for discretion. "I'm following up leads. Got a witness who saw three boys running down the alley about the time you heard them rummaging around."

"I appreciate your diligence, Sheriff."

"Sure thing." He jammed his hands in his pockets. The wind was up tonight, and clouds sped across the star-strewn sky, gathering strength, draining darkness. One by one those stars winked out, leaving the street dark as Hades.

The town of Moose was smaller than most, but well enough off. It hosted a main street full of thriving businesses, and the mill north of town kept a lot of folks employed most of the year. On an ordinary walk across the nighttime streets, he often felt a sense of satisfaction at being part of a place like this. It was a good decent place. Solid. Storefronts were clean and tidy. Come morning, people he knew by first name would call out to him as he passed.

But tonight his heart was too numb to feel much of anything. No, that was wrong; he wasn't numb, he was used up. The sap and life burned out of him. It was the dream. It was the time of year. It was anything, sometimes everything that would bring up the dream. It would spark like a stray ember in dry grass and flame out of control before a man could stop it.

"Over this way." Jeb hiked through the drifts and up onto the loading platform. Instead of heading over to the storage buildings, he arrowed straight to a railroad car where the engineer stood silent, haloed by the drift of his cigarette smoke.

"We didn't wanna wake 'em." Jeb dropped his voice, and gestured toward the cracked boxcar door.

"Not another stowaway?"

"Well…not a usual stowaway." Jeb stepped aside.

Not again. Mac didn't think he could stomach it on this night, the longest of the year. Another old man hungry and alone with no family to care for him, or, no family that cared. Probably some old war veteran, wandering and homeless. It always got to him.

Mac tipped his hat to the engineer and, with no reason to delay, stepped inside. He'd make the arrest as was his duty, and with as much respect as possible.

The instant his boot met the iced floor of the boxcar, he sensed it. Something wasn't right; he heard the quiet rhythm of breathing instead of the snoring draw and pull of a man sleeping. And the scent; he didn't detect cheap whiskey or cheaper tobacco.

What he sensed was peace. A somber quiet radiated like light within the confines of the pitch-black car. Lost in shadows, hidden in the inky blackness in the far corner was something, he could feel it, sense it like the blood warm in his veins.

He took the match tin the engineer handed him and struck a light. The flame flared and fought back enough darkness for him to see her. An angel's profile, wisps of ebony hair, a soft rosebud mouth, and then the match faded in the wind and flickered out.

Leaving only night shadows. A woman. He couldn't get over the sight of a nice woman in a place like this. But the soft moan low in her throat told him she was waking, and he lit another match quick before she could panic. But as the spark struck and light erupted, her rasp of fear echoed against the low ceiling.

He was too late. The last thing he wanted to do was to scare her, a woman alone. She was young—not too young, somewhere in her twenties, he figured, but far too tender to be traveling like this alone. And she knew it, judging by the flare of her eyes, a jewel green in the match's flare. In an instant she was sitting up, her hand moving beneath the single blanket covering her.

A bowie knife was his guess. "Easy now, ma'am. I'm not about to hurt ya."

Beneath the wool blanket, her hand became a fist around the handle of a blade.

He didn't take another step. No sense panicking her. She was within her rights to be afraid. Disoriented. Alone. Vulnerable. So he held up the match and his free hand. So she could see he wasn't armed. And he wasn't coming any closer. "I'm Mac McKaslin, ma'am. The sheriff of this town. You want to let go of that knife you're holding?"

"No. I'm quite fond of my blade." Her words came low like the alto chime of a bell, and the sound of it moved him back in time, to another woman's voice and another woman's fear that was tangible as snow on the wind.

He swallowed hard, feeling the starch go out of his knees. It had been years since he'd let himself think of Amelia in the waking hours, to allow her brief image to flash across his mind's eye, and there it was, he saw the gold of her hair, the blue of her eyes, the delicate features and her voice, calling for him for help, trusting him to save her.

"Here's a lantern, Mac." Jed's down-to-earth western drawl brought him back.

Mac was grateful for it and for the light. He wasn't the kind of man to let emotion, memories or anything else get the best of him. He was tougher than that. A good man had to be. "They're gonna need to load up, miss, so you'll have to come with me."

The woman's hand remained clenched beneath the thin blanket, every muscle tensing up visibly beneath the worn wool coat draping her like a hand-me-down that was two sizes too big. Something else was off, and Mac sensed it a moment too late. The bulk beneath the blanket he'd assumed was from the bulk of a skirt and petticoats shifted. The softest voice came muffled from beneath the wool and loaded with fear. "M-mama?"

Well, I'll be damned. Mac understood better now—a mother protecting her young, and he took another step back. And another. Until he was far enough away that the dark-haired woman relaxed a tad and laid her free hand on the child's shoulder.

"It's all right, baby."

There was no mistaking the love in her tone, and it changed the timbre of the night. The ruthless wind gusted with an arctic force stirring the random bits of straw on the car's frosted floor, yet it could not dispel the softness in the air that gleamed like the gentlest light. Something rare, and it was this woman. His heart might be ashes, but those ashes well remembered the warm crackle of love's flame. Mac closed down the places of his lost heart and barricaded them well.

What kind of world was this, where a mother and child huddled alone beneath a single blanket, and on a frigid night? The woman's eyes met his, dark pools that spoke not of naiveté but of disillusion. What could have put that in a young mother's soul?

"Change of plans, Jed." He saw the same shock on the depot clerk's face. "She has a child with her. We're gonna take 'em to the inn."

Jed's surprise turned to remorse. "I don't think so, Sheriff. That's not railroad policy."

"He's right." The engineer took a deep drag on his cigar. "There's only one way to handle stowaways. The company can't afford to let folks ride for free. They gotta pay."

"This isn't your usual stowaway situation." Mac couldn't remember ever coming across a mother and child. Not like this.

Crystal snow fluttered from a heartless sky to dust the floor at his feet. The woman was watching him, her voice too low to discern what she was saying as she comforted her little girl. She was too lost in the shadows for him to see how old the little one was, but one thing was certain. She was far too young to be without a home. Much too young to know uncertainty and fear.

"We can't toss 'em in jail." His words cracked like winter thunder. "It just isn't right, Jed."

"I don't care if it's right. It's the way it is. A stowaway's not better than a thief."

A thief. Carrie Montgomery's chest squeezed hard at that horrid truth. Is this what she had become? What her life had unraveled to? She'd seen the pity in the lawman's steeled gaze. It was hard to miss. She hated to think what she looked like, bedraggled from travel and from sleep. It took every ounce of dignity she had to lift her chin, even the littlest bit, and not give in to the despair closing in on her.

She'd not come this far to fail. To be called and judged a thief. This was the end of the line—they'd been found. She'd accept this the best way she could, as a setback and not as defeat.

With a handful of change weighted in her skirt pocket, she gathered her child in her arms, bundling her as well as possible against the frigid cut of the wintry gale. It took but a moment to loop the fraying satchel handle on her arm.

"Mama, I'm c-cold." A tiny sob seemed to shatter the night.

And Carrie's heart. "I know, baby. Just a few minutes more." Where she would find shelter, she couldn't say, but find it she would. A storm was heading this way and she'd rip these mountains down stone by stone to find a safe place for her child.

She faced the three men blocking the doorway. This wasn't going to be easy. She felt the fist of it in her gut. "Excuse me."

"I don't think so." The man in full uniform beneath his wool jacket closed the small gap between the men and the doorway, barring her from escape. "You're a stowaway, ma'am."

"And as soon as I step foot off this train, then I'm not any longer. So, please, step aside."

"It's not that easy. You're trespassing."

Shame burned hot on her face and pulled downward inside, making her feel smaller. Diminished. But she had a daughter to fight for. A child's welfare at stake, so she put some steel in her voice. "Move aside and I'll gladly stop trespassing—"

None of the men moved.

She studied one grim face after another until finally she came to the sheriff. The big commanding man, not beefy like the man in uniform or lanky like the local man, but a solid, dependable cut of muscle and authority. He'd been the one who'd backed off, and she put her hopes in him now. "I don't want trouble, sir. I just want off this boxcar."

"I think that's reasonable enough." The lawman's eyes were cold, not warm, and haunted when she expected them to be full of judgment. Good. Perhaps he had larger concerns. And he'd leave her be.

To her relief, the lawman stepped aside and gave her room to pass on the other side. She took it, moving with as much dignity as possible when the deepest of instincts screamed at her to run and run fast. Her hold on her child tightened as she took those last few steps toward the door.

Almost free. Standing in the doorway, the punch of wind and snow struck her. The downfall came quick and thick, with an icy sting on her unprotected face. Her muffler had sagged low, but she didn't take the time or effort to worry about that now. She turned her shoulder so most of the gale struck her in the side and back, shielding her daughter from the worst of it. She went to step off the train.

"Hold on, there! Sheriff, this isn't right. She pays for her passage or the company presses charges."

"Throwing a young mother in jail isn't right and you know it."

Her attention wavered. Press charges? She thought of all the hobos and wanderers who'd caught rides in the freight cars when she'd been at the train station in Minot. Well, more accurately, tucked away in a row of abandoned boxcars trying to get up the courage to steal a ride. It's not hard, and most never do get caught, several of the more gentle-seeming hobos had told her. She'd never thought to ask them what happened on that rare occasion when one was caught.

Now what? She could run away and be lost in the thick curtain of snow in no time—unless the sheriff came tracking her. It was tempting, because as she held her daughter against her heart, she had so much to lose and so much at stake.

But it was not in her to run. Even as her gut instincts urged her to go, she planted her feet and sought out the steely lawman and his hollow gaze. "I'm sorry to have stowed away, but you have to understand that I was desperate."

"Are you running from someone? From some harm?" There was a note of hope in his voice. As if there was a legitimate legal reason for her to be fleeing at all.

"No." She could have lied—but that wasn't in her, either. "Since the train was heading west, I'd hoped it might take us to a better situation."

The lawman—Mac was his name—stood with his feet braced, shoulders straight, as unyielding as a mountain peak. Her last hopes fell like the snow at her shoes. Whatever faint chance she'd had to escape this situation had already passed.

Too late, she stepped onto the platform where snow was already accumulating. The night seemed heartless and desolate as the wind began to howl, and the thick shroud of snow twisted and whirled, hiding all but the boxcar from her sight. The light of the lantern the sheriff held traveled toward her.

　As well as the uniformed man radiating with anger.

Chapter Two

Mac couldn't believe his eyes. One moment the woman hopped onto the platform as if ready to escape into the night. And the next, Bose leaped out after her, his beefy hands reaching as if to grab her by the shoulders.

Oh no, you don't, man. Mac shoved the lantern at a surprised Jed and bounded into the blinding snow. He nearly broke his neck when his boots hit the iced platform, but rage held him up and kept him going. Rage was all he noticed, all he felt and all he saw as he caught the brakeman by the collar just in time.

"Let go of me, Sheriff!" Bose howled like a trapped bear. "This is railroad business."

"This is my business." Fury burst out of him like cannon fire. He struggled to hold the man back, to keep him from grabbing the woman who'd planted her feet and stood her ground. Bose was more than het up; he was like a rabid dog. "We're gonna let this one go, man."

"Over my dead body, Mac."

"I can't arrange that. But I can toss you in a cell."

"*Me?* She's the thief!"

"What'll it be? Back down, or it's jail." Mac watched the realization dawn in the engineer's eyes.

The violence went out of him but not the attitude. "I want restitution. I have to do right by my employer."

"Do right? How could any part of this be right?" Mac let go of the bastard. "She's a woman."

"So? The company's got a right to charge her and the kid."

Disgust left Mac reeling. Shaking his head, he rubbed the snow out of his eyes, aware of the woman quietly watching, a willowy figure even with a child in her arms. Gilded with snow, it was a beautiful thing the way the gleam of white haloed her. Snow clung to the round of her hood to frame her face, and dusted her shoulders. Stardust clung to each flake that fell and added a glow of the softest blue-purple haze. And the sheen of it enveloped her, and made his heart hammer hard.

Mac felt his boots pulling him toward her, as if he had no choice. Who was this woman who did not make excuses or cry or blame? "Are you all right, ma'am?"

She didn't answer or blink. She didn't appear to so much as breathe. She was deciding if he was friend or foe.

He was good at reading people. Wouldn't be much of a lawman if he wasn't. She was no trifling woman, for there was an air of quality about her. Not hoity-toity, but genuine decency. Her gaze was honest.

Not the usual stowaway.

Since she was such a small thing and he was towering over her, he kept his voice subdued. "I'm here to help, ma'am. You'll see that soon enough. Let's get you and your little one someplace safe and warm. How does that sound?"

"Are you pressing charges?"

"I don't want to, ma'am—"

"That man wants me to pay. What if I can't?"

"Well, I suppose that's a problem."

Exactly. Carrie waited for the answer she knew was coming and refused to shiver or bat away the flakes clinging to her cheeks and eyelashes. The sheriff stood as if made of stone, more of an impression than anything in the shades of night.

They wanted to press charges? Fear burrowed deep within her. She was in big trouble. As she listened to the snow tap everywhere around in quiet symphony, she felt nothing but the cold heartlessness of a world she knew too well. There would be no mercy from the sheriff or the railroad men.

They were arguing with one another, their low angry voices rising. The wind's gust tore apart their words, but the man in uniform was gesturing violently at the sheriff. Lots of money. Of course that's what was so important to them; it was what they wanted and the one very important commodity she was short on. She doubted that these men who stood between her and a jail cell, who had eaten a good hot supper until they were full, could understand. How could they?

They continued to argue, and she saw her fate as easily as the tumble of snowflakes freezing to the platform at her feet. Inevitable. They were right—she had been taking use of the train without paying for it. And while she had no notion of what passenger fare for the two of them would be, from the Dakotas to the middle of the Montana Rockies, she knew it was far more than the handful of coins tucked safely in her pocket. So, if they took her to jail, what would become of Ebea? Would they take her child?

She could run. Now, while the men were busy. The uniformed man had worked up into a frenzy, and it would take them some time to notice that she'd slipped away. But even as she took a few steps slowly back, silent as the snow, she knew the tracks she would leave could lead them right to her, wherever she ran. *And so what do I do now?*

As if in answer, the brush of snow against her cheek felt like a touch, like an unseen presence, and she knew. There was one thing left, one item worth nothing of great monetary value, but it was all she had to pay with. She slid the mitten from her right hand and the gold band off her finger.

She chose the sheriff because he seemed like a decent enough sort, for a lawman. For a stranger. "Sir. I know this is far from enough, but it's all I have. At least, for now."

The sheriff's sharp gaze told her he'd not been surprised by the ring she held. Maybe he had been watching her more carefully than she'd suspected. But there was no harshness when he spoke. "Perhaps it's best you keep your wedding ring."

No, this was not her ring. Her wedding band had been the first thing she'd sold when hard times hit. "No, take it."

"Ma'am, I don't want your ring. Bose, you can see she has no way to compensate the railroad. It's Christmastime—"

"I don't give a rat's ass if it's the holy night. She's a stowaway and I'm under strict orders. I don't like it, but there it is. That ring, is it gold? What else have you got?"

Was it her imagination, or had his voice dipped with lust? She couldn't keep her disgust out of her voice. "That's why we borrowed a ride on the train. Because I could not afford anything else. If I had the money, then I would have paid for a passenger fare."

Couldn't he see that? Couldn't any of them? Perhaps the sheriff did. She saw a hint of pity in his eyes. She couldn't stomach pity.

The uniformed man, Bose, as the sheriff called him, snatched the ring from her fingers. Carrie couldn't believe how he looked over the ring as if it was far below his expectations, when it was so much. It was a symbol of love that meant far more than its weight in gold. She saw delight in Bose's gesture and her blood turned cold. What if he was going to keep the ring and arrest her just the same?

Panic squeezed the blood from her heart, the air from her lungs. Time slowed down as she watched Bose's delight turn to a twisted smile. *Carrie, you should have run while you had the chance.* But where? And how to escape with a small child in tow?

Bose weighed the ring in the palm of his hand. "This ring isn't much. Hardly worth the trouble of melting it down. I'm gonna need more. Why don't you go on home, Sheriff? It's late and it's cold. This is likely to turn into a blizzard soon. The woman and I can take it from here. As long as she's willing to deal. This is a start."

Her fury came colder than the arctic winds, icier than hell frozen over. "I do not deal. The ring will have to be enough."

"This isn't worth more'n a quarter of what passenger fare is worth."

"This is not a passenger train. We did not enjoy a warm nor comfortable ride. I say it is enough."

"The lady is right, Bose." Mac fisted his hands, careful not to act on his rage and break the laws he upheld. What was the engineer thinking, propositioning this woman? "Take the ring as payment or leave it be."

"I can't do that." Bose's gaze traveled over the length of the woman, and it was an ugly leer that flashed briefly across his face. "It's my way or jail."

You are a bastard, aren't you, Bose? Sometimes Mac hated what he saw of humanity, the underbelly of the wrong side of decency, and it was all he could do to keep his fury in check. There was no mistaking the mother's protective stance.

In the lantern light, even shadowed by the falling snow, he read the resignation in the cut of her jaw and the challenge in her eyes. She was ready to wage battle and well aware of the hardship she was in. There was nothing he could do about that, he thought. Unless…

Mac snatched the ring back from Bose. "I can't stomach the sight of you. Get back on your train and out of my town."

"You're gettin' soft because she's a woman. Or maybe you're gonna make a different arrangement with her behind my back."

"Enough! Do you want me to toss your ass in jail?"

"The company accountant will be expecting the money." Bose backed toward the waiting train. Other company employees hurried away from him, their loading of the freight cars complete, and a long warning toot from the engine hurried all of them along. Bose headed toward the front engine. "I'm writing up a report on you."

Instead of rising to the man's bait, the sheriff lifted a shoulder in a careless shrug. Maybe he wasn't such a bad sort, Carrie thought—he was doing his job. She knew he had responsibilities to his town and to the businesses that supported it. She knew how things worked in the world. She wasn't so sheltered, not since she'd become a bride, to know the hard truths.

The sheriff held out the ring to her. "Well, ma'am, I suppose you'll be wanting to keep this."

"It won't keep me out of jail?"

"No."

So much for small hopes. Not in these long dark night of winter. Carrie accepted the ring he returned to her, the gold tarnished and worn but more dear for it. She slid it into place on her finger and pulled the mitten over it.

"Mama, I'm s-so c-cold."

"We'll get warm in a moment, baby." Carrie pressed a kiss to her daughter's forehead and tucked the blanket more tightly to keep out the wind that was stubbornly batting at the blanket.

"I don't think a widow ought to have to sell her wedding ring," the sheriff was saying kindly, and somehow that made the shame inside her all the worse.

"It's my mother's." Her throat closed tight and a revealing gasp of pain slipped out and only embarrassed her more. Her death was still too new to think about, but to feel the ring again on her finger was a comfort. *If* there was comfort to be had on this bitter night.

"You lost her recently?" He gestured toward the darkest part of the platform as the train behind them began to chug and grind.

She could only nod as she followed him down some icy steps and onto a snow-covered boardwalk. Some losses were too deep to talk about, and so she said the only question left to be asked, since her fate had been sealed the moment she climbed aboard that train. "When you lock me up, what will become of my child?"

"There is no orphanage in this area to take her. You're afraid of losing her."

"I am." She could not give name to the terror. Every hour of every minute since she'd been on her own, she'd feared nothing more. Her sweet, good girl alone and helpless, without anyone to take care of her, to protect and defend and provide for her—she couldn't stand to think about it.

Panic began to claw in her chest, like a wild trapped creature struggling to escape. "She has no one else. Is there any way I could do work of some kind—*decent* work? Anything? I'm not afraid of hard work. I can cook. I can clean. I have a strong back. Please, sir."

And, as the town buildings came into sight and the jail had to be among them, she heard the sheriff's silence and all he didn't say. There would be no escape. His hand brushed her shoulder as if to catch her in case she slipped or ran. They stepped down onto the street and down a dark lane, and the wind howled and became cruel, shoving her along as if to hurry her to her fate.

Carrie pressed a kiss to her dear Ebea's forehead, but only kissed ice on her hood. "You did not answer my question. What will happen to my child?"

"Your daughter can't stay the night in a cell meant for prisoners." He stopped and seemed to check his bearing in the blinding storm. "Follow me."

"I overheard you when you were speaking to that man, Bose. You said that throwing a mother in jail isn't right. Could you let me go? Could you say I ran and you couldn't find me? I won't cause any more problems. I'm not a thief, not at heart. And I—"

"I can't do that, ma'am. A blizzard is blowin' in. I can't in good conscience leave you to become lost in it. Think of your little one."

Ebea's teeth were beginning to chatter, her little body shivering despite the layers of flannel and wool. *I'm so sorry, baby.* Carrie pressed a kiss to her child's forehead again and put a wish in her heart that somehow, someway, there would be some good coming their way.

Buildings rose up to shadow the brunt of the wind and snow. Carrie's grip tightened even more, her fingers clutching the blanket so that the backs of her knuckles burned. How had it come to this? Everything she had done, every thought and every action Carrie made had been to protect her little girl. To keep her safe. *And I've failed.*

As if in disgust, the snow slapped and stung at her face between her muffler and her hood. She'd never felt such cutting snow. There would be no help from above or from the sheriff. Carrie wasn't looking for a handout. Just a touch of grace.

There would be no mercy. Why did she hope there would be the chance of it? I'm not yet that bitter, she thought, wishing, just wishing she could rub out the last few years like a mathematical problem on a child's school slate, wipe it away until it was as if it had never been. A clean slate, and she'd never have known her husband's decline and her mother's death. She never would have been here, following a sheriff up a set of steps to the jailhouse.

This was it. As she watched him unlock the door, and the blizzard hit full force, stealing all of the night shadows so that she saw nothing but black. Then a golden spear of light appeared, growing ever wider as the door opened. There was no escape.

She stood trembling for a long moment, letting the lethal winds pierce like a thousand sharp teeth into her skin. The warm light and safe harbor of a lit hallway beckoned, and she could not resist.

Carrie followed him through the narrow hallway and through an arched door where there was no light. The drum of shoes on the wood floor did not tell of a cold, empty jail cell. She had to be imagining the faint whiff of lemon polish and fresh, sweet pine.

The embers in the fireplace centering the room were too low to cast more than the faintest shadows over a braid carpet set between what looked like two deep-filled sofas. Sofas. She watched while the sheriff knelt to poke the embers to life. "What is this place?"

Wicked orange light writhed and twisted on the hard, unforgiving planes of his face. But there was forgiveness in the rumble of his baritone. "This is my mother's house."

"A house? I don't understand."

"Do you want your child to spend the night in a jail?" He added wood to the fire, the greedy flames flaring and lashing waves of light across his face.

It was kindness she saw. Kindness she did not believe in. He meant to leave Ebea here with his mother, but she'd come to know the way of many men. "And what do you want for this? You don't mean to make the same offer as that railroad man?"

Her blood turned cold as he turned and straightened. He rose over her, all six feet of raw, powerful man. There was no mistaking his strength; the room vibrated with it. Her nerves tingled with it.

"No, ma'am. I aim to do the right thing. Now, why don't you sit and warm by the fire. I'll see if the kettle in the kitchen is still hot for tea."

The right thing? Whatever she'd been expecting from this man, this stranger, it was not this. As she watched him shoulder past her and disappear through the archway, she felt the fear drain out of her like water from a leaky bucket. She slid onto the corner of the nearest sofa cushion. He could not have shocked her more if he'd reached out and struck her.

She rocked her child and listened to the blizzard turn feral outside the walls. A vicious force in a wholly cruel night.

But there was small mercy in this world, after all.

Chapter Three

All she had of worth on her was her dead mother's wedding ring. Mac didn't think he would ever forget the sad determination etched on her face, a face lovely and too young for that depth of sorrows. But just add that image to the thousands that were lodged in his head. Being a lawman, and a retired Range Rider, had taught him about life in a way he had never figured when he'd been a green recruit. A young man hoping to do some good.

He wasn't sure if he'd ever had the chance to actually do that, but he'd surely tried. And kept trying. Some days, it felt like a lost cause.

Maybe he needed a change. Of scene. Of job. Of everything. Yes, that's what he wanted.

The thought of starting over again somewhere—anywhere—calmed him. To get away from his past, that would be a relief. It would be best for him. Best, but not right. No, he thought as he ambled through his ma's kitchen, it wasn't right at all. His folks were getting on in years and they needed him.

The clatter of the stuff on his mother's serving tray made him sound like a herd of drunk elk let loose in the parlor. China rattled, glass tinkled, flatware clinked. If he wasn't careful, he was going to wake up his parents. They would think a thief was loose in the house.

"It's just me," he told the young woman who stared at him with wariness in her big jeweled eyes. "You thought I was bringing along my chains and shackles, judging by the sound of things, huh?"

"You make a lot of noise for just one man. I thought lawmen were supposed to be quiet. Stealthy. So they can creep up on the bad guys."

"That would be the good lawman. The ones worth their salt. I'm just a small-town sheriff. No need for sneaking around. Much." He didn't add that he could be as quiet as a silent winter's night if he had to be, as long as he wasn't carrying a loaded tray. Not something he had a lot of practice with. "I'll leave you two to warm up, and get a room ready. That is, if this'll do."

"It's wonderful. Thank you. Is there a chance your mother is still up?"

"She and my father are upstairs asleep, ma'am."

"Carrie Montgomery. Since I'm your prisoner, I suppose you should at least know what to call me."

"Then just call me Mac."

She'd learned long ago thinking of a man in that way only got a woman into more trouble and heartache than she bargained for, but for some reason she couldn't help the way her gaze followed him through the room. It was an easy gait he had. Not exactly carefree, but not militant, either. A nice comfortable step that made her look and keep looking. Even when he was more than shadow in the dark edges of the parlor, his tough male presence made her heart kick up a little faster.

No, that wasn't from watching him, it *couldn't* be. And if it was, she wouldn't let it be. It was just gratitude for this warm room for Ebea. A gratitude that did not fade but grew like the fire snapping brightly in the grate as Mac set the tray he carried on the short wide table between the sofas. She'd smelled the comforting aroma of sweet tea, but when the sheriff returned with a plate of iced gingerbread men, it surprised her.

At the sight of the neat little men with their candy buttons marching up their chests, their smiling face and candy eyes, Ebea gasped. Her tensed little body relaxed. Her child who had burrowed so deeply inside the blanket and huddled hard against Carrie relaxed for the first time since they'd been found in the boxcar.

The sheriff's eyes were kind as he knelt close. "I raided my mother's cookie jar, so if there's trouble, I'll be the one getting it, okay? You like gingerbread?"

Ebea nodded, still silent, but she grinned up at the lawman.

"They're all for you, then." He held out the plate for her to take one of the delicious-looking men. "Go on."

"Thank you." Ebea's voice came small and thin like the tiniest silver bell, and then her hand shot out and took the closest cookie by the iced foot.

"You are most welcome, little lady." Mac set the plate on the table and stood, moving away, moving on to where the raging fire needed tending.

His long wide shadow fell across the couch, across them, and it was oddly intimate. She wasn't afraid. Maybe it was the tree tucked in the corner, where evergreen needles and graceful branches held candleholders and delicate crystal figures. An angel at the top seemed to watch over the room. Over them.

She'd nearly forgotten it was that time of the year. Maybe on purpose. She brushed the palm of her hand over the top of her child's head, her skin rough and callused catching on the silken strands of fine hair.

Christmas. Carrie squeezed out the images of home, the good ones before she'd married, of Ma's house filled with the scent of baking and the excitement of the gifts to be laid on the hearth come Christmas morning. Of Ebea's delight on the

Christmases more recent, and of the hope that the year to come would be better.

Surely this was the year things could not get worse.

"Those bed irons ought to be hot in no time." The sheriff didn't miss much. His gaze followed hers to the tree. "Were you trying to get home to family?"

"No, that wasn't why I was on the train. We've lost all our family."

Mac noticed again the ring on her right finger, and none on her left hand. Widowed and alone in the world. "Well, it looks like you'll be stuck here for Christmas. I hope you don't mind if your girl gets a little spoiled by my mother."

"Spoiled?" The tense line of the woman's shoulders, as straight as a soldier's, eased. First a little, then, as the words sank in, a lot. No longer rigid, she relaxed against the sofa's cushioned back. "That would be welcome."

"Why don't you have one of those cookies, too? Take off your wraps and stay awhile."

"I s-suppose." The tension snapped back into her spine as she reached with her free hand, the one that wasn't holding her child protectively, and tugged off her dark woolen hood.

The dark fabric fell away to reveal the richest brown mane of hair he'd ever seen. Gleaming with deep burnished reds, chestnut warmth and silken beauty, those lustrous waves could not be tamed in a proper lady's knot. They had swept down out of numerous pins to tumble in a riot around her face.

Just the way a woman's hair looked when she'd been well loved and pleasured by her man. The surprising longing to do just that raged through him like a chimney fire. A yearning he'd thought long dead but here it was, roaring to life like banked embers exposed to air.

It surprised him there was any spark of desire, of want left. Maybe it was because he wasn't prepared for her beauty.

Fair of face, with an angel's heart shape and carefully chiseled features. She was a striking woman.

But when she pressed a kiss to her daughter's brow, she became even lovelier to him. For hers was an inner loveliness, as well.

It was goodness he saw, and that was something he didn't run into much in his line of work. He knelt before the fireplace and pulled the heating irons from the hearthstones. "Will your girl need more to eat? There's makings for sandwiches in the kitchen."

"No, thank you. This is a real treat."

"How about for you?"

"No, I couldn't eat."

Gratitude warmed the emerald in her eyes. Maybe it was the bleak night or simply the darkness that made his soul twist to life in a way it never had before.

Or maybe it was the endless loneliness for what had once been good in his life. It had haunted him tonight in dreams and in this very house.

He escaped into the shadows of the hallway, but it was no refuge. His chest ached and tightened as if an illness was coming on, but this was no illness. It felt as if the woman, Carrie, had tossed a noose around his chest and pulled it tight, holding on to him even as he headed up the stairs.

Just goes to show how tired I am. He dismissed it; how could he do anything else? Even if it seemed as if the rope binding him pulled tighter and tighter, and made him more aware of the woman in the room below.

You're gonna get in over your head with this one if you're not careful, man. He made up the bed in the spare room, the one reserved for his sister's boys when they came to stay, and slipped the glowing warmers between the sheets. The bed would be snug in no time.

He left a lamp burning, to guide the way.

* * *

Here he comes.

Carrie cringed inwardly at the first knell of his boots on the top of the stairs. She heard the creak of wood, the groan of the runners and knew her time had run out. *One thing I can't do is frighten her more,* she thought, holding the plate steady as Ebea grabbed the last of the gingerbread men. Somehow she would have to keep her terror inside.

She would feel better about this if she'd had the chance to meet the sheriff's mother. But the mantel clock had chimed one at least twenty minutes ago, and Mac's steps came closer, tolling through the house like a funeral procession. Somber. Grim.

This feels unreal, she thought. *Me, going to jail. Being arrested.*

The dark tree in the corner, decorated with bits of crystal and finery, bows and candles, drew her gaze. Her heart ached with longing. She missed her mother.

It's not the same without you, Ma, she thought, so grateful for all the times her mother had been there to understand, to help out or at least to offer her gentle advice. While Carrie always prided herself on being independent, it wasn't the same as being utterly alone.

How is this going to be all right? How could she let her child go, even when the law forced her? Everything she'd worked for, every hope was gone.

While the wild notes of the wind worsened outside, she awaited the sheriff's entrance into the room. It seemed to take an eternity with her pulse thrumming in her ears loud enough to drown out the storm, but he came from the darkness and the shadowed hallway and through the door into the light where she waited.

"Go ahead and take your girl up. Unless you want me to carry her?"

"Uh…no, I can." Determined to do this with as much dignity as possible, Carrie gathered her daughter in her arms, made sure to catch hold of the satchel and stood.

The lawman was there, taking the satchel from her. She let him. Why not? Most of what was inside was for Ebea, and it was nice to concentrate on holding her child this last little bit. She feared the moment she was taken from this house, her arms would be so empty, her heart aching with the chance to do just this, hold her daughter again.

And so as she ascended the stairs, she breathed in the sweet scent of gingerbread and tea. Memories she would hold on to through what remained of the night.

A faint light glinted when she reached the top of the stairs, like hope in the night, and she followed it. Closed doors on either side of her seemed to make the place more austere, but when she reached the middle door where the lamplight glowed, she saw not a simple stark room as she'd expected, but a chamber bright with a handmade quilt draping a big feather bed and molasses-rich wood posts. Lace hung at the windows, where pillows stuffed against a seat promised a sunny daytime sewing spot.

The braid rug softened her step and the toll of the sheriff's step behind her. He shouldered by her to deposit the satchel on the bed, where pillows were plumped and waited like something out of a fine store window's display.

"Ma, do I getta sleep here?"

"Yes, you do, baby. Isn't it nice?"

Ebea gasped with delight. "Oh, yes. Yes, it is!"

Come to life, the child struggled out of her mother's arms and plopped onto the thick down mattress. Her faint squeal of awe was unmistakable.

Mac didn't need to ask. This humble home of his mother's was nicer than anything this child had known. And yet anyone could plainly see how well she was loved.

Her clothes were neat, and although she'd spent most of

the night in a freight car, her hair was carefully pulled back and her pins and ribbons matched the yellow plaid of her pretty, clean flannel dress. Her sturdy shoes looked handed down, but neatly polished.

And the unguarded joy on the child's angel's face when the mattress bounced her up into the air, told him she'd lived a protected life, as a child should be.

"No jumping, baby. Come, let's open the satchel and find your nightgown."

It was then Mac noticed the resemblance between the young mother and her small daughter as they worked side by side to unwind the length of knotted rope holding the satchel closed. She let her child dig through the depths to find her nightgown and a battered brown stuffed rabbit.

He deposited the last item he carried onto the bedside table and turned away. *She's a good mother.* He knew why it hurt. Knew why it was easier to head out the door without saying a word.

The past was heavy within him tonight, on this long night of the year. It was as if the extra minutes of darkness had crept inside his bones and deeper, into his soul. And as eyes did that had been left too long in the dark, it blinded and burned when a lamp was lit.

"Uh…excuse me, Sheriff?"

Even her voice had a hold on him, not like lethal talons of a predator hawk taking hold but with the force of it and the pain. He had to will away the image filling his mind, the one that would not quit haunting him, of another woman who'd wanted to be a mother. Who should have had the right to be one.

If he hadn't failed her, his wife. He froze, choking with torment, not willing to gaze upon this woman, whose future depended on his actions and his decisions.

"What is it?" He heard the hollowness of his words and grimaced, hating what he'd become.

"I'll get her ready and asleep. It shouldn't take long. And perhaps you'll want me to bring down the tea. Ebea has had enough."

"But I brought it for you."

"I—I don't think I could stomach any, and I won't be here long enough anyhow—"

"Why? Did you want a separate room? I'd assumed you'd want to spent the night in the same—"

"What?" She felt the flannel nightgown tumble from her grip. *"What did you say?"*

The granite line of his shoulders tensed. "Then this room is all right for you?"

"I'm to stay here?"

"Yes." He sounded exhausted. Annoyed.

"But I thought—"

"It can't be right to put you in a cold jail cell. Good night, ma'am."

"I—" She couldn't seem to talk, to think, to thank him. Shock left her paralyzed as he ambled across the threshold and into the shadows.

For a brief moment the strong outline of him lingered against the absolute darkness of the long hallway, and then just the sound of his gait tolling steadily away until there was nothing at all.

She thought she heard the outside door slam against the wind, but she couldn't be sure. She only knew he was gone and she was safe in this snug room with her daughter.

Surely this was only for the night, she thought, afraid to believe that any more good could come her way, for it felt as if she'd used up her humble portion. But Ebea was sparkling with happiness as she crawled on the soft flannel quilt, her smile as pure as a morning star.

"Ma, ooh, it's warm." Ebea vibrated with wonder as she slipped both hands beneath the pile of covers. "Look!"

It took only one feel of the sheets. Blessed, bone-melting warmth seeped into her. She hadn't realized how cold she'd become. Or tired. It felt like decades since she'd last slept in a real bed, safe and warm, although it had only been three weeks. Three long, infinite weeks. The weight of endless worrying and constant responsibility slipped off her shoulders for this moment.

As she helped Ebea into her nightgown and into that toasty, luxurious feather bed, she caught a glimpse of her old self— before her husband's drinking and her mother's death took their toll. And again in the mirror as she brushed out her hair. Maybe somehow she could make this right. She'd come this far already. If she could salvage this, maybe there was still a chance to start over, to build a new and good life for her and Ebea.

At least, she thought as she climbed into bed beside her sleeping daughter, it was something to wish on.

And, remembering the tree downstairs, silent and waiting, it was the right time of year to dream.

Chapter Four

"Mac, get in here before you catch your death, do you hear me?"

How was it that no matter how old a man was, his mother was still his mother? And nothing could motivate him like her friendly scolding. "I can't hear you over the storm, Ma."

"If you know what's good for you, you will." Selma McKaslin hadn't raised five strapping sons and a wonderful daughter by letting anyone push her around. She knew how to stand her ground and give orders. "Get in this house this minute or you'll regret it."

She tugged the door shut loud enough to give her threat emphasis, but Mac wasn't worried. She was trying to get him to come in to keep her company, and to get the real news about the visitors he'd left her a note explaining.

Not that he was worried Ma would cast out Carrie and her child. Nope. He'd learned the mettle of his mother long ago. She baked the best cookies in the county, everyone said so, and she had a sweet heart to match.

His ma was always someone he could count on. He made sure to knock the snow from his boots before he walked through the door and hung his snowy coat and hat to dry on

the pegs near the stovepipe. The stove was crowded with siz-
zling pans being managed by his efficient mother. Dressed in
her usual flowery apron pulled over her work dress and her
hair poofed up into a knot, she hardly spared him a glance as
she flipped golden buttermilk pancakes.

"That's a lot of cakes. Any of 'em for me?"

"Maybe. Depends on whether I like the reason you brought
strangers into my home."

"You will." He stole a browned sausage link and bit back
a curse as the grease scorched his fingertips, but it was a sacrifice he was willing to make. He blew on one end of the link
to cool it enough so he wouldn't burn off his tongue. "How
mad are you?"

"Son, you've never done a thing like this before, so I figure there must be some reason behind it." Sparkles lit up her
gray eyes as she took a platter from the warmer and heaped
on the last of the pancakes. "I trust you with my life. You
would never bring harm to us. Your father thinks the same."

"Never." If he had a heart, if any small bit of it had managed to survive, it would be warm as the red-sided cookstove
with a son's love. But as it was, he felt hollow as he turned
away, for he knew that glimmer of hope on his mother's face.
The hope that he'd be able to leave Amelia buried in the past
and marry again.

Some things were not to be forgiven.

"Is Pa at the shop?" Woodenly, he took a cinnamon roll
from the plate on the counter.

"He wanted to get the place warm before I got there, the
dear man."

"It's damn cold out there." Mac dragged a chair out from the
table with the toe of his boot and settled into it. He considered
the impenetrable snow that writhed and whirled on the other
side of the window and ate the sticky sweet roll with his fingers. "You shouldn't go out in this alone. I'd best go with you."

"I'm perfectly capable of finding my way, storm or no. Besides, you need to wait for your guests upstairs." More glints twinkled in her hopeful gaze, and her face gentled with love as she came, untying her apron as she went, to press a kiss on his brow. "Son, here's some good advice. Take care with this day given to you. They are numbered for each of us, and should never be wasted."

He squeezed his eyes shut, willing down the pain. The ashes within him scattered. While he knew what his mother meant, how she always wanted to remind him that life went on, it did not for him. "You're off in a hurry."

"You wouldn't believe the orders! Stop by the shop and bring our houseguests with you." She hurried on her way, lifting her hand in a wave even as she disappeared through the doorway and down the hall.

But he wasn't alone. He felt the whisper of her presence before he heard the brush of her step in the archway behind him. He hadn't been able to catch more than a wink of sleep thinking about her. And not wanting to think about her.

The tug within was there too, as if she'd given a good yank on that invisible lasso, and even his emptiness seemed less when he looked upon her.

This was Carrie? He knew it was. The bulky coat was gone, and the weariness had vanished. The woman in a sedate gray wool dress with black buttons marching from her chin to hem did not look homeless or penniless.

She looked like a dream. Her silken chestnut hair was drawn simply back at her nape in a braid. There was no mistaking the rich emerald of her eyes or the delicate cut of her porcelain face.

"Good morning, Sheriff. I heard voices, and I wanted to come and thank your mother. I can't remember the last time I've had such a good sleep. The room was so comfortable."

The height of color ebbing into her soft cheeks told him

she was referring to the bed. He felt his face heat, too, at the image of her slim woman's form stretched out on that wide feather bed. With her hair loose and untamed, and his fingers aching to wind through it—

Whoa, tighten the rein on those thoughts, McKaslin. Realizing his blood was hot, his breathing changed and a heavy want was drumming like a heartbeat within, he bolted from the chair and headed straight to the stove. What was wrong with him? He'd seen lovely women and hadn't reacted like this. Was he no better than Bose?

His fingers shook as he grabbed down a clean cup from the shelves. "Coffee?"

"That would be wonderful."

It was the way she'd said it, as if he'd offered her something rare, that made him realize the comforts surrounding him. And all he took for granted. And, he thought as he filled the cup, all he did not. "Is your little girl still asleep?"

"Fast. Oh, this is a beautiful kitchen. And it smells so good, the way a home should."

Coffee and baking and wood smoke, and beneath it all the lemon polish his mother used. He tried not to remember the last time he'd had a real home—the house he'd built for his wife—and the emptiness inside him, where not even the ashes remained, stirred as if a wind whirled there. And brought with it pain.

Firmly, he set the cup on the table, determined to stay right here in the present. He had no notion why his nightmares had crept into his waking day. "Help yourself to the food in the warmer. My mother made enough to feed a small army."

"Where is she? I want to meet her. I mean, we're strangers, and surely she must worry what kind of person is in her home."

"She just left to join my father. They own a shop in town and are apparently very busy with Christmas orders."

Add to the equation the fact that his mother wanted him to

enjoy time alone with Carrie, and that was the real reason she'd run for the door.

What was he going to do with his poor hopeful ma? "Here's a plate. Come, dish up."

"Oh." She simply stared at the array of food.

"How long has it been since you've had a home-cooked meal?"

"You mean that wasn't made over a campfire?"

"This is winter. How long have you been cooking outdoors?"

And with a child. Carrie could hear his unspoken question. In her defense, she'd worked hard to make sure her little one was warm enough, surely not as snug as she'd been this last night, but comfortable enough. Surely, a county or territorial orphanage was no warmer. She'd heard horror stories of the cold dormitories where there was no heat at all in the entire building.

Likewise had been true with the boardinghouse where she'd last stayed. There was no heat in the individual rooms, no coal heaters, no stoves, no fireplaces.

"This is why I was on the train." She had so little dignity left, but she clung to it because it was all that was keeping her from a desperate life. "The work I was able to find was temporary— most jobs in this part of the country are, you know that."

"Because of the hard winters. It's the same story around here. No farming, no logging. Except for the town stores, work comes to a standstill."

Relief filled her, for she heard understanding in his words. "I was hoping to go West. To Idaho or maybe Oregon or Washington Territory where the winters are mild and there are jobs year-round. I need to find work so I can take care of my child."

Since he handed her a serving spoon, she took it and dug into the hash potatoes in the bowl in the oven warmer. With a tap of steel on ironware, she dropped a scoop of buttery and steaming hash browns on her plate.

"That's all?" He took the spoon back but not unkindly. "That just isn't going to work. Not in this house. You'd offend Ma if she saw that measly little serving."

He plopped a second, enormous scoop of soft, crispy potatoes next to the first. "I can see how this is going to go, so you'll just have to suffer with me filling your plate. Sausage?"

"Those are real links."

"I'll take that as a big yes." Mac forked half a dozen before she protested, then went on to the scrambled eggs.

It was an odd thing, he thought as he dished up a big helping first on her plate and then on his. Somehow it felt intimate, familiar, having her at his side by the stove.

It was a strange comfort that wrapped around him like the heat from the fire, driving away all coldness and dispelling the darkest of the shadows. After he dished up a big stack of pancakes, she thanked him and moved away to the table.

You've gone a long time without a decent meal, haven't you? While the coat she'd worn last night had been large, there was no mistaking the too-big dress she wore. From the back, where her braid met the back of her collar, he could plainly see the thin column of her neck and the obvious, painful bumps of her neck bones. She did not fill out the dress. Last night, he'd mistakenly believed she'd worn secondhand clothes, but that had to be wrong.

This was her dress, made for her, for the hem was the right length, offering glimpses of her shoes, but it did not fit her. The loose fabric whispered over the tiny cinch of her waist and, when she turned to slide her plate onto the table, he could plainly see the outline of her shoulder blades and, he feared, ribs, through the soft wool. He thought of the child upstairs with her soft cherub's face. The girl had eaten while the mother had not.

Sadness ebbed into him like a slow cold wave. Carrie was a young mother with no family and no help, no job and no money. She said she was hoping to find work. That was all. She did not deserve a stint in a jail cell. He no longer cared if the railroad threw a tantrum over this or if he even lost his job.

He saw that he might be able to do some good after all. "What job did you used to have?"

"I cleaned and cooked at a boardinghouse." She accepted the sugar bowl he pushed her way and spooned two generous scoops into the steaming coffee cup. "It wasn't a great job and it didn't pay well, but I could keep Ebea with me while I worked."

"And that job ended?"

"Yes. The workers who'd come to hire on to the farms went back on the trains and the mines closed down, and they didn't need me anymore." She thought of the day she'd walked away from the boardinghouse, with Ebea's hand so small and trusting within hers and a fear she could taste gathering on her tongue. There hadn't been money enough saved up. There hadn't been anywhere to go or anyone to help. She said no more.

The blizzard did not seem to blow so fierce as she cupped her hands around the ironware cup and let the coffee's heat soak into her. She breathed in the rich fragrance, and the first sip was an unbelievable luxury. She let the sweet bitterness roll over her tongue and down her throat. It glowed in her stomach, warming her.

"You seem to be enjoying that. I have a weakness for coffee, too. Can't get moving unless I have my usual three cups. On mornings like this, four."

"It is one of my favorite things."

His wise eyes didn't move from her face. "How long has it been since you've had any?"

"My mother gave me a five-pound bag of beans for Christmas the year before last. Ebea was just a wee thing toddling about, and times were lean then, too." She could read the question on his face; it wasn't hard, for she could feel it in the air as if he'd written it in smoke. *Two years without a cup of coffee?*

She didn't say another word about it but simply took a second slow, satisfying sip. Mac was a decent man, it seemed to radiate from him, but he had a good-paying job, a home and family. He had people who loved him—surely he was married—and comforts all around him. He couldn't understand. Especially the part about her Ebea's future hanging in the balance.

"Will you be taking me to jail after the meal?"

"No." He didn't look her way as he picked up his fork and dug into the pile of eggs on his plate.

The hard ball of fear dead center in her chest began to unravel. "If perhaps the rail company will agree not to charge me a passenger fare, but something lower, then I can pay part with my mother's ring. When I find work, I could make payments on the balance of the debt. I would be good for it."

She waited, heart pounding while the sheriff chewed, swallowed and took a long gulp of coffee. His silence remained. The penetrating heat of his gaze seared her, as if he was trying to peer deep into her heart. She wrenched away to stare out the window where snow whirled and warred.

Finally, he spoke. "The problem with that argument is that you don't have a job."

"No. But I will find one. You know I have to. I have my Ebea. I will not fail her."

Although it felt she might already have. Desolate, she watched the white screen of the storm on the other side of the window. Pure white as spun sugar, the gales of snow did not seem so thick.

Perhaps it was just wishful thinking or the brightness of the sun somewhere beyond the heavy mantle of cruel storm clouds that made the snow all the whiter. Through the veils of it, she caught sight of a white-draped fir's bough, heavily weighted, and then it vanished.

She felt like that tree, sagging beneath the weight of what she could not stop or escape.

"It's cute, but what kind of name is Ebea?"

"It's short for Elizabeth Beatrice. My mother made it up." Carrie set down her fork. Her stomach fisted and she could not eat.

He only stared at her with serious eyes she saw were gray. Not a cold and uncaring gray like a storm, but warm, like sun on steel. "The storm's letting up, do you think?"

"Maybe."

"Sometimes we get lucky and a blizzard is only a day. Two at the most. But not often." He took the small pitcher in the center of the table and poured thick maple syrup over his stack of cakes. "I suppose being from the Dakotas you're used to a blizzard or two."

"Wouldn't be much of a woman in these parts if I wasn't."

"True." She hadn't touched her meal. "The food's gonna cool off if you don't get busy. The good part about the storm is that if the winds keep going, the railroad will be shut down until it ends, what with avalanches and snowdrifts on the tracks. It takes half a day or so for crews to clear the way."

"Are you saying that I have some time?"

"That's what I'm saying." He picked up his plate and cup, now that they had that settled.

The vastness in his chest hurt and did not stop no matter how hard he willed it. Something like when men lost their limbs to accident or war and they could feel the hurting pain of the arm or leg that was no longer there. He could still feel the shadows of his heart, and the longing.

And since it had been some time since he'd shared a morning table with a pretty woman, one who made him wish just a little, he found it easier to leave the room. He could make no excuse, and decided it couldn't matter to her. She had her own problems.

So he took refuge in the parlor where last night's fire was nothing but black ashes in a cold grate and listened to the sounds of the storm outside, instead of to the one within.

How long would the blizzard last? Carrie wondered as she wiped the last dish in the drainer. How long did she have? As the morning ticked by, the blizzard had seemed to lessen in intensity, but the white veil of snow continued to fall in a thick, unbreakable curtain.

"Ma, Molly's tummy is full." Ebea looked up from cradling her baby doll on the floor before the cookstove.

"You are a good mother, baby girl?"

Ebea nodded as she cradled her doll, rocking her gently. Her sweet voice lifted in a familiar lullaby, and love warmed Carrie more than the wonderful heat from the stove ever could.

Please, she thought, please let the blizzard last long enough. So I can figure out where to go from here. How to give her the future she deserves. The weight of it, and the hope, tugged heavily on her as she emptied the dishpan outside the back door and then wiped it down and the work counter.

The sheriff had left as soon as he'd emptied his plate, with promises to return. So when she heard the front door wrangle open, she wasn't worried.

After wrestling with the wind and shaking the snow from his wraps, he ambled into the kitchen looking like a legend in his Stetson, buffalo coat and denims. "Howdy there. I see you ladies have been keeping busy. Carrie, you didn't need to do the dishes."

"Yes, I did. I'm a guest here. It's the least I can do to repay your mother's hospitality."

"That's exactly the point. You're a guest." Although he sure appreciated what she'd done. The kitchen shone. He guessed she'd cleaned the floor, too, judging by the look of things.

Mac tucked his gloves into his pocket and held out his hands to the stove. He'd been out most of the morning helping folks who were more stubborn than the storm. He'd helped secure the ropes across the ends of the boardwalks, and assisted the shop owners needing help with clearing snow. Freeing a stuck sleigh that had been blocking Mountain Street had kept him out in the weather for hours.

"I meant to come by earlier, but a sheriff's job is never done. Are you ready to head out? My ma made me promise to bring you and your little one by the shop. She'll box my ears if I don't."

"Box your ears? If she does, I'm sure it's no less than you deserve. I can have us ready in a few minutes."

"Fine, then." The ache remained within him, lodged in the center of his chest, and it was a sharp, keening pain that made him wish he had a deputy on duty to handle this situation. Hand her off to someone else so he wouldn't have to feel. But Larkin was out of town visiting family. *And she's your responsibility, anyway.*

He wasn't surprised the silverware remained untouched in the bottom of the glass cabinet. Or that the child on the floor chanting a lullaby in a singsong voice was as neat as a picture with her hair so like her mother's falling in a cloud of innocence. With her head bowed, she continued to sing, rocking her baby doll wrapped in a tattered length of pink cloth.

Footsteps heralded Carrie's approach and he knelt before the fuel door and grabbed the poker from its iron hook. He was busy breaking down the fire and banking the chunks of glowing embers when she tapped into the room, a reticule clutched in her hand and their wraps piled over her arm. Her skirts swished and the flannel petticoats beneath them whispered in a hush that was so distinctly feminine and somehow alluring that it set his teeth on edge.

Why was she affecting him this way? He did not want her

to. He did not wish it. He stubbed the last flicker of flame and covered it in ash. If only he could smother this feeling within him as easily.

The little girl tipped back her head to gaze up at her mother, her soft face pinched with worry. "I wanna stay here."

"We'll be coming back, baby girl."

"Okay."

How one simple word could hold so much joy Mac didn't know. It only made the sharp edges of the pain within him cut deeper like a serrated blade that chewed instead of sliced cleanly.

Carrie knelt, deftly plucking the girl's muffler around her neck. "How about you, me and baby Molly go take a look around town?"

"No." Her small fingers turned white as she gripped her dolly. "I don't wanna go anymore."

"I know, but we have to." Carrie cradled her little girl's chin in her palm, and the love that shone in her eyes made it clear. She knew exactly how rich she was, how blessed.

Alone, Mac stood, forcing away the ghosts of the past. The ones that reminded him in silence and emptiness of all he had lost.

At least she knows how lucky she is, he thought as he watched her brush a kiss to her child's forehead. "Come, I think I have change enough for a cookie."

"A cookie?"

"We'll find the town bakery and when we do, you get to pick any cookie you want. Okay?" She brushed her little one's bangs out of her eyes, and there was no missing the love and sorrow and lost wishes all rolled up together and leaving him changed inside.

Maybe he could do something about that sorrow. About those lost wishes. He stayed, when he wanted to turn on his heel and retreat to the safety of the outside world, where the frigid winds could chill this ebb of emotion.

He lifted the coat from Carrie's arm and held it for her. Felt the warm lap of feeling within him grow like a water spring at the bottom of a newly dug well, rising in a slow steady flood.

She smelled like roses and cinnamon and wood smoke from tending the fire, and something else, something wonderful and rare he hadn't sensed in what felt like a lifetime: home. His throat cinched up tight, leaving him silent. The garment he held by the collar tugged and moved as she slipped into it.

She was so close, he could see the burnished red highlights in her hair. Smell the silk of her skin. See the fast beat of her pulse in her neck beating as fast as—and in time with—his.

Chapter Five

This is like something out of a storybook. Carrie felt breathless and not from the shocking cold as she stepped out of the white fury of the blizzard and onto the covered boardwalk. Here the wind did not seem so brutal and the brightly lit windows of the shops marching along the walkway cast a welcome, fairy-tale glow.

"Mama! Look!" Ebea pointed with her little pink-mittened hand at the mercantile's display.

The windows glittered with lamplight, casting a golden pool over the porcelain snowy village on display, with a toy train winding through it. Inside the store, shoppers were plainly visible hurrying about with full baskets, checking their lists.

As they passed other shops—the candy maker, the general store, a hatmaker—they found the windows just as festive. All were decorated in pine garlands and strings of cranberries. The dress shop had a small Christmas tree lit with tiny taper candles and bright, cleverly made ornaments for sale.

"Pretty," Ebea breathed, transfixed. She'd been too exhausted last night to notice the McKaslins' decorated fir tucked in the dark corner of the parlor, and she'd never before seen a real Christmas tree.

There was no mistaking the sheriff's inquisitive gaze. He had so much—he probably had lost sight of what was truly important in this holiday season. And in life.

The shop's door glided open and a handsome woman in the most lovely dark green wool coat emerged, holding a decorated basket. The seamstress took one look at Ebea. "Oh, what a pretty little girl. I haven't seen you two before. Are you relatives of the sheriff's?"

Carric was at a loss. How could she explain? "No, I—"

"They're visitors," the sheriff interrupted easily. "They'll be staying with my mother for a few days."

"For Christmas." Brightening, the store owner smiled, meeting Carrie's gaze directly. "I'm giving out hair ribbons to all the little girls who stop by today. Would your daughter like one?"

"Oh!" Ebea's gasp of delight was answer enough.

The seamstress knelt with her basket so that the child could easily look at all the pretty handmade bows and decorated ribbons. "Go ahead and pick whichever one you like."

It was the loveliest assortment Carrie had ever seen. "Ma'am, you had to have spent hours making those."

"I work on them throughout the year when I have quiet time here at the shop. I'm Candace."

For an instant it was as if they could be friends. They were not so far apart in age, Carrie realized. It had been a long time since she'd had a real friend or the time to spend with one.

But maybe, thanks to the sheriff, she would one day. A person never knew what good was in store for them around the next bend.

If she could figure out a way to reach the Northwest, then who knew what good things could come her way? "What do you say, Ebea?"

"Thank you."

"You're most welcome. You'd better get a matching one for your baby. What's her name?"

"Molly. My grammy's named Molly, too. 'Cept she died."

"I'm very sorry for that. Molly is a lovely baby. You have a merry Christmas, all of you." With a genuine smile, Candace slipped back into the warmth of the store.

The sheriff cleared his throat, and he sounded gruff as he gestured down the snowy boardwalk. "My folks' shop is this way."

With Ebea's hand safely within hers, Carrie followed Mac past storefronts where tenacious shoppers braved the storm and busy store clerks waved or called out wishes for a merry Christmas in such a friendly way, it was clear the sheriff was well thought of. Some places were real communities, where folks knew one another by name.

Mac pulled open a frosted-glass door. The sign hanging overhead said in pretty blue lettering: McKaslin Bakery. A musical bell chimed cheerfully overhead as Carrie stepped out of the storm and into wonder.

What a beautiful place. Welcoming lamplight shone on polished oak floors and counters and little tables, which were set up by the wide windows and the red-hot potbellied stove. Such inviting places to sit and relax and, she imagined, watch people go by when a blizzard was not blowing. And the scents of baking chocolate, warm yeasty doughnuts and baking cinnamon rolls made her mouth water.

"Oh, good, you came!" A pleasant-looking woman cornered around the counter. Her silver hair was puffed up in a soft chignon. A crisp apron covered the red dress she wore, emphasizing her matronly curves. She moved with confidence and energy and cheer.

Mac's mother. Carrie didn't need an introduction. Mrs. McKaslin had the same gray eyes, but hers sparkled like sunlight on the clearest lake. She adored the woman immediately. "Mrs. McKaslin, it's especially good to meet you, I can't thank you enough—"

"Goodness!" she interrupted, waving her hand away. "I didn't do all that much. It was my boy here who brought you."

Her boy was a big strapping man, but Mrs. McKaslin didn't seem to notice that, even as she went up on tiptoe to give him an exuberant motherly hug. The top of her head came only to the center of his chest, so she had to tip her head back to see him as she released him. "I can't begin to tell you, my boy, how happy this makes me."

Carrie wasn't sure what the woman was referring to, but happiness seemed to radiate from her, the quiet, contented kind, and it grew. The affection between mother and son was unmistakable, and it heartened her to see it. Now she understood why Mac had helped her last night and this morning. Family was important to him, too.

"Call me Selma, and you're Carrie? And who is this?"

Ebea studied the grandmotherly woman with somber eyes. "Elizabeth Beatrice. Are you Mrs. Santa Claus?"

"Goodness me, dear, I wish I were. Because surely Mr. Claus wouldn't be such a procrastinator as my dear Fred is. Tell me, Elizabeth Beatrice, do you like cookies?"

"Mama said we had money enough for any one I want!" Delighted, Ebea squeezed her doll to her chest. "Can I pick now?"

Out of the mouths of babes. Mac watched Carrie's face turn from pink to red, and she was lovely when she was blushing.

"You can pick now, baby." She knelt to loosen the secure ties of the girl's hood.

Mac couldn't help watching the way Carrie's hands moved. They were long and slender, her fingers tapered and looked made for playing a piano instead of the hard work that had reddened and roughened them.

Still, her touch was obviously gentle as she loosed her child's wraps, kissed her on the cheek and said, "Go along up to the display, but don't touch the glass."

"'Kay. Do you think there are gingerbread men here, too?"

"Possibly. Go see." Carrie straightened, her fingers lingering on her daughter's cheek, a normal, affectionate gesture of a mother to her child.

So, why did he feel as if he'd been struck in the chest with a .45-caliber bullet?

His ma seemed extraordinarily pleased as she held out her hand to the child. "Come, sweetheart, I'll show you where they are. Carrie, I'm sorry I'm so busy. Heavens, are those more customers, too? Please, help yourself to a cup of coffee and find a place to sit. Unless you want a cookie?"

Carrie shook her head, her hand tightening on the small cloth reticule she carried, as if thinking of the little money she had inside. Mac knew that his mother had meant a free cookie, and it was interesting that Carrie hadn't seemed to make that assumption.

Mac concentrated on taking a clean tin cup from the shelf and pouring two cups of coffee. It was as if the bullet in his chest remained, creeping deeper as Carrie swished up to him, her skirts rustling around her slim ankles. He could see glimpses of her dark stockings as her skirt swayed. Not that he ought to be noticing something that personal.

"Here." He knew he was gruff; it was the best he could do. He didn't want to explain, his past was private, but he couldn't go around letting her affect him like this. If only he could stop the tingle of awareness in his chest as he handed her the cup and their fingers brushed.

Skin to skin. He felt her warmth; he was near enough he couldn't miss the warm rose scent of her. Then the contact went from comfortable to scalding. His hand jerked back as if he'd touched a scorching flame. What was that? He couldn't explain the kick of his pulse and the jittery feeling as if he'd had two pots of coffee. Needing to get away from her, he poured a second cup for himself, not that he needed it. No, he just had to get away.

But did she? No. She remained at his side. Her sleeve brushed his as she reached for the sugar canister, and his body betrayed him like a randy, undisciplined youth. Blood thrummed in his veins, and he wrestled down thoughts he had no right having. He wanted her in the worst way, just like that, and this couldn't go on as if he were a man with a heart. A woman's love was something he could never have again. Not that his body agreed.

Add that to the look Ma kept sneaking in Carrie's direction and he was in big trouble. The absolute worst kind. If he wasn't careful, his mother was going to start trying to match-make, when she knew the way things had to be. And why. She knew the darkness was more unbearable this time of year, for Amelia had died on Christmas Eve.

What I need to do is to help Carrie to get on her way. It seemed the only choice. She had plans that would take her far from there. She simply needed a little mercy—and help—to do it. He was in a position to give her both.

"Goodness, I should have known you would have gone for the pink one!" Ma's voice chimed like a silver bell above the hubbub of the customers chatting with each other and Pa, who'd come from the back to help out.

Carrie, who was only a few steps away, swept to the counter, untying her reticule. Her little girl was holding an enormous gingerbread lady in one hand in a square of waxed paper, gazing at the cookie as if it were the most incredible thing she'd seen yet. Even better than the Christmas tree in Candace Day's display window.

Mac turned his back before his mother could shoot him another hopeful look or his father joined in with the same hopes. The coffee was hot and fresh and he slurped it down without sugar. The scalding heat on his lips and tongue helped him to forget the woman standing behind him.

But not well enough. He could hear the gentle tone of her

alto words. "No, Selma, I'm sorry. I can't accept more of your generous hospitality. How much do I owe you?"

The bell jangled behind him as more customers stumbled through the door, drowning out his ma's response, although he already knew what she was saying. Good luck to Carrie in trying to get his mother to accept her three pennies in payment.

"Howdy there, Sheriff." Jed swept off his cap. "Sure is blizzarding out there. If it gets much worse, folks'll be in a bit of trouble tryin' to get home."

"Everyone I've come across today lives right in town. Besides, that's what I'm here for."

"That ain't the little lady from last night, is it?" He squinted in what looked like disapproval. "I thought she was supposed to be locked up."

"Tell me what's a reasonable fare from Minot to, say, Seattle." Mac took another scalding gulp from his cup, his eyes tearing at the burn. What he was thinking was lunacy. But what else in blazes was he to do?

"Uh, well, a good hundred and fifty, two hundred. Depends on the class of car you want."

"That's a lot of money." Mac set down his coffee, watching Carrie as she took her daughter by the hand and led her through the gathering crowd at the counter. Her chin was up, her shoulders tensed, and she marched with a quick, angry pace that told him she'd failed to convince Ma to let her pay.

His groin thrummed—yep, he was in big trouble. "Two hundred. That's for passenger fare. She sat in a boxcar with no seat and no heater. Could you figure that into things?"

"You asked for fare to Seattle."

"Just figure out what she owes the railroad for getting here. And then get me an amount for the rest on a passenger train."

"I'll do my best. See ya 'round, Mac."

It was more than lunacy. He'd lost his damn mind. And for a woman he didn't know, would never see again and didn't

want to. Not that he could see her with the crowd backing up.
The bell above the door jangled again, announcing more business. Where was Carrie? Well, he'd best find her and figure
out what to do with her for the rest of his workday. His folks
were busy here, and—

"Uh, can I help you?"

Why her soft alto rose above the noise from the kitchen and
the din of customers talking amongst themselves he couldn't
say. He only knew he heard her as if she'd spoken right beside him. He pivoted toward the front and there she was. Behind the counter.

That can't be right. His eyes were playing tricks on him.
Ma didn't let just anyone back there. Hell, how many times
had she banished him? More than he could count. But his eyes
weren't deceiving him. She was behind the counter with an
extra apron of his mother's tied around her slender waist. She
was smiling as she listened to the request of the next customer
in line.

Well, I'll be. The noose she'd left tied around his heart gave
a long sweet yank. That was worse than the desire strumming
in his veins. Yeah, he needed to help her on her way the instant the trains were running.

It wouldn't be soon enough.

Carrie watched the sheriff shoulder out the door, keeping
his back firmly turned toward her. Or so it seemed that way.
He powered through the billowing snow in the doorway like
a man with a fierce amount of determination. Just like that,
he was leaving. Without saying goodbye.

Remembering how he'd jerked his hand from hers over the
coffee cup, it all made sense. Maybe he thought a young
widow down on her luck might be looking to catch herself a
husband. He was probably used to women wishing on him.
Now he thought she was one of them.

Not that she had time to worry about it. Even more people had crowded into the shop with last-minute orders for Christmas treats. She'd concentrate on helping Selma, that's what she would do, and keep her mind off Mac McKaslin.

Except it wasn't her mind that was troubled. It was her heart. It felt as if she were lost in the blizzard and didn't know which way was home.

After being alone for over a year, since she'd buried her mother, she'd never quite felt this lonely. Not that she had time to think about why she felt this way after the precise moment Mac had left. She tried to focus her attention on the customer she'd offered to help.

"I'd like a dozen iced cinnamon rolls, the large size," demanded a severe-looking woman on the other side of the counter. "And a Black Forest cake, decorated like last time. Fred will know what I mean—"

Fred being Mac's father, Carrie guessed as she spied an extra tablet on the counter and grabbed one of the lead pencils lying beside it. She wrote as fast as she could, although the woman kept right on talking.

"I'll need this by tomorrow, no later than noon. I have family coming in, if this dreadful storm blows out. Are you the new hired girl?"

"You could say that."

"Then you'll need my name, and make sure to give this order to Fred personally. I'm Mrs. Brickman."

"Yes. Thank you, Mrs. Brickman."

"Don't you lose that order, now, or I'll have your job."

Perhaps Mrs. Brickman had been a schoolteacher for a long length of time, because she had that intimidating, nononsense stare. "I promise, ma'am."

The instant Mrs. Brickman stepped aside, another customer took her place. "I believe I'm next. Goodness, you're busy. My little Annie would like one of your gingerbread ladies, please."

Carrie had to stand on tiptoe to see far enough over the counter, but there was an angel-blond little girl, hugging her rag doll in the crook of her arm. "Oh, of course. Do you want the lady with the pink dress or the yellow?"

"Yellow." Annie clasped her little hands together.

Carrie knew how important cookies were, so she chose the nicest one from the tray in the display case. While she handed over the treat carefully wrapped in waxed paper, the mother gave a start of surprise. "Why, is that your little one?"

"Yes. Our girls look to be about the same age." Carrie couldn't help the shine of pride when she gazed upon her child. Ebea, the good girl she was, was seated in the corner, safely out of the way, pretending to share bites of her cookie with her baby.

"Say, Annie is having a Christmas party. No gifts, nothing like that. It's just for her little friends to come and have apple cider and treats, like a tea party. Would your little girl like to come, too? She would be most welcome."

"But you don't know us."

"The McKaslins have hired you, and you're working here in town. That makes you one of us. I'm Lena Cowan. We live above the leather shop. That's my husband, he's the leather worker in town. You bring your little girl by this afternoon at one, and I promise she'll have the best time. We have games and goodies and—oh, I'm holding up the line. Let me pick up my order then."

If she hadn't met Mrs. Brickman, Carrie would have thought everyone in this town was unusually friendly. She hurried to the racks filled with packages and boxes along the side wall, tossing Ebea a smile as she swept by. Maybe a Christmas party would be just the thing her child needed. To have fun and to just be a little girl.

"The orders are alphabetized." Fred McKaslin emerged from his work at the big tables, a big man and built like his son but apparently shy as he jammed his floury hands into his pockets and stared at the floor. "Sure is nice of you to pitch in. It's our busiest Christmas season yet."

"It's the least I could do for your hospitality." She spotted the Cowan order right away, two cake boxes and a huge pastry box, and gave thanks that the prices were written right on the boxes. It was a simple thing to total them up, accept the greenbacks from Lena and make change from the tray Selma kept right beneath the counter on a little shelf.

"One o'clock," Lena reminded her, with her arms full and the crowd pushing around her. "We'll be expecting you!"

As Carrie hurried to write out the next order for fudge, divinity and two dozen decorated sugar cookies, Selma sidled up to her on her way to the order racks. "I saw Lena Cowan talking to you. You ought to take your little Ebea to the party. She'll have a fun time. And believe me, you won't find nicer people than the Cowans."

"Unless it's your family."

"Oh, pshaw! We aren't so much, but I tell you, both Fred and I sure appreciate the help. You and I will settle up as soon as the rush is over."

"There's nothing to settle up. And if you think you're going to pay me, then you and I are going to come to blows." She added a smile to her harsh words, although she meant them.

"We'll see about that!" With a wink, Selma bustled off.

More customers waited, and so Carrie dived right back in, her tablet and pencil at the ready.

On the other side of the counter, an elderly man glanced down at his shopping list. He laid the list on the counter and tapped at the written items as if he was half-amused. "The wife said to give this to you so I don't mess up and get it wrong."

"We'll make sure we get the order right, then."

That made the man grin, and in his day he must have been

a handsome one. It was his kindness that shone through as he handed over the list. "Might as well copy it down since Selma is busy. Me or the wife will be by tomorrow to collect everything. You look like a good worker. You liking this job?"

"It's nice." It wasn't her job, but that would take too much time to explain with so many waiting. She copied down the order. "What name do I put on this?"

"McKaslin." He winked, making the family resemblance unmistakable. "I'm the grandpop. Can you believe it? It seems like just yesterday I owned this place, but then they ran me off."

Selma arrived with the pie boxes and handed them over to her customer. "Oh, Shamus, you know we didn't chase you off. Not with a broom, anyway, or any kind of weapon."

"See how they treat me?" There was no mistaking the joke between them, for there was only clear abiding affection. "You be good to this young lady, Selma. She looks like a keeper. Has Mac met her yet?"

"Oh, has he! He's the one who brought her to us."

It's not like that. Carrie cringed, because the look they exchanged was clear. "I'm only here for a few days."

But Shamus McKaslin seemed to know better, for he waved her comment away. "No, I have a feeling you'll be here longer than that, missy. It just goes to show that miracles do happen. That would explain why Mac refused to come inside with me. Now, I'd just best be on my way because if I'm late for lunch, the wife'll take a broom to me. You lovely young ladies have a fine afternoon."

And with a lift of his cap he turned away, drawing her gaze with him. That's why she noticed the figure standing on the other side of the frosted window, shrouded in snow. More of a silhouette through the frosty glass, but she recognized the solid, dependable cut of those iron shoulders and proud head.

Mac. Her heart squeezed. He'd chosen to stay outside

rather than to come in and face her. She couldn't forget the sensation when their fingers met. Maybe he couldn't, either, and that's why he wanted to keep his distance.

And then she realized how it must seem. There was another reason he was watching her with his steeled scrutiny. She was behind his parents' counter, taking orders and handling money. She, a woman who by all rights ought to be sitting in his jail charged as a thief. She, who was letting his family and their customers think that she was something she was not.

The bell over the door chimed as it closed behind Shamus. The grandfather and grandson were clearly exposed for a brief moment as the gusting wind tore apart the snow and she saw the two of them amble away, side by side, their backs both straight and strong. Unshakable.

She cared very much what Mac thought of her. And she knew that this horrible feeling burrowing into the pit of her stomach was her troubled conscience. She had never lied about who she was or pretended to be something she wasn't.

As more customers streamed through the door, she sighed. She could not leave Selma to handle all this alone, not when she had the power to help, but neither could she let this charade continue. She did not deserve the McKaslins' generosity and their trust, for she was not the miracle they were hoping for their son.

Chapter Six

At least his office was warm. Mac huddled by the potbelly and took a deep breath. The storm was thinning some, the wind not as fierce, so that was good. That meant most townsfolk could get out and about pretty safely. But it was the heavy snowfall that was giving him trouble. He'd been helping with shoveling, keeping alleys and the entrances to businesses clear, and the day was already half done.

His stomach gave a bearlike growl. Lunch would have to wait until after he was done mulling over the problem of Carrie Montgomery. Jed had been good enough to stop by with the information he'd asked for.

The figures were higher than he would like, but they weren't impossible. He'd been tucking away most of his paychecks for years because he had no one to spend the money on. His folks refused help. His grandparents merely thought his attempts to offer to spend his money on them was insulting, for they'd always paid their way. What good was money if it was sitting untouched in a bank account forever?

None. And who better to help? Carrie had sure impressed Pop, when she'd taken Grandma's order. In the shop, she had looked like a different woman yet again; it was as if the layers of weariness and anxiety had been peeled back, and he could see her more clearly. The gentle-voiced woman with a lovely manner and the kind of beauty that could drop him to his knees.

He knew the rap at the front door came from Carrie even before he glanced up from the note Jed had left. A tight sensation swelled in his chest as she pushed open the door and blew in with a cloud of sugary snow.

He folded the note and slid it into his shirt pocket. "Howdy, there. Did my ma give you time off for good behavior?"

"Ebea was invited to a Christmas party. I just left her at the Cowans'. I promised Selma that while I was out, I'd bring you lunch." Clearly unaware of her beauty and her effect on him, she pulled off her hood, revealing the soft cloud of her hair. She plopped a little pail on the edge of his desk. Lunch, made by his mother.

Not that he was hungry for food. No, only hungry for the sight of Carrie. The cold had pinkened her cheeks, and her mouth looked as succulent and as sensual as a midnight dream. She shed her gloves, revealing her slim, delicately made hands. He remembered the brush of her fingertips and it was enough to thicken his blood. She was everything he hadn't even known he wanted; everything that he could never have again.

Sensibly, he got up from the chair and did the right thing, which was to keep the conversation neutral. It was best that she never know how she made him feel. "Come sit here by the fire. Warm up before you head back. Although you're probably used to this kind of weather."

"The blizzards seem different from the ones in Dakota Territory. Maybe it's just that I know we're high up in the mountains, but the snowfall seems much heavier." She unbuttoned her coat as she went. "Your town seems to do well enough during a storm. Minot, at least the part of town I lived in, closed up tight during a blizzard. No one ventured out."

"Our founders put some thought into where they put the main street, for instance," he said. "The winds run from the northwest, so when the storm breaks, you'll notice they ran the road southeast, in the lee of the mountainside, which means we're protected from the worst of the winds. Doesn't mean it isn't cold, though." He offered her the chair.

She kept her distance and didn't move toward the warmth. "I've got to get back. But before I do, can I say something to you?"

"Sure."

She hesitated. A furrow crinkled between her eyebrows, an endearing gesture, and he had to fight down the urge to rub that spot with the pad of his thumb. Her soft bangs tumbling over her forehead would feel like fine silken threads against his callused fingers. And her skin would be sun-warmed rose petals.

Hell, he couldn't keep thinking like this. What he needed was a little will, a bit of self-discipline, and he'd be fine. That's all. He laid a hand on his shirt pocket, feeling the reassuring outline of Jed's note. Simple enough now that he thought about it. "What do you have to say?"

"I hope you don't think I'm trying to take advantage of your parents." Her chin shot up, and there was no mistaking the pride and intense dignity that held her up.

"What? Where did you get that notion?"

"I know what it must look like with the way I just invited myself behind their counter. But your ma refused to take payment for Ebea's cookie, and I did what I thought was right."

"I noticed."

"I don't meant to worm my way into their lives or into a job or anything. I know how it must look. You know that every customer who came through those doors thought I was the new hired girl. I don't want you to think I was encouraging that. The shop was so busy and it just wasn't worth the time to explain."

"That's not what I thought at all."

"No?" That was a relief.

She could see the steel bars of the jail cell through a doorway behind him, and she shivered at how close she'd come to being there. "I owe you something I cannot begin to ever repay. Ever. I know what you've done for me. And I thought that a way to pay you back for your help and your parents' hospitality would be to volunteer in their store, so—"

"Whoa right there." He held up one hand. "You don't owe me a thing. What you do for my folks is between you and the two of them. As for the railroad, I think I may have found a way to do a little negotiating on your behalf."

"Really? What? Do you need the ring?"

"Not just yet. You leave it on for now."

It was the way he said it, with all the assurance of a man used to solving problems that made her relax. She could trust him. "I haven't had a lot of luck go my way in a long time. Until I came here. I'm afraid to believe in it."

"It's easy, Carrie. Just believe. It's my job to help people. I intend to help you and your daughter all I can."

"What a fine man you are, Mac McKaslin."

"You would be wrong." He twisted away as if she'd struck him, turning his shoulder hard and marching straight to the stove where he knelt to shovel in more coal. Determined and busy, and as distant as the western shoreline.

Why? He'd turned from her so fast. After she'd been praising him. Mortified, Carrie jabbed her fingers into her handmade mitten and spun toward the door, her face flaming hot. She seemed to have a talent for leaping out of the frying pan and into the fire. There wasn't any disaster that she couldn't make worse. Now Mac thought that she was *really* sweet on him.

Great. It was an excellent moment to leave. She wrestled the door closed behind her without looking back to say goodbye. The last thing she needed was one more look at that ir-resistible sheriff—and risk having him notice.

She had her pride. She had her dignity. She wasn't look-ing for a man to save her.

After the sadness of her marriage dissolving into her hus-band's alcohol troubles, she had to stand on her own two feet. It was up to her to make a living, to solve problems and make things right. She would hope for leniency from the railroad company and work hard until she'd paid them back every penny owed. And she would do so hundreds of miles away from this storybook town, where she could no longer embar-rass herself in front of Mac McKaslin.

Or notice that the more she was around him, the greater he became in her view.

I hope you don't think I'm trying to take advantage... Car-rie's words haunted him for hours. The note Jed had left seemed to increase in weight, making him more aware of it tucked in his pocket.

No, it had never crossed his mind that Carrie would try to take advantage of his parents. He was a sheriff; he tended to see the bad side of life and of people on the job every day. He knew the woman she was. That was the problem.

The day passed in slow, stretched-out increments. Minutes and hours he struggled not to think of her. Working helped. He kept busy by completing his check; all townsfolk were ac-counted for.

After he'd helped two elderly ladies with the snow drift-ing against their front doors, he had to attend to a chimney fire over on Rocky Road, and then he had to fetch the doc when Dunn Larkin cut his thumb with an ax. He worked all day in frigid winds and hazy shadows. He ached with those shadows, as if the darkness was gathering inside him, too.

As he grabbed hold of the rope that tied the end of the

boardwalk that would lead him safely across Mountain Street to the steps up to the depot, he caught sight of a woman pushing out of a shop down the way. He knew it was Carrie even though he could not see more than a hint of her shape and height.

He couldn't help watching the sway of Carrie's hips beneath her coat. Or the long smooth line of her gait. Her legs would be long and smooth too. And what was he doing thinking like that? It felt as if a mule had kicked him hard, right behind the sternum. His feet nearly went out from under him. The wind knocked him sideways and he lost hold of the rope.

Standing breathless, he watched as she ambled around the corner with her little girl by the hand and out of sight, hurrying back to his parents' shop. Her words disturbed him. *I thought that a way to pay you back for your help and your parents' hospitality would be to volunteer in their store.* Volunteer. She wasn't doing this for a wage.

He found the rope and oriented himself. He probably looked like a fool for losing hold of the rope in the first place. It was a good thing no one could see him due to the blizzard.

At least, not too many. He waved at a teamster making his way cautiously down the only open street through town, hauling freight from the depot to one of the merchants down the way. This was his life, looking out for folks, keeping them safe and enforcing the law. That's all he was doing for Carrie. If his sister was down on her luck and in a strange town, he could only hope that someone would do the same for her.

And once Carrie was on her way West, he could go back to being as frozen as the storm and as dark as these long bleak days of winter.

"Well, what a day we had." Selma's good cheer remained, even by the worsening storm, whose gusts knocked them against the porch railing. "I can't remember when we've had a rush like that. Fred, can you?"

"No'm." The big strapping man balanced the glass-enclosed lantern while he unlocked the front door. "Not a rush like that. Most of the town seemed to be in today."

"What we would have done without you, I can't say," Selma went on, despite the cold and snow. "I am sure grateful we didn't need to find out."

"I'm glad I could help."

Carrie blocked the howling wind with her back and ushered Ebea across the threshold first. Her poor baby. Ebea's teeth were chattering and she was covered from head to foot in a layer of crystalline snow. But beneath the thick muffler, her cherub's face was still flushed with joy from the fun time she'd had at Annie's.

Baby Molly and the new doll blanket Ebea had received at the party needed to be properly swept free of snow and sent safe in Ebea's arms to warm in the kitchen, where Fred was stacking cut fir chunks into the cookstove's fuel door.

The welcoming heat and merry snapping and crackling told her someone had been by to uncover the banked coals and build a roaring fire—Mac, no doubt. It was just the sort of thing she could see him doing, coming by the cold house to make sure the kitchen would be toasty when his parents came in from the cold.

By the time Carrie had hung all of their wraps, including Selma's and the ones Fred had slung on the entry bench, on the pegs to dry in the kitchen, Selma was lifting a bubbling teakettle from a trivet. Apparently Mac had done that too, and set a big kettle of water to heat.

"A good hot cup of Irish tea is just the thing on a night like this." Selma returned the kettle to the stove with her easy efficiency. "Why Mac didn't stay around, I can't imagine. Where else has he got to be but alone in that little house he lives in?"

"Where else would Mac be? I wonder." Fred adjusted the damper and closed the fuel door. "I imagine some work may have just come up." With a wink, he added, "He *is* the sheriff."

"Oh, I know that." Selma rolled her eyes, laughing so carefree. "I just mean this time of year, it's not good for him to be alone. A man needs a home and a wife to love him."

"That surely makes a happy man." Fred rose and caught his wife in a hug. With a smacking kiss to her cheek, he released her. "I'm off in search of sweetener for my tea."

"Whiskey, you mean!" Selma waved him away as if she'd had enough of him in her kitchen, although her eyes were bright and merry. Ebea was right, Carrie realized, she did look like Mrs. Claus as she reached small plates down from the sideboard. "Mercy me! You've done the morning dishes. And not just that—why, the entire kitchen is clean."

"No, I heard that Christmas elves had stopped by while you were away at the shop." Carrie took the plates from Selma and gave her a little nudge in the direction of the table. "You've been on your feet all day. Let me do the work."

"You've done enough already! This is my kitchen, and I'm the boss of it."

"Not tonight." The parlor clock knelled eight times as Carrie grabbed the canister lid Selma was reaching for and then the entire jar before the older woman could do a thing about it. The sweet scent of macaroons made her mouth water. "Ebea, come to the table, baby."

"I get more cookies?" Wonder shone in her words, and she skipped to the nearest chair like a little girl should, not weighed down by uncertainty.

Shame lodged like a rotten apple in Carrie's throat and she couldn't speak, couldn't even swallow as she filled two plates with various treats from the different canisters and carried them to the table. Selma was busy pouring china cups of tea.

"Like a real tea party! Again!" Ebea squeezed Molly tight, her happiness contagious, as she offered Selma her most dimpled grin.

Selma set a cup, breakable and fine, on the table in front of Ebea. "We'll have a tea party, you, your mother and I. We'll leave Fred out of it. He's better off reading the paper."

Carrie feared for the teacup, for it looked very costly, but before she could pluck a pretty but less delicate mug from the sideboard, she felt the air change, the way it did before thunder struck.

Before he moved out of the shadowed hallway, she knew Mac was there. She was already reaching him down a cup before he strode into the light.

The instant their eyes met, she felt lightning flash a spark from her heart to his. The cup slipped from her hand and clinked to a stop on the work counter. Deep winter thunder rolled through her and in the reverberation of that sensation, she felt a complete and wonderful silence.

Selma's chair scraped against the floor as she hopped to her feet. "Mac! I didn't hear you come in. That storm just rested up a bit to give us a harder blow. You must be chilled to the bone. Come up to the stove."

Every step he took toward the stove was nearer to her. Carrie felt the edge of the counter jabbing into the small of her back. The silence pealed in her ears and in her very core. It swelled in a crescendo, fading out every other detail until there was only Mac. Her soul ached with longing.

So, she was gazing at him again, but Mac McKaslin was the most exceptional man she'd ever met. He was strong. True. Noble. And how did she know? She had taken a deeper look. She could see the real man inside, down to the shadows that swirled like a blizzard in the darkest of nights.

"Mac, you're half-frozen. Look at your hands, they're as white as could be. And your face!" Selma's loving concern lapped at the edge of Carrie's senses, and she shook her head, rousting herself, and turned to fill more plates.

She felt Selma's probing interest and thought, I'm not the right woman for your son. I wish I was.

"Would anyone like a touch of the Irish?" Fred appeared in the archway with a fancy squat bottle of whiskey in hand.

"A touch of the devil is more like it, imbibing in spirits." Selma marched over to her husband and snatched the bottle from him, schooling her face so she actually looked almost stern. "Selfishness is a deadly sin, Fred. I'll save you from yourself by making you share this with me."

Fred landed a sweet kiss on his wife's cheek. "I'm lucky to be saddled with you, honey."

"Don't you know it." She added a generous dollop to her cup.

"C'mon, son, let's leave the women to their talk." Fred led the way through the archway and out of sight.

Carrie felt frozen as Mac's broad back and granite shoulders disappeared around the corner. The low rumbling of men's voices could be heard above the snap and crackle of the fire and the low-noted whistling of the kettle. The McKaslins' rare affection for one another lingered in the room in the cookie-scented air.

"A little of the Irish for you too, Carrie, and you'll sleep well and deep."

Since Selma tipped the bottle over the extra cup on the table, and rich liquid sparkled out of it, Carrie didn't protest. It was too late, and it wasn't the few drops of whiskey that troubled her.

Selma went on as she pulled out a chair and patted the seat. "Come, sit. I know exactly how hard it is to get a good night's sleep when you're traveling. It's a different room, a different bed, and the sounds and shadows are all wrong. That's always been my experience. Mac said you were stranded when the train came through the blizzard. It's a good thing you got off when you did—you would be stuck on that train between here and the summit."

Carrie slid into the chair. Stuck? She'd never considered that a train would be stopped for a blizzard. What would have become of her and Ebea if they hadn't been removed from that train? She shivered in horror thinking about it.

"Now, I knew right off that you were something special, you and your girl. Why else would my son bring you here?"

It wasn't right to let Selma continue to believe in what could never be true. "Mac wasn't exactly honest with you, Selma."

"Then it's what I suspected! The train didn't close down, did it?"

"No—"

"He brought you here to stay on purpose instead of by accident."

"No." Carrie laid her hand on the older woman's, hating that she was going to take away Selma's hope. "You have been as kind to me as my own mother, and it's not right for you to believe that Mac and I are involved. Mac never met me before. I was a stowaway. Ebea and I were stealing a ride in an empty freight car."

"You were stowaways? No, why, that can't be." Selma's face wreathed with confusion. "That doesn't sound right at all. I don't believe it."

"It's the truth. I've never stolen anything before in my life, and I'd never do anything to you and Fred." The wind batted at the window and scoured at the eaves, and she well remembered how bitterly cold it had been outside. What if she were tossed out? But there was dignity and integrity. What was a person without that? "If you want us to leave, I would understand."

Selma stood, her hand trembling. "I'm sorry, Carrie, I just don't like this. Not one little bit."

Chapter Seven

Mac froze in the doorway, not meaning to eavesdrop, but he couldn't seem to move forward or back or to turn off his hearing. He couldn't believe what his ma had said. His generous, loving mother sounded about as upset as he'd ever heard her.

A sinking feeling pulled him down, and he swallowed hard.

Carrie's soft words came next, quiet, and with nobility. "Then please give me just a moment. I'll go upstairs and gather our things. If you'll watch Ebea?"

Mac couldn't believe it. Where would she go?

"I noticed there was an inn not far from your shop." Carrie sounded sad, but there was no mistaking her strength. She cared about his mother; even when she was facing being cast out in the cold, she remained kind.

I've never met anyone like her. Admiration beat within him, slow like warm molasses. And it wasn't helping dim the physical attraction he felt to her.

Then his mother spoke. "Goodness, sit down. If you leave, that will only get more of my temper up. What kind of world is this, where women and their children have to stowaway on freight trains? And in this cold."

Mac leaned his forehead against the door, his pulse hammering through his skull. And he knew now why he had wanted to help Carrie and her child. Because he could not save another woman with a gentle manner and a kind heart.

The storm gusted, the howl of the wind wild and eerie like a woman's scream. Like a ghost from the past haunting him. Carrie was the reason Amelia had risen from the depths of his dreams and had begun troubling him during the waking day. The bundle in his shirt pocket was the only answer. The only way to right this.

He intended to go back and join his dad by the fire, when he heard Carrie's answer. "Selma, I want you to know that I'm not an irresponsible person. That's not why I was traveling with my child on a freight train in the middle of winter. I'm widowed. My husband was a teamster and died while doing his job."

"He was the bread earner and he left you with a small child and not much else, if my guess is right."

"True. Ebea was three, and there was no one to leave her with. My mother had fallen ill, and so we moved in to help take care of her. Her new husband never took a liking to me. The day after she died, he put us out of the house. I was lucky enough to attend her funeral, but I'd had no warning before we had to leave, and I had no money and nowhere to go."

Nowhere to go. Mac's chest squeezed with sympathy. He already knew what happened next, how she'd looked for work, but with a small child to care for and no family to leave her with, her choices were limited. Her wages would be too low to make more than a meager living.

Her troubled sigh said he'd guessed right. "We've been managing ever since, but right before I made the decision to stowaway on the train, we were camping in an abandoned yard of old boxcars. We weren't there long, only a couple of days, but I had to make a decision to find better circumstances. There were no jobs I could have—or would do—left in Minot."

"Honey, I don't need a confession. I see the way you take care of your little girl. I watched how hard you worked today, and my kitchen has never been this clean since it was new, thanks to you. No wonder you wound up where you did. Lord knows we can't get through this life alone. Not one of us."

"I just want you to know the truth. I don't want you to find out about my trouble with the railroad from someone else."

Mac felt the punch all the way to his soul. He ached for Carrie. Well he knew that no one was immune to adversity and tragedy. Life treated everyone the same, it was simply a matter of what and when. But like cream rising to the top, the quality of a person did, too, regardless of hardship. Carrie was one of those people.

He thought about that as he went back to the sofa and took the cast-off section of the territorial paper his pa had set on the cushions. The comforting rattle of the newsprint and the scent of ink settled him a little, but he had a hard time concentrating enough to read. He kept an ear to the kitchen, although he was too far away to hear anything.

He was waiting for her. It wasn't long before her footsteps padded in the hallway between the kitchen and parlor. He caught a brief glimpse of her through the archway as she carried her sleeping child in her arms, and then she was gone. The creak of the stairs marked her progress.

Then Ma came hurrying after her with warming irons, and her quick knell on the steps drowned out the sound of Carrie's gait. Mac swore he could feel her move overhead, as if that invisible lasso he'd felt last night was still tight around his chest. Right where his heart used to be.

Pa crinkled his paper, folded it for later and moaned as he straightened his tired back. "I suppose that's my hint. Time to get upstairs while I'm not too stiff to make it."

"Want me to bank the fires?"

"That would be a help, son." Fred McKaslin was no one's

fool, and he could read people well. What he sensed developing between his boy and the young lady Carrie was a true Christmas gift. "You stay as long as you like. That new territorial magazine came in yesterday's mail, if you wanna take a look at it. Or not." It was hard to sound offhand. Especially when an old man had hope.

Yes, he thought as he headed from the room. He'd seen that look before, about the time Mac was gettin' ready to propose to Amelia. Maybe time had healed the wounds in him. Maybe it was time Mac came in from the cold, from his self-banishment, and started living again.

A father always wanted the best for his son.

His wife of forty-two years gave him that smile he loved so well as she came from the extra bedroom. "Ebea's already out like a lamp. Had a busy day. Isn't it good to have a little one around again?"

"Sure is." He knew what she didn't say because he could feel her dreams. They were his, too. "It's a cold one tonight. Why don't you and me snuggle up under the quilts and try to get warm."

Desire was sweeter as time went by, and so was the feel of his wife's hand in his.

He had time to halt in the open doorway and spot Carrie inside the room, who was turning down the bedside lamp. A father had to matchmake where he could. "The fire's warm. Why don't you go down to the parlor and put up your feet. You've had a hard day, too."

It was the night before Christmas Eve, he thought as he escorted his wife to their room. It was the season for miracles to happen and for dreams to come true.

That's one thing off my chest. Carrie felt enormously lighter as she padded down the stairs, warm inside for the first time in more years than she could count.

She'd cleared her conscience, she'd put in a good day's work and that always felt right. Ebea was safe and warm and tucked in bed, exhausted by her fun day, as little children should be.

Tomorrow was Christmas Eve. Carrie tamped down her excitement. While Ebea had been at Annie's party, she had managed to sneak in a little shopping with the little bit of tip money Selma had insisted she keep. There were a few small but nice surprises for her girl's Christmas. And for the McKaslins, as well. She'd slip those under the tree now that no one was watching.

When she was just outside the archway, she heard the fire pop as if a handful of buckshot had been tossed on the flame. Imagining sparks showering out of the grate and onto the beautiful braid carpet, she bounded into the parlor.

She wasn't alone. Mac knelt before the hearth, broad of shoulder, sure of movement, flicking the fiery embers back into the grate. For the span between breaths, his back tensed. Aware of her.

Maybe I can manage not to gape at him. "Can I get you more tea?"

"Nope. One cup of Pa's Irish is enough." He sent the last coal skipping back into the hearth and he kept his back firmly toward her. "We need to talk."

"We do." She had things to say to him, too. While he was busy stirring the coals, she eased around the sofa and slipped the small packages beneath the tree. They were easily lost among so many brightly wrapped presents.

She chose a seat on the end of the sofa, waiting while he rose from squatting before the hearth, all six granite feet of him. He should have been a hard man, but he was not. She felt the shadows within him, saw the sorrow. And wondered.

"I got a telegraph from the railroad's Missoula office." Mac didn't sit; he didn't even come close to her. He remained standing at the hearth. "The agent there said they would rather receive some income instead of nothing. So arresting you wouldn't get them much of a profit."

Relief cracked through her like ice in a melting pond. She couldn't say anything. She eased back into the cushions, covered her face with her hands and let the realization shatter so many of her worries. Mac's help was one thing; the rail company's cooperation was unexpected.

"Now, there's another part to this. They want money."

"I know. There's the ring. I'll sell it at the jeweler's tomorrow first thing—"

"No, I can't let you part with your mother's ring." Mac's slow and easy gait padded on the carpet toward her. "They have agreed to let you make payments. And you have passage to Seattle."

I don't believe it. Some good luck at last. She'd been alone for so long. When Teddy started drinking heavily, and then her mother's long illness, she'd had so much work to do and responsibility to bear, it seemed that there had been no break. Only working and worrying without anyone to lean on or anyone to ask for help.

Mac cleared his throat. Her hands slipped from her face and she saw him there, on the other side of the couch, his big hands holding what looked like a train ticket.

A ticket to her new home. To hope. To a good future. She could feel it like the warmth in the air, scent it like the wood smoke from the fire. "This ticket is part of the debt I'll be paying off, right?"

"Uh, not really." He laid the envelope on the table between the sofas. "I paid for it. You and Ebea will be leaving when the tracks are cleared. Merry Christmas."

There were no words. She could think of none. The heart of this man awed her. Her regard for him carried her away like the force and fury of an avalanche roaring down a mountainside. It could not be stopped. It could not be outrun. It knocked her down and left her helpless as he simply walked away.

She had her pride. She had her dignity. She had respect for him. "I wish I could accept this, but I can't."

"Why would that be?"

"Because I believe a person pays their way in this world, one way or another. I appreciate the arrangement you made with the rail company. That is miracle enough for me."

"And this—" he tapped the envelope with his fingertips and knelt before her "—is this too much good coming your way?"

How did he know? She gasped at the pain it caused, this keen way he understood her. Hot liquid built behind her eyeballs and she blinked hard, willing those tears away. "I would rather not tempt fate."

"What if this is your fate?" He gathered the envelope and pressed it into her hands. The sorrow in his eyes was like the storm outside, growing darker and despairing as the night deepened.

If only you could be my destiny. The wish came like the first powdery flakes of snow in a winter squall, falling gently, peacefully and true. Her soul squeezed with the rhythm of her heart, with the music of it. It was as if her entire being ached for this man.

For the impossible. Suddenly she realized that the pain within her was not only her pain, but it matched the storm of grief she saw in his hopeless eyes. In his spent heart. In his broken soul.

"I cannot take this ticket, Mac. It's a lot of money."

"It's no great deal."

"It is to me." She laid the packet unopened on the cushion beside her. "Do you know how many hours I have to scrub floors to earn this?"

"No idea." Nor had he ever heard of a woman refusing money. But then again, Carrie surprised him in all kinds of ways, the good kind of surprise, and it heartened a man who was in sore need of it. "How much money do you have on you?"

"Uh…" She bit her bottom lip as she thought. "Not enough. It's upstairs—"

"I don't want it. That's not why I asked." Couldn't she see? Didn't she know?

How could she, he realized, when people took for granted what they had every day. It was only human, he supposed, to not realize what you had until it was gone. "You have less in your reticule by far than I have in the bank, and yet you are the richest person in this room."

Her eyes filled. And he could see she understood. She could comprehend now what he could not say. What he could never speak of for fear it would break him, and he would be nothing but shattered pieces.

"For your daughter's sake." It was all he could get out, for his voice cracked.

He strode from the room without stopping to read on her face what she thought of him. Without pausing for anything except to grab his coat and hat on the way out. He stood, teeth chattering, on the porch, struggling into his wraps rather than stay one second longer in that house.

To remain one second longer with her.

He gave thanks for the vicious winds that scoured him with the coldest of ice. It drove out the fire of feelings.

And the pain.

When he was as cold as the storm, as dark as the night, only then did he stride out into the gale. Half wishing the dangerous blizzard would knock him off course, leave him wandering the mountainside until he froze to death. Anything. Because he could not go back to that house and that woman.

Nor could he go to his house. There was only emptiness there lurking in the rooms, in his bed.

In his soul.

* * *

Carrie held the envelope for a long while. The weight of it, the reality of it was no reassurance. It felt wrong to accept so valuable a gift, and yet whatever loss Mac had endured made it clear why she had to: Ebea.

Inside the crisp white parchment were two third-class tickets to Seattle, an adult and child fare. Meal tickets. And a hundred-dollar bill.

She'd never been given such a valuable gift. The envelope became heavier in her hand, taking on weight as the fire in the grate burned down and the icy shadows took over the room. She didn't know what to do. Finally she slipped the packet onto one of the branches of the Christmas tree.

The house echoed around her as she cleaned up the kitchen and banked both fires. Then, leaving the cold and darkness behind her, she carried the last set of warming irons and a small lamp up the stairs.

Mac's gift of the tickets troubled her. Now everything felt wrong. Out of place. She didn't know why or how to make it right as she eased open the bedroom door and shone the edges of light onto the double bed where Ebea lay on her side, her brown braid curled on the white pillow slip behind her.

My own sweet angel. Mac was right. She was rich. Ebea was everything that mattered.

Love so bright it blinded her nudged her to the edge of the bed. She resisted the need to brush a kiss against her daughter's brow and to whisper more sweet-dream wishes. Ebea slept so soundly, without worry or cares. Her cherub's face was relaxed in sleep and her rosebud mouth was drawn with a hint of a smile as if she was lost in a good dream.

Carrie set the lamp on the bedside table, slid one warming iron at Ebea's feet to keep her toasty, and the other in the space on the mattress for her own feet. As she shivered out of her clothes and shook out her nightgown, she thought of Mac. He was out in the weather. Was he cold? Was he alone?

And then she realized what had been troubling her. It was the silence. The blizzard's winds had stopped.

The storm was over.

Mac stood in silence at the edge of town. Starlight gleamed down on him, the softest, lightest bluish glow as the thick mantle of clouds broke apart, sweeping to the southeast, racing fast with the wind. Leaving him in a growing brightness he neither wanted nor needed.

The town stretched out before him, polished like a black pearl. The snow reflected darkly the black sky, and the shimmer of stardust iced the slopes of roofs and the crests of snowdrifts piled along the hitching posts. The power of the night made him feel mighty alone. The contact of his boot against the hard-packed snow reported like rifle fire and echoed along the far spread of street ribboning out before him.

Like the snow beneath his feet, like the frozen earth beneath the snow, he did not feel. Not even the gusts of wind skating along the snow and sifting up whirlwinds of powdered sugar. When he headed off Mountain Street and onto the lane where he lived, the silent guard of fir and cedar that marched down the road seemed to come alive.

But it was only the wind stirring the snow-laden boughs and sending down soft chunks of flakes. Something cool brushed the side of his face, just above his muffler, and he saw a mist of white in his peripheral vision. A fan of blowing snow, nothing else was visible, but he *felt* a presence like moonlight, like wishes and dreams. Amelia. His heart was lost and he turned, staying his hand from reaching out to grasp what he knew could not be there.

Only thin air. The crisp icy snow swirled from the boughs to the earth. He kept on going. One foot before the other, while the night whispered through the trees. He passed homes on both sides of the street, their windows golden and curtains drawn, and inside families gathered.

He tried not to think of the husbands and wives, children and grandparents who lived in those homes. Were these families bursting with secrets of presents bought or made and hidden away? Were they celebrating tonight? As his parents had, snacking on the sweets made special every year for Christmastime and sharing them with Ebea and Carrie.

She'll be gone tomorrow. That would to be an odd relief. She was the only woman to stir his soul since Amelia. When she was gone, there would be no more of this agony. No more of this remembering and feeling.

But it was no victory.

He walked deep into the shadows and did not feel alone, although there was no one else stirring, no creature or human, on this lonely night. Every step he took, it was as if the past he'd buried had come alive. It was whispering in the night air. Echoing in his footsteps. Moving in the sift of snow drifting in eerie white snow devils.

Or maybe it was her voice—Amelia's voice—that lingered just beneath the tone of the wind. Words he could not let himself hear. She was a ghost he could not listen to, and the emptiness within him shattered like ice. It made no sense that something that no longer existed could break.

But it was as if the past was no longer silent. The first glancing beams of moonlight peered from behind the last of the retreating clouds like an accusing finger. Overhead, the great white orb watched as if from the heavens, scouting out the shadows, driving out darkness from the frozen land.

The guilt that haunted him took him back to that night when there was no peace or hope. To that exact moment when Amelia's screams ended at the abrupt blow of a rifle. His mind hadn't accepted it. He could still hear the echo of her scream, as he'd willed it to continue, for if her scream continued, then she could not be dead. She would be waiting for him somewhere in the dark and storm, waiting for him to rescue her. To keep his promise to always protect and love her.

He stumbled and saw not the past, but the cold path to his steps. Snow obliterated the walkway. Drifts leaned lazily against the side of the porch, blocking the brunt of the wind. At first he didn't see the footsteps trampling the more protected snow at his front doorway.

Someone was waiting for him. It was a woman huddling beneath a too-large coat. She tugged off her muffler when she spotted him and smiled.

Chapter Eight

Carrie clutched her coat around her, seeing Mac tense until he looked as harsh and unforgiving as the mountains spearing up into the sky behind him. He didn't want her here. She'd made a mistake. *I shouldn't have come.*

"You didn't go inside? You just stood out here in the cold?"

"I wouldn't invite myself into your home—"

"The door's unlocked. You could have frozen to death. Good thing for you I didn't take a longer walk. My mother. She told you where I lived, didn't she?" Fury, that's what he seemed to radiate like bitterness on the wind as he shouldered past her to push open the door. "Folks know to wait for me here. Build a fire or something."

Not only was he furious with her, but he refused to meet her gaze. His back remained squarely turned to her as he knelt in the dark cave of his home. She heard the rattle of a stove door and the clank of a metal poker. Light flickered to life as he stirred the coals, and grew, while he added slivers of kindling and then thick chunks of wood.

She shivered, debating. Was it better to leave now? Or to try and explain and anger him more?

The envelope in her pocket felt too heavy to run off with.

She simply could not take the coward's route and leave. No matter how cranky his mood.

"Are you comin' in?" He didn't sound as if he wanted her to as he banged the stove door shut.

Well, it didn't matter. She'd come here for a reason, and it would only take a moment to do what she had to. Somehow, she made her feet move forward and take her out of the frigid night and into the utter darkness. It was too dark to see anything. Not even Mac as his footsteps knelled away from her and more deeply into the house. She slipped the envelope from her pocket.

"Don't you have a child you should be with?" A clank of a lantern hood punctuated his words like anger.

"She's fast asleep and safe as can be in your parents' home. I intended only to come for a moment."

He struck a match and lit a battered lantern. Orange flame flickered to life and he adjusted the wick so it wouldn't blow out. "Shut the door, would you?"

"Sure, on my way out." Her words came crisp, not harsh or sharp or shrewish, and the only sign she was pissed at him was the knell of her shoes on the wood floor as she headed for the open doorway.

She meant to leave. Well, good riddance. He couldn't tolerate this, seeing her alone like this. He had to hold on to his anger because without it he had no other shield to protect the places so broken within. She'd dismantled everything else, shattered them like the ice chunks beneath her feet. He grappled around in his mind for the right combination of hard words to send her from his sight forever.

Then he noticed the white envelope on the edge of the table. The envelope he'd left with her. Damn it, didn't she know this was best for all of them? How much more did he have to explain? How much more of the past would I have to feel and in the feeling of it, tear himself apart? What good would come from that for either of them?

Because rage was safest, he wallowed in it. Snatched the envelope and struggled down the need to toss it at her. "I thought you agreed to take this."

"Not take, no." That chin of hers hiked up, determination and steel. "I'm returning the hundred-dollar bill. I don't feel right about that. I know you mean it in the nicest way, but I refused to accept payment from your parents for my work in their shop, so how can I take money from you?"

"It's not like that."

"Then what is it like?"

Couldn't she understand? He needed to get her away from him before he shattered and not even anger could protect him. He'd been in that place before, holding Amelia's lifeless body, and he did not want to feel that killing sorrow again. He could not let her close, let her in. For he had no heart left to give. Even the places where it had once been ached with torment.

"Just leave." It was what he needed. The moonlight was magical this night, and if he believed in miracles and happily-ever-afters, then he would give credence to the way the light painted her with a platinum glow. Rare and beautiful and everything precious in this world. Everything that was tearing him apart.

"Not until you know this, too." She stood like a priestess of old, draped in light and honor. "I can accept the train passage only because I intend to pay you back."

"No!"

She was unbowed by his thundering outburst. "It will take time, but I *will* do this."

"I won't accept your money." His fists bunched. "I won't."

"Fine. But if you do not, then I will send the payments to your parents to hold for you." Calm, she refused to be swayed. "It's the right thing."

He wavered inside, for the anger was not enough to protect him from this. From her goodness. From a woman who would do the right thing no matter what, the same as he. He felt the moonlight shift in the room, infinitesimally, but a shift all the same.

When he looked down the edge of the shaft was nudging his boot, as if reaching out to him, as if inviting him. He felt the darkness within him crack apart like deep drifts on a mountainside. The rumbling reverberated through him, shaking his soul. He could feel the last wall begin to crumble apart. He did not want it. Could not survive it.

And then there was darkness and she was there, her fingertips cool against his face. "What's wrong? You need to sit down."

"I need to stay far away from you before I give in to this." He fisted his hands so tight, the bones burned, stretched to the limit.

"Into what?" She gazed up at him with guileless eyes, unaware.

How would she not know the torture she put in him? His last defense was crumbling now—there was no more anger. And like the thick layers of snow giving way down a mountain, he felt it fall. Felt the sheer down to his soul.

He was exposed, with no way to hold back his soul. The sorrow he'd never been able to face, the loss that haunted him so on this night broke way and tumbled, too.

She was speaking; he could not make out the words, only the tenderness of her alto voice. Her hands were on his shoulders nudging him backward.

He only knew he was sitting when he felt the edge of the chair digging into the backs of his knees. Her fresh female scent, her rose shampoo and the rustle of her flannel petticoats filled his senses until his head echoed with those sounds, with her. Only with her.

Her kiss brushed his cheek, and it was a touch of heaven. A touch he had no defenses against. With a turn of his chin, their lips met in a tentative caress that made every exposed piece of him yearn. Her mouth was warm satin. Her taste like sweet cream and temptation.

How could he resist? His hands unfisted and he plunged his fingers deep into her chestnut hair, cradling her nape as he tipped her head back. It was no polite kiss, but rather a thorough kiss that he gave her. The way a man kissed the woman he desired more than anything.

She responded with a helpless moan, the kind that said she desired him, too, and wanted him in the same way. That was not what he expected. He tore away, breathless, his blood burning. His gaze had adjusted to the darkness so he could see the deep pools of her eyes. The shadows of her face.

But he could see more of her, into her, to her secret wishes.

"I cannot make promises." He choked out the words. Longing raged within him. He had to be smart. He had to do the right thing. "I have nothing to offer you but tonight."

She pressed a kiss to his cheek and did not answer. The seconds stretched like minutes. Her hand splayed against his chest, as if to feel the rise and fall of his breathing and the crazy speed of his pulse.

"I have been so lonely for so very long." Need shone in her words like a small, forgotten light. "I have been lonely for you all of my life."

She didn't care if he could not give her forever. She could feel the wound within him that pulled and tugged at her with its darkness and torment. Carrie didn't know how it was that she could feel his heart like her own. She only knew that she could. What a rare connection they had.

When she found his mouth with hers, it was her answer. She would love him no matter what. For this night only.

"I want *you*," he choked out, his hands at her shoulders tender. "No one else. No one has ever done this to me."

"Or to me." Whatever this force was rolling through her, it could not be true love, could it? Real love was something nurtured over time, grown like a seedling to a flower; not created suddenly out of circumstance and need.

But it *was* true love that spilled through her. And wonder that left her breathless as she surrendered to his hands tugging at the buttons of her coat. To the weight of his big granite body easing her back onto the pile of their coats. To the nudge of his knee between her thighs, so he could move between them.

How amazing it was to hold him like this. To cradle his jaw in her hands and truly kiss him. To be lost not only in need, but in rare affection. She'd been lonely for so long that it did not feel wrong to let this happen. To accept the cool air on her skin and the heat of his mouth on her breasts. Or the weight of him over her and then, wonderfully, inside her. He joined their bodies, and more, on this night of darkness.

And of light.

She came back to herself slowly, and it was like drifting on a summer cloud. Complete.

Mac had drifted off, his head pillowed on her breasts. His dark hair tumbled everywhere and was black against her skin. The moon had kindly managed to ebb around a crack in the curtains, giving her enough illumination to see his face. To memorize the hard shape of his mouth. The cut of his chin. The slope of his nose.

She'd never known what a dear thing it was to hold a man she loved so entirely like this as he slept naked upon her. She didn't want to move or wake him. She wanted the night to go on without end.

But that was impossible, and she had responsibilities. It was one thing to leave her daughter sleeping in a house she knew was safe and with reliable grandparent-types just down the hall. It was another to spend the night away making love to a man who was not her husband. She could not stay much longer.

But how can I leave? Her heart wrenched even as she thought about slipping out from beneath him and leaving for good. Forever.

Not yet, she thought, clinging to him. *A few more minutes and then I'll go. Then I'll leave him.*

She learned by heart the feel and curves of his shoulders. She let her fingertips memorize the muscled plane of his back. He stirred in his sleep, rubbing his face against the inside curve of her breast, and love exploded ever more, ever brightly within her. How was she going to let him go?

She had to. It was only sensible. He wasn't hers to keep. But that didn't make it easier as she took one last moment to savor the privilege of being with him. She breathed in the winter-night scent of him, pressed a kiss to the crown of his head, and moved carefully out from beneath him, cradling his head. Laying him down in the soft pile of wool and sheepskin.

As the night deepened and the hint of moonlight moved away from the gap in the curtains, she tugged on her clothes. He slept so deeply, he did not dream or stir, so she left her coat on the floor beneath him and took a lighter winter jacket of his that hung on the pegs by the door.

Quietly she added wood to the stove to keep him warm while he slept the rest of the night through and pulled the quilt off the top of his bed. Covering Mac was the last loving thing she could do for him. She tucked him in, ignoring the twisting of her soul.

Time to go. Every piece of her yearned to stay with him forever. To keep this night from ending. *I love this man so.* She felt the strength of it fill her and give her the courage she needed to open the door. She took one last look of him asleep and at peace.

Then she walked into the night, alone.

The brush of a kiss woke him. He didn't bolt awake; he didn't feel suffocated by a nightmare he couldn't end and couldn't forgive. When he opened his eyes, he saw the hint of a shadow and thought he heard a woman saying goodbye.

But the door was already closed. The first graying of dawn crept through the curtains to diminish the shadows in the house. The fire was nearly burned out. There were no woman's clothes on the floor where he'd tossed them in his rush. No sign of Carrie or her footsteps hurrying away.

He stood, naked, ignoring the cooling air in the kitchen, and pulled back the drapes. There was no one. Nothing. A faint dusting of new snow fell, and the steps and walkway from his house to the lane looked unbroken by tracks. Whenever Carrie had left, it had been a long while, and yet her love remained.

Chapter Nine

In the early hours before a winter dawn, Carrie tried to keep her mind on her work in the bakery's kitchen. It wasn't easy. She might have walked away from Mac, but her heart had not. Love that should have been easily extinguished was not. It burned more brightly within her as the minutes turned to hours. A love that Mac did not want. A love he could not give back to her.

Concentrate on your work, Carrie. Rousting herself, she first checked to make sure Ebea was still sound asleep and then went back to spreading festive red frosting across the almond-butter snowmen, adding color to row after row of red Santa caps. She worked until the cookies laid out across the entire table were red decked.

Selma bustled by, reversed and peered over Carrie's shoulder. "Oh, you've got a talent for this."

"I've made a lot of mistakes, but luckily I've been able to hide them with more frosting."

"Not even I can tell it. We ought to hire you on." Selma hurried along and disappeared out of sight around the partition to where her husband worked at the ovens. Soon, the low murmur of their conversation filled the kitchen as pleasantly as the scent of the baking cinnamon rolls.

Wouldn't it be wonderful to work here? Carrie traded the red frosting for a bowl of green and settled it into the crook of her arm. Wouldn't this be a fun job to have? A person would spend all day decorating cookies, taking orders, talking to customers and enduring the kindness of the McKaslins. Yep, it would be a hard row to hoe, but she would love to have the opportunity.

Except for Mac, she would stay and accept Selma's offer of a job. But he didn't want her to stay. As sad as that was, he had been very clear. He had nothing lasting to offer her.

If she stayed, there could only be disaster. She loved him; that could not be helped. Love wasn't something logical or practical or governed by choice. But a woman's behavior was. While she'd made love to a man she wasn't married to, and even if it had been the most thrilling joy she'd known, it was not something she would repeat. She had her dignity and her reputation and her daughter to think of. And her future would be based on what was best for Ebea.

Surely she could find something like this in Seattle? There were bakeries there. And diners and hotel restaurants and even logging-camp cooking opportunities. She need not scrub floors and other people's bed linens for a living.

She dipped the spreading knife into the frosting and began to ice the snowmen's jackets. The work was pleasing, and the almond scent of the frosting made her stomach growl. She worked fast because she wanted to get these dozens of cookies finished before she had to leave. The work crews had gone out in the night; she'd heard from Fred, who'd gone to the depot to ask. They were expected back by midmorning.

The train would soon follow, and she and Ebea would be on it.

Selma returned. "Lovely. I couldn't have done the job better myself. You know, if you stayed on, you could get to know Mac better."

Carrie felt the older woman's probing gaze. There was no way she could know what had happened last night, was there? No, surely it didn't show. Although remembering the wonderful experience of lying naked beneath the man made her face burn. "Stay on? I don't know if that's a good idea."

"I think it is. He's so alone, you know." Selma shifted the bowl of sugar icing she carried to her other arm so she could lean in close. "He was a Range Rider, you know. He lost his wife six years ago. She was seven months pregnant when she was shot by a fugitive who wanted revenge on him."

No. The knife fell from her fingers. Mac had been married? No wonder he was so wounded inside. "A loss like that could destroy a person."

"It nearly did." Selma patted Carrie's wrist. "But you have put a spark into his eyes that hasn't been there in some time. It's like he's coming alive again. Do you know what that means to his mother?"

Carrie's gaze slid to the corner where her little girl slept bundled warmly on a cushion. "I can imagine how much you want Mac to find happiness again."

"That's right. And you, my dear, ought to stay right here. It's not good for a woman to be alone in this world, and with a little one to raise. If you stay here, you'll have us. We'll help you look after her. You can work right here. We'll fix up the upstairs rooms so you'll have your own place."

"What would Mac say about your generous offer?"

"He'll come around. And in the meantime, it'll be good for you to stay. Good for Ebea."

"I'm sorry. I wish I could accept. There's nothing I would like more than to be here. But—" Carrie's mind was spinning. No wonder he couldn't get close again. She hurt for him. She grieved for him. She loved him enough to give him what he needed. "I'll remember you always, Selma."

"Oh, we needn't lose touch. We can write. Surely you will

want to let me know how your Ebea is doing. I'm awful fond of her. Only my daughter has made me a grandma. My sons are too busy, off chasing their dreams, to settle down. Maybe I could be an honorary grandma to your Ebea. If you would let me."

"I couldn't think of anyone better." Her heart melted as Selma brushed a kiss on her cheek.

No, she would never forget these people. She would always be grateful to the forces of nature and of fate that had brought her here for a brief time.

Mac eased the shop's glass door shut behind him, careful not to ring the bell. The jingle would bring his mother, and she was busy enough on this Christmas Eve morning with so many orders to prepare. Besides, he wasn't quite ready to see Carrie. Or to tell her the news. So he was careful to keep his boots from making much noise as he hung her coat on the hooks by the door.

And then he saw her. She was like the first light of morning after a bitter December storm. When the nights are the longest and darkest of the year and the dawn sky is all the more crisp and clear. When dawn comes like magic over the frozen land and the world is utterly still.

That's how she makes me feel, he thought as he unbuttoned his coat and watched as she worked at decorating. She brought to him the still, refreshed peace of a winter's dawn.

Wanting a better view of her, he angled toward the potbellied stove and began peeling off his mittens and muffler and cap. Yep, he could see her better from this vantage, over the end of the counter, through the doorway and into the kitchen where she worked at a table with dozens of cookies spread out before her.

He could not deny he cared for her. He could not deny he thought her beautiful. Her thick, chestnut hair was back in a braid and wrapped in a coronet around her head, and her thick bangs curled across her forehead and framed the wide brilliance of her eyes.

Yes, he could look at her for the rest of his days and only want to gaze upon her more. This morning, her face was soft and relaxed; the circles beneath her eyes were gone. She looked happy with her cheeks flushed from the heat of the kitchen, and she cradled a big mixing bowl in the crook of her arm.

Why his gaze remained on the bowl had nothing to do with the red-tinted frosting she was scooping out with a spreading knife. No. The rim of the bowl was pressed against the round curve of her breast. Longing thundered through him. Images of last night, of loving her, caressing her and being joined with her hit him like a punch. Tenderness for her thrummed through him hard and sweet. *I want her again.*

The toll of his father's gait hammered from the back of the kitchen, and Pa's bellowing baritone carried easily through the shop, although he remained out of sight. "I got more boxes folded up for you, my lovely wife. Will you let me grab one of those buns?"

"Oh, you! Keep your hands to yourself."

"You can't blame me. Yours are the sweetest buns I've ever seen."

"Stop! You may have one of the iced ones *if* you will be decent!" Her laughter came like lark song and there was a smacking sound, and Mac could easily picture Ma playfully swatting his pa.

He was surprised how he could feel their happiness wrapping around him. It came warm and comforting, instead of something too intense that made him want to head for the door. Strange how he no longer felt hollow or empty, and he knew just who was responsible.

He felt bright. And the brightness within him intensified until it was pain the closer he came to her. She was absorbed in her work, and the furrow in her forehead and the way she bit her bottom lip in concentration only made him ache all the more. He couldn't keep staring at her like this. Ma would be coming in from the ovens any minute and she would know with one look what had happened last night. And how he felt about Carrie.

But the truth was, even if he was again painfully alive, he had no heart to give.

He cleared his throat and hoped he would sound as he always did. The sheriff at work, in control, as hard as stone and not a man falling in love. "I see my folks are keepin' you busy."

She did not startle. There was no hitch in her movements. She'd known he was approaching all along. Did she, he wondered, feel this connection, too?

"I knew exactly how many orders your parents had to have ready today, since I helped take them. I thought that it was the least I could do to help out until the train comes."

"That's why I'm here."

"The crews are in?"

"They sent a telegraph to Jed. I happened to be over checking on their progress."

Had he been over there checking to see how soon I could leave? Carrie set the bowl down with careful diligence. Her hand was shaking. Her entire being was unsteady. He didn't want her.

You knew that last night before you stayed, Carrie. She couldn't deny it. He'd been honest with her all along. And with what Selma had told her about his wife's death, it was understandable. Sometimes a heart broke too deeply.

She loved him; it was that simple. She could not help it. She could not will her heart to stop feeling and to stop filling with longing for this man. The most loving thing she could do was to give him what he needed. And unless he showed any sign of needing her to stay, then she would be on that train.

It was hard to believe that the man filling the door frame as easily as he filled her senses would one day be only a fond memory.

Since the icing was finished, she turned to the final touches on the cookies. The tiny black candies made perfect cheerful eyes, and she added them to the blank snowman faces. "How long before the train arrives?"

"You have a half hour or so."

There was nothing in his tone to give her a clue. He sounded relieved that she was going.

"Good," she said brightly. Falsely. "I'll have time to finish these cookies."

"Fine then." He jammed his hands in his pockets and his gaze strayed to the front door. "I'll…uh…carry over your bag for you. I'll stop by the house in about fifteen, twenty minutes."

"I have my satchel here, and anyway, I can carry my own bag." She held her heart still. It was the hardest thing yet she'd had to do. But she was no weak woman, and if she cried at losing him, then it would be in private. "As much as I care about you, Ebea and I are not your responsibility."

He reeled back as if she'd struck him. For a moment it seemed as if he was hurt. As if he truly cared for her. For an instant, hope flamed to life within her soul. *Does he want me? Is it possible last night has changed his heart?*

Then his face turned to stone, his stance to steel, and she had his answer. She watched him pivot on his heel and walk away.

Every knell of his step rang through her like a funeral bell. The door whispered open and closed with a swift bang. He was gone. And since she would be leaving in thirty minutes' time, she would never see him again.

She could hear the sound of her heart breaking, piece by tiny piece.

"Goodness, is Mac gone already?" Selma appeared from the back of the kitchen, her cheeks flushed from the oven's heat and an armful of packed boxes to go on the racks. "He came with news of the train, didn't he? Oh, of course he did. I just can't stand you leaving us. Can't you stay, at least until after Christmas?"

"I would love to, but I have to take this train."

"Alone is no way to spend Christmas Eve. I'll worry for you dreadfully."

"No, please don't worry. Ebea and I are on our way to a better future because of you and your family. We will be just fine. Have a merry Christmas, Selma."

Tears filled the older woman's eyes. "You too, sweetie."

It was Christmas Eve. She gathered up a wish in her heart, one for staying here with these people and for having Mac's love. But she made no wish after all.

She and Ebea would spend Christmas Eve on the train instead of in the McKaslins' parlor with the lovely tree and even lovelier people. They would light all those beautiful candles come dusk, and she could only imagine how each crystal ornament would twinkle like a star of wonder on this sacred night when miracles were possible.

But she'd already been given a gift of grace. Ebea lay still sleeping, wrapped warmly in the corner. A child was not a gift to take lightly, and so there could be no more wishful thinking. Not when she had so much.

Not even a frigid walk through town, with the windchill slicing through to his bones, could rub out Carrie's words from his mind. *As much as I care about you, we are not your responsibility.* Maybe because it was an insult, and because he was a man who took responsibility seriously.

Or maybe her words stung his conscience because she hadn't said them cruelly. He could still see the lift of her chin and the quiet dignity that seemed to hold her up as she'd spoken.

Her words reminded him that she'd been taking care of herself and her daughter alone for a long time. And he'd come along and helped her with the railroad and with finding shelter. He'd behaved as a friend to her and, last night, as a lover. When in truth he had no heart to give her. He'd been honest about that, but he'd made love with her all the same.

It hadn't been enough. He needed her still. Not with a selfish physical lust that was easily slaked, but with all the emptiness within him that had hurt for so long. When he'd made love to her, joining his body with hers, he'd felt joy like dawn come to an endless night. Like calm come after an endless storm. Like color to a life of gray and shadow.

The town was busy, yet the tone of the train's whistle blasted like the wrong note above the clatter from the busy road. From his vantage just north of downtown, he could see the black locomotives gleaming in the bright morning sun, the pair of stacks billowing coal smoke like thick black snakes undulating across the cold blue sky.

"Merry Christmas, Sheriff," Tom Farley called as he swept off the boardwalk in front of his mercantile. "Hear you're a courtin' man these days."

"You heard wrong, my friend."

"Well, the rumor is you've taken a sparking to the new gal your folks hired. She came into my store yesterday and picked up a few things. Nice as could be. It's wise for a man to take his time when he's courtin'. Marriage is a grave matter."

Not at all in the mood to continue that conversation, he tipped his hat and kept walking. "Merry Christmas to you and your family, Tom."

Now he'd have to live down the gossip that would probably go on for a good month, or at least until something more interesting came along.

It was to be expected. It was hard to keep secrets in a small town. And it wasn't as if Tom had been wrong. He *had* taken a sparking to Carrie. She was good and decent and kind. She worked hard and with dignity. And she was the only woman who could make the places gone dead within him come to life.

Because that was what she'd done. He could no longer deny it. No longer lie to himself. What he'd thought was impossible had happened. He'd grieved Amelia long and true, and he would save her now if he could. But he no longer wanted to live like a condemned man. His heart yearned to be let loose from this guilt.

The trouble was that the only person who could forgive him was buried.

"Mac!" His ma jabbed open the bakery door. She must have been watching him come down the street. "Do you know what I noticed hanging on the hook at the house this morning? Your other coat."

How was it that a mother's voice didn't need to rise in anger to carry the full weight of accusation? His step faltered. He spun toward the depot. Between the line of buildings at the intersection, he could clearly see the train loading up passengers from the platform.

Carrie would be in the crowd. And the thought of her seared his heart like noon sunlight on snow. It was too much, too intense, and he wanted to close up against the brightness.

"Mac." Ma squinted at him, not fooled, and if a look could kill, hers would at least inflict a serious wound or two. "You love her."

"No." His denial came quick. Too quick. "Love her? I barely know her."

"Love is about *knowing*…here." His mother covered her heart. "Why are you letting her go? After losing Amelia, I would have thought you would know how rare it is to find true love."

Across the way, the train gave two long blasts, a warning of its impending departure. *Just let her go, man.* He only had a few more minutes, and then life could go back to the way it was. The way he wanted it.

Except it's never going to be the same, you know that. The instant he'd reached out to her in need, she had changed him. In loving her, she had changed his life. Healed him. And like the sun rising in the sky, more bright and bold with each incremental step, Mac could not pretend he lived in shadow. Not anymore.

He gazed at the train with longing. Wishing, just wishing he could hold on to her forever.

"Forgive yourself." Ma pressed a kiss to his cheek. "Please. It's not forsaking Amelia. Don't you think that wherever she is, she would want you to be happy? That she doesn't grieve over every day of life that you're wasting?"

Maybe that's why he could feel Amelia and the past so strongly lately, clinging to him like a damp fog. Was it her he had felt last night? Her kiss to his cheek, releasing him from his failure?

"Son, love is the greatest miracle. And it's Christmas Eve, the very day of miracles. Forgive yourself, for Amelia's sake. And grab hold of this new chance for love and a life with Carrie. It's a Christmas gift from above." Ma kissed his cheek again.

Go to her. It was not his mother's words he heard. It was Amelia. It was forgiveness.

It was summer's touch in the heart of winter.

The train's long bellow called through town. As the wheels began to grind on the metal tracks, he took off at a dead run. He dodged horses and sleighs on Mountain Street and did not yield to the teamsters at the intersection.

Running like crazy, he leaped onto the boardwalk, circled a gaggle of women shoppers chatting and hiked up the steps two at a time until he was pushing past the crowd leaving the train.

He skidded to a stop. The last cars were pulling away from the end of the platform, leaving with a thick cloud of smoke behind.

And nothing else.

His heart fell as he watched the last car of the train's procession speed away down the tracks. His heart, alive and beating full of love and hope, took another mortal blow.

She was gone. It was as if the sun overhead went out and would never shine again. The shadows in his soul seemed to thicken.

And then he heard the smallest sound, a woman's voice, dulcet and low like a hymn on Sunday morning. Like forgiveness and second chances all rolled up into one perfect gift.

The smoke thinned and he saw the faint outline of a woman in a too-large coat, huddling in the crisp wind, with a small child at her side.

No, it can't be her. He didn't believe his eyes. The smoke had lifted more and *she* was there in full color, adorned with sunlight, tears glistening on her cheeks.

"Carrie." She'd stayed. Joy exploded within him as she flew into his arms. He lifted her up, swirling her around, holding her close to his heart. Her love filled him like the first shards of sunlight so welcome and amazing, it blotted out all darkness, every shadow, every sadness.

"I saw you running to us from my window seat." She swiped at her eyes and laughed as her feet touched back to board plank. "I was sitting there, so sad because we were leaving and you didn't want me. And then there you were, running like a wild man down the street, and I thought maybe it was worth the risk of getting off the train while we could. Because I've never known this kind of love before."

"You really love me?"

"Yes. More than I know how to say." She glanced down at her daughter, who had sat on the satchel, watching with big, questioning eyes as if she knew, too, that so much depended on Mac's answer. "What I don't know is if you feel the same way for me."

How could she even ask him that? Mac thought of last

night, how desperately he'd needed her, and how at peace and whole he'd become after lovemaking. With every breath of his being, he needed her as his wife, his lover, his best friend. "You don't know? You came like a miracle and breathed life into my heart. I love you with all that I am. Forever."

"That's how I love you." Joy lifted her up like the clouds floating by. She knew exactly how lucky she was to have this man to love and cherish.

The brush of his lips to hers was like magic. A cold wind blew her into the shelter of his strong arms. His embrace was like coming home after a long journey to a place that was safe and warm and dear. And remembering that desperate night she'd first stepped foot on this platform, she gave thanks for the miracle of his love.

Tiny, crystal flakes sifted from a clear sky, brushing her cheek, as if with the sweetest answer.

Epilogue

Christmas Eve, one year later

"Would you like some eggnog, sweetheart?"

Carrie stirred from her thoughts to take the offered cup and smiled at her husband towering over her. Mac returned her smile, without shadows. Only with quiet, assured joy. It was a comforting sight, as always. Deciding to marry this man two months after meeting him was the best decision she had ever made. "Come sit with me, handsome."

"I'd love to, beautiful."

He glanced over his shoulder to check what the rest of his family were doing. His grandparents were playing chess in front of the fire. Ebea was with Ma and Pa, who were busy in the kitchen. His nephews were busy shoving each other beneath the tree, trying to count all their presents. And his sister was thumbing through sheet music at the piano.

Mac gave his beautiful wife a full-fledged kiss that came straight from his soul. The kind that he knew would curl her toes and make them both anticipate hurrying home to their new house when the celebration here was through. They would put Ebea to bed and head down the hall to their room together.

"Making a Christmas wish?" Carrie was laughing, her face pink with pleasure. "Because I may be making the same wish."

"Babe, that's what I'm counting on." He set his cup aside and knelt before her, the palm of his hand settling on her slightly rounded stomach. "Isn't that how we got you into trouble?"

"I don't think it's trouble. It's more of, well, proclaiming how in love we are. Have I told you lately how happy you've made me?"

"It couldn't be as happy as you make me." Reverently, he cupped the side of her face with the palm of his hand. Ten months ago he'd made her his wife, and each day of their marriage had been better than the last.

"Ma, look! I helped with these." Ebea came running from the kitchen, for she was pretty much inseparable 'from her grandmother, and showed off the gingerbread man she'd decorated. "Pa, I made mine with a badge just like yours. The gingerbread village we're makin' needs a sheriff, too."

"You've done a great job, sweetie." Carrie beamed with pride. Her daughter had flourished over the last year here with a real extended family to love her and a father who took his job of providing for her and protecting her seriously. "Are you going to make more?"

"Yep!" Ebea ran off, and the ornaments on the tree swung at her passing, a few clinking together as they swayed.

The first notes of "Jingle Bells" pealed from the corner, a lively, skilled rendition of the cheerful song that seemed to send joy spiraling through the house. In the kitchen the oven door slammed. The boys stopped rummaging and wrestling beneath the tree and dashed to the piano to shove and push each other there. Ebea followed her grandparents from the kitchen out into the parlor.

"The ham is almost done," Selma announced with holiday cheer. "Should we light the tree?"

"Yes! Yes!" Ebea clapped her hands and Fred lit the first candle.

Like magic the soft candlelight burnished the pine needles and graceful boughs. Light gleamed off crystal and sang off porcelain and filled the entire room with an angel's solemn glow.

"Merry Christmas, my husband." Carrie leaned into his touch. "May every Christmas find us happier than the last."

"On my honor, my love." He searched her lovely face, seeing clear into her soul, and then he kissed her, long and sweet.

* * * * *

THE CHRISTMAS GIFTS

Kate Bridges

Chapter One

British Columbia
December 19, 1887

Even from a distance too far to see his face, Maggie Greerson knew who he was. She recognized the swivel of the broad shoulders beneath the ten-pound, buffalo-fur coat, and the sheer strength of him as he gripped the lines of his husky dogs and urged the dogsled team to go faster. It figured he'd be out in a storm when everyone else in the town of Goldstrike was waiting for it to subside. He thrived on danger and sought solitude while Maggie did everything she could to avoid it.

"Look at that." Maggie's nine-year-old niece, Rebecca, pointed out the window of Maggie's store, the Spice Shop. She stood on a wooden crate beside Maggie, peeling orange rinds for the citron basket. "It's Saint Nicholas from the North Pole. He's bringin' Christmas gifts."

"No, darling, it's much too early for Saint Nicholas."

It was near closing time and Maggie rushed to finish. Up until this point, it had been a wonderfully busy day. So busy that Maggie hadn't had a chance to stop and think about what was missing in her life. But sooner or later, this time of year always brought out those sentiments.

Behind them, Maggie's two sisters, their mother and five other nieces and nephews were rehearsing for Maggie's busiest day of the year—December twenty-fourth. The children were softly laughing and singing "The Twelve Days of Christmas."

Maggie was looking forward to the twenty-fourth, when she'd have carolers in her store and mulled wine for the shoppers. They'd all pitch in to make charity boxes filled with food and firewood for the poorer families in the valley. Maggie was proud that her store was a neighborhood gathering place, packed with flavorings from the Orient, a place for women to exchange recipes and try her version of plum pudding.

Maggie hummed along to the children's voices. Surrounded by customers and the fragrance of cinnamon sticks she was arranging at the front windows, she peered into the snowstorm. Red-velvet ribbons dangled off the curtains, framing her view. Ice, a quarter-inch thick, glazed the bottom lip of the windowpanes while a crackling fire kept everyone warm.

At first he appeared as a distant blur on the windswept horizon. Moving along the east bank of the Kootenay River, cradled by the jagged Rocky Mountains, he was a lone man racing behind his dogsled team.

James Fielder of the North-West Mounted Police.

Maggie often saw him dashing across the countryside. Now, as the team plodded closer and he loomed larger, she could see him pressing a gloved hand beneath a bulge in his fur coat. What was he carrying?

He'd probably been ice fishing or checking his traps or a dozen other reckless things that could have waited. And soon it would be dark. Already, the sun was sinking behind the western ridge, and long blue shadows crossed the snow.

Maggie tapped affectionately at one of Rebecca's blond

pigtails and tried to get into the spirit of ten lords a-leaping. "That's Sergeant Fielder," Maggie explained.

"I guess he's going to the fort."

"That's likely right."

The Spice Shop sat on the outskirts of town, sandwiched between the bootmaker and tinsmith shops, facing an open field with a good view of the athletic Mountie. Although the gold rush of twenty years ago had long since dried up, the town of Goldstrike remained a vital link for the lumber camps and coal mines farther north.

It would take several more minutes for James to pass Goldstrike on his way to Fort Steele, which was located a mile south in the smaller town of Galbraith's Ferry. Because it was difficult to watch him without thinking about the past, Maggie went back to rearranging cinnamon sticks. Then she wiped her hands on her apron and shook the bowl of orange peels.

"Rebecca, you did a wonderful job with this orange peel. Would you please help your mother at the till, wrapping the packages, while I measure peppercorns for the schoolteacher?"

As slender as a stalk of growing corn, Rebecca gave her a wide smile and tore off while James barged back into Maggie's thoughts. Five years ago on an afternoon as windy and stormy as this, he had laughingly sung her this very song, and then unexpectedly at five gold rings and four calling birds, he'd lowered his face and brushed his lips across hers.

It had lasted right through to the partridge in the pear tree.

But at that time she had been engaged to another man, and James had quickly backed off.

He'd enlisted with the Mounties and trained in Edmonton, returning only recently to serve in the temporary outpost of Fort Steele. The fort had been set up by the Mounties from Alberta district to peacefully settle tensions between white settlers and a band of Indians, which they'd accomplished. The company of roughly eighty men would likely return to Alberta in the coming year because British Columbia had set up their own police force. She wondered where James would go.

He had a nice singing voice, she recalled.

She tingled at the recollection of his kiss. Swallowing firmly, she slowly raised her chin to glance outside. She still couldn't see his face but knew in these past five years, his looks hadn't changed much. He was still as dark from the wind and sun, his black hair as thick as it had ever been, his jaw as resolute. He looked taller as he raced along the snow, but it was maybe because of his big boots and his massive proportion to the dogsled.

With a clap to her apron, Maggie walked behind the counter.

"Are you sure you should be letting the little one handle the vegetable peeler, Maggie? It's sharp." The schoolteacher, Mr. Furlow, adjusted his peak cap over his gray hair and watched Maggie scoop peppercorns into a burlap sack.

"Absolutely." The pepper smelled sharp in Maggie's nostrils. "Rebecca's been handling it for a year now. Last year, she was cooking over that fire to help me fill my applesauce orders, and the year before, she could handle a knife to chop walnuts. You know, she's been with me for the whole three years, and I don't know what I'd do without my little nugget."

"But the child…"

"Yes?"

"She's flourished with you here, Maggie. That's all I meant to say. Merry Christmas to you all."

The gentle words of praise brought a flush of comfort to Maggie. Mr. Furlow tipped his hat and paid at the other counter where Maggie's mother served him. Every year for the busy month of December, Maggie hired her family to help in the store. She loved their company and they loved helping. She smiled as her oldest sister, Tamara—Rebecca's mother—held up a kissing ball.

It was made with two barrel hoops looped one inside the other and covered with evergreen branches and mistletoe. Tamara had been in charge of mistletoe at dances and get-togethers ever since Maggie could remember, and she was assembling this one for the twenty-fourth. They'd hang it in the corner near the fire, above the mulled wine. It always caused laughter and excitement in the store, from adolescents to grandparents.

Tamara was also seven months along, her skin as smooth as a ripe plum. Maggie's other sister, Anna, graceful and the tallest of the three as she weighed coffee beans for the banker's wife, was only three months along. If you looked real close, you could tell her waist was getting thicker.

Maggie's heart trembled. The whole world was full of children, but she and Sheldon hadn't been married long enough to have any.

She turned to the wall and lit two lanterns. Still, she thought, pushing back the blond hair that had fallen loose from her braid, that was no reason to settle for just any other man to replace him, despite her sisters' thrusting. No-settling Maggie had become her nickname in the family.

Maybe Maggie didn't have children of her own, but she had her sisters' little ones to love. Rebecca was Maggie's best companion and permanent store helper. The soft-spoken girl had a knack for cooking and flavoring foods. She was dexterous with her hands and precise in her measuring, and such a happy girl.

Walking toward the door, Maggie fingered the loose threads of her skirt pocket. She wondered what had gotten into her this week. Perhaps the Christmas carols were making her reminisce.

"Fare well through the blizzard, Mr. Furlow." She opened the door a crack and was nearly propelled backward by the onslaught of wind. She braced her shoulder to the door.

"Who on earth is that?" Mr. Furlow wrapped his woolen scarf around his hat and throat. "Sergeant Fielder?"

"I—I think so." Maggie heard the huskies barking softly in the distance.

"I wonder what he's got under his coat. He keeps checking on it." Mr. Furlow left and she closed the door, but other customers had heard his comments and rushed to the windows.

"Look. He just passed the cutoff for the fort, which means he's heading this way instead," someone said.

Maggie let out a rush of warm breath. She slid to the window to watch, peering over the shorter heads into the purple shadows of nightfall.

James was a hundred yards away in the fields. His huskies, ranging in color from pure white to gray and speckled, pulled the sled across an icy patch. He was moving very slowly, as if exhausted.

What could he possibly want in her store? He had all the food he needed at the fort and never bought from her. The last time they'd spoken had been three months ago when they'd accidentally come across each other on the boardwalk. He had softly offered condolences on her husband's unexpected death three years earlier. The complete kidney failure had come suddenly, Maggie had told him, although she'd known it was coming for a year. How could that be? It had been unexpected, yet she knew it was coming.

Maggie straightened the button on her lace blouse. "Sergeant Fielder's probably headed to the tinsmith next door."

"Maybe he needs something for his sled," offered one of the boys.

"But what's he got under his fur coat?" asked another child.

"Maybe he caught a fish."

"He wouldn't be carryin' it under his coat."

Their mother, Anna, spoke up. "Come along, it's five o'clock, children, time to go. Supper needs to be prepared."

Anna rushed the children to the back hall to don their coats and hats. Their grandmother, permanently bent at the waist with old age, but still energetic enough to help the littlest ones, hushed their complaints.

Maggie hugged her mother goodbye. "Careful on the ice."

"I'll hold on to Anna," said her mother. They slipped out the back door as Maggie watched. Their mother had been living with Anna, her husband and three children for over ten years now, ever since their father had passed on, and thankfully didn't have far to travel in this weather because they lived across the street.

Maggie whirled around to watch the others. Tamara's two youngest boys raced to Maggie, chasing around her long navy skirt. She laughed, trapped them both and kissed them. "Stay out of trouble."

Maggie gave away handfuls of sweet raisins to the children as her older sister's husband, Cliff, appeared at the back door. They had a bit farther to walk than her other sister—two blocks and over to get to their home.

"Will you be all right without our help for the next hour?" Tamara tugged her coat over her large belly.

"I'll be fine with the last few customers. The storm has slowed the shoppers."

An elderly couple, inspecting candles on display, glanced up and nodded from across the room.

"Cliff, I feel much safer now that you've arrived." Maggie adjusted the little girl's bonnet then wiped another child's nose. "Please hold on to my sister tightly. We don't want her to fall."

Cliff smiled beneath his damp Stetson. "Don't worry, I won't let her go. And if the weather's like this tomorrow, I'll insist she stay home with me."

"Thank you."

They were about to leave, when the front door burst open. The bell above the door jingled rapidly.

With a kick to her heart just as rapid, Maggie wheeled around. There he stood. James Fielder.

Something was terribly wrong. Black soot stained his face. He hadn't shaved for days. Blazes, he looked as if he hadn't eaten. His lips were parched. The edges of his coat were streaked with dirt and ashes. And the storm had wet everything, including his fur hat, giving everything a muddy appearance.

Clawing at his coat to undo it, he quickly glanced around. He dominated the room with his massive coat, dark looks and probing brown eyes. His husky voice came in rapid fire. "I didn't know where else to come. The fort's so far and I don't know if the doctor's in. Your shop's always full of women and children and I thought you'd…you'd know what to do."

Stricken with fear, Maggie stepped forward. "What is it?"

James pulled hard on his coat and it fell open. Inside, guns were strapped around his lean hips, but above that, strapped to his wide chest in a makeshift harness was a moving bundle.

He pulled at the blankets and rushed the bundle to the counter. "It's a baby, Maggie. And she's having trouble breathing."

Chapter Two

Shaking from exhaustion, James placed the little angel on the pine countertop, propping her up, blankets and all, to make her breathing easier. The five adults and three youngsters in the store crowded around him.

He thought it astounding that the baby's entire chest fit into one of his soiled hands. She had short, soft black hair. He'd never been this close to a baby and her size scared him. She made grunting noises when she exhaled, as if struggling. Thank God she was pink and moving normally. Clenching her fist, she shoved it into her mouth, at the same time closing her eyes against the lantern's glow and letting out a soft wail.

James's deep voice crackled in the silence like a newly struck match. "If I lose her now after coming this far with her...please help."

Maggie lifted the rasping baby into her arms. "Who is she and what happened to her?"

Others chimed in. "She looks to be around three to four months old, judging by the way she can hold up her head."

Maggie cooed to the baby, and James, in a woozy fog and feeling weak, thought he heard the angel respond. The raspy groans subsided. Maybe the baby was just as stunned as he to be back in a safe, warm room. Maybe she thought Maggie looked like her mother, whoever that was.

Maggie opened the baby's mouth and checked inside, but found no obvious obstruction to hinder breathing. She called for bottles and goat's milk from the back storage room, and a pot of water to be hung over the fire. As she took over, his grip on the situation slackened. He'd made it here. Hallelujah, he'd made it.

Thank God for Maggie. She knew what to do.

The room's warmth penetrated his face. The heat and the calm felt good after hours of frigid, pounding wind. His legs ached from running behind the sled. His biceps felt as if they'd been whipped, and his neck, from the weight of the angel, felt as tight as his fists.

He parted his dry lips. "I don't know whose child she is. She was in a fire at High River Landing."

Various gasps escaped the adults. He recognized Maggie's sister, Tamara, and her lumberjack husband, Cliff Meese. There was also the elderly couple who gave grammar lessons across the street, the Billings.

Mrs. Billings, in a dainty lace collar, peered at the baby in Maggie's arms. "Was she hurt in the fire?"

"No."

"Were you?" Maggie asked James.

He peered down into her soft face, the light streaks of hair that framed her arched brows and the warm brown eyes that glistened with concern. He hadn't been this close to her since… A lantern behind her started to swim in his vision. He suddenly realized he must look frightful from the fire he'd escaped. Tamara's two boys raced around the counter and were spying at him in scared silence.

James pulled off his fur cap. He ran his fingers along his forehead, trying to suppress the dizziness. "I'm all right. I saw the fire from a long way off. By the time I got there, the old barge house—the one they deserted when they built the bridge—had burned to the ground. I don't know who was staying there…it was still smoldering. I found the baby in the shack that contained the spring pump. The burning house must have kept her warm."

He took a deep breath and forced himself to finish. "I figured by the amount of crying she was doing, she'd been there for a few hours and she was hungry, but she hadn't been there long enough to suffer. She was wrapped warmly in fox skins."

"Who was she with and what happened to them?"

"I searched the charred logs but there was no evidence to speak of. A couple of minor things I'm still contemplating. There were faded tracks in the snow, but nothing I could recognize because the wind was covering it up fast." He yanked off his fur coat. Wobbly on his feet, he meant to toss his coat on a corner rocking chair, but it slipped to the ground. Someone else picked it up.

"Has there been any word in Goldstrike about the fire?" James asked the group.

They looked at each other. "No," everyone agreed.

Maggie pressed her ear to the baby's chest and listened. "Her lungs sound clear on inhalation, but she's definitely groaning when she breathes out. She feels warm enough. Maybe she's just lacking fluids and needs something in her tummy. When's the last time she drank milk?"

"I didn't find any baby bottles in the shack, and never had any milk to give her. I had my canteens of water and soaked a rag with it, letting her suck the water through the rag."

"Water? She needs more than water."

"I know. I had some hard biscuits, so I softened them with water and gave them to the angel to suck on. The whole way here I was petrified she'd choke."

"How long have you been with her?"

"Since noon today. But I was away from town for three days. I got trapped by the storm and tried to wait it out."

"You've been going steady from High River Landing since noon?" From across the room, Cliff gently dipped the filled milk bottles into a warm cauldron of water. "That's normally an eight-hour trip by sled. It took you less than six."

James nodded. A wheeze escaped him. He slouched onto the counter. A moment or two must have passed, for the next time he looked up, Maggie had the bottle in the baby's mouth. She was sucking on it and closing her eyes in sheer delight. She'd be fine, he could see it.

Every bit of tension melted from his body. He felt light-headed, but managed a smile. "If she were a kitten," he said softly, "she'd be purring."

Maggie's lips parted into gentleness. Everything about kids had always come naturally to Maggie, and so unnaturally to him. She was the first one her sisters called for help in their own deliveries, and then the town doctor, James had once heard. Maggie took easily to the skills the doctor demonstrated.

Maggie's cheeks glowed in the streaky light. "You saved her life."

"I think you just did."

Cliff put on his hat and spoke to his wife. "It's safe and there's plenty to eat here. If you're okay with the kids for an hour and a half, I'll go notify the doctor."

"He's not there," said Mr. Billings. "He went to visit Chester Simpson yesterday on account of Chester's heart ailment. Likely stayed where he was when he saw the storm kick up today."

"We might not need a doctor in such haste," said Maggie, burping the baby over her shoulder. "Her breathing's relaxed. It could have been simple dehydration—a loss of fluids. Fluids are important to a child, much more than to an adult. They can't last as long as we can without drinking something."

It seemed to James that Maggie was right. The baby's raspy breathing could no longer be heard.

Maggie's niece, Rebecca, came around the other side of her. Maggie lowered herself into the corner rocking chair. "You see, Rebecca, the baby's fine."

"She's fine," Rebecca repeated.

James watched the girl hold the bottle, marveling at how much she'd grown since he'd last seen her. This was the girl everyone in town had called "slow," the one the doctor had said would never be able to read or write, the one who'd failed the first grade twice before Maggie had insisted on homeschooling and training her in the store.

As the first grandchild in the family, Rebecca must have unknowingly brought great joy but also great concern to her family. Something was wrong. She got her numbers and letters all switched around and couldn't seem to get them straight in her head. She'd never learn to read or write, but it was apparent to the whole town now, thanks to Maggie, that Rebecca was smart. While Maggie worked to make the child independent, her parents, Cliff and Tamara, seemed to be working on creating an army of brothers and sisters to love and protect Rebecca in her old age. Both plans were working.

Maggie had never, of course, explained her way of thinking to James, but he could see it. Maggie had shown everyone, including the doubting schoolteacher, Mr. Furlow, that Rebecca could indeed learn practical business procedures and with her talents in cooking and baking, help in the store. She wasn't school-smart, but she was quick in other ways, and Lord help anyone in this town if they dismissed her as simple. They'd have Maggie to deal with.

Seeing Rebecca with Maggie now, feeding the baby, stirred him. He felt sorry for Maggie, not Rebecca. Her husband of two years had been taken from her before she'd been able to conceive. It was apparent to James how much she wanted children of her own. But life had a way of pulling the rug, rich or poor, deserving or not, and no matter what time of year it was.

The young girl looked up at James. "I thought you were Saint Nicholas."

The others in the room chuckled, but James sighed. Still dizzy, he looked around. Christmas. He caught glimpses of it around the store, noticing details for the first time since entering. The scent of roasted chestnuts coming from the brick oven of the fireplace; red ribbons wired to the till; a wooden painting of Saint Nicholas displayed on the counter.

Why was the Christmas season so easy for some folks but so hard for him? Christmas had never filled him with a sense of magic, not even when he was little. *Especially* not when he was little. What he remembered about his Christmases was his mother crying for the lack of food, and his father begging for an extra shift at the mines. The year he'd turned thirteen, James had signed up to permanently work in the coal shafts alongside his father, hoping to contribute to the family's Christmas that year, but he'd only made things worse.

"I'm sorry, James," said Maggie, looking at him strangely. "We've all been so concerned about the baby we overlooked you. You must be hungry and thirsty."

"Right," he said, but the room began to tilt. Then spin. He felt himself sliding.

Someone thrust a chair underneath him. He sank onto firm wood.

"He's been on the road for three days," someone said. "He needs sleep."

"Well, he can't sleep here. Not alone with Maggie in the same house."

"We can't lift him and drag him out into a storm," said Cliff. "He's been through hell already. I could get—"

"No," said Mr. Billings. "You've got to take your wife and children home. I'll stay to chaperon. I'll walk my wife home across the street, get a few things and come back. I'll sleep in the back room and Maggie can take the baby upstairs with her. James can sleep in the parlor area of the store, over there, by the woodstove."

"We've got to notify the other Mounties. Someone's got to know something about the baby's folks. Where could they have gone in a storm?"

"I'll help," Maggie promised. "By looking after the baby. She can stay here with me till they're found."

James drifted off and the next thing he knew, he was sitting in the rocking chair trying to force his eyelids open.

He looked about. The front room of Maggie's store was divided into two areas—the merchandise section with its shelving, bins and counter, and the sitting parlor with two sofas, upholstered chairs and woodstove, where Maggie's family and customers could sip a cup of coffee. In the far corner stood a tall pine Christmas tree decorated with nuts, candles, dried fruit, glass ornaments and plaid bows. It smelled good, even from the distance where he sat. Several packages wrapped in brown paper tied with red ribbons lay beneath the tree.

He must have slept for hours, for the wind had stopped howling and the sky behind the windows was painted midnight black. The fire was scorching, the heat penetrating his tingling toes, and Maggie was crouched low beside his rocking chair, holding the baby in a swath of fresh blankets.

Maggie wore a night robe and James could hear someone—likely Mr. Billings—snoring loudly from the next room.

"You found her and brought her here," Maggie whispered to him. "Do you believe in miracles?"

"No," he murmured. "No such thing."

Chapter Three

"Why would a man prefer to spend three days out there *alone* rather than in town, where it's dry and warm and folks are celebrating the holidays?" Maggie asked the question of James as she stood at the storefront window thirty minutes later. She could hear him moving behind her, the tin plate she'd placed his rye sandwich on rattling on the pine table while he ate. Firewood snapped and popped in the blazing heat of the cast-iron stove.

Maggie cradled the sleeping baby in her arms and gazed over deserted countryside. The sky was thick with clouds, but occasionally the full moon slipped out. It scattered light across six-foot-high drifts. It would take men days to horse-plow the roads.

James spoke behind her. "Not everyone is good at holidays."

Maggie turned slowly toward him. He took a long look at the sleeping baby nestled in her arms.

After eight straight hours of sleep and something in his stomach, he looked stable on his feet. The crisis of the baby's arrival had passed, which left Maggie with time to let his presence sink in. It was physically impossible, even in the darkness, to tear her gaze away from his wide-shouldered stance and the riveting curiosity in his eyes. Passing time had etched lines into his face and had thickened the bristles of his shaven jaw. She'd always been attracted to older men like James who was a good ten years older than she, in his late thirties; he had experience and wisdom on his side.

Despite her guarded reservation toward him, memories washed through her, of a time when the most pliable part of her had been exposed to James. It had been just one brief afternoon of tobogganing and caroling with friends, but that kiss had been enough to send her mind reeling in pleasant daydreams for months afterward.

She gazed at him and felt a tug of unwanted affection. He still felt like a stranger, though.

Snoring loudly from the other room, Mr. Billings had been kind enough to bring a spare toothbrush, comb and razor blade. He'd left it in the spring room, with the water pump and basin for James when he awakened. Now, freshly shaven with his long dark hair combed back to brush against his denim collar, James made an unforgettable figure in the firelight.

"I should—I should light a lantern," she offered. "It's dark in here. I can barely see."

His hand came out to stop her. It was firm on her upper arm and left a trace of heat beneath her red flannel robe. "Leave it," he whispered. "I like it like this."

His voice was deep and sullen and caused gooseflesh to rise at the back of her neck.

His figure looked rough beneath his white shirt and denim pants. He'd changed into fresh clothes from his pack, and dry cowboy boots. Earlier, the men in the store had tended to his dogs. Mr. Billings had penned the team across the street inside his small barn for the night.

Searching for a safe place to look, she gazed down at the sweetly pressed lips of the sleeping child. As she did, Maggie's hair, a mess of uncombed curls, fell over her shoulder and made her wish she'd taken the time to tie it with a ribbon. And good heavens, her robe was five years old and tattered from wear.

She should have stayed in her bedroom with the baby and not worried about James downstairs, about whether he was hungry or if any part of him had suffered frostbite.

What made her most nervous, being alone with him, was that their conversations had always gone straight to the point. His honesty was something that both captivated and scared her.

Even in a crowd, even with Sheldon standing near, she and James had always talked about important matters that concerned them, nothing light that others shared. He'd ask about her plans for the future and if she ever thought of traveling the world. What did she think of the current government and the situation with the Indians. Or what they could do, as a community, to raise money for a proper school.

Here, standing with James at two o'clock in the morning trapped between the moonlight and firelight, Maggie trembled. What might he say this time, that might turn her stomach inside out?

She brushed past him. The baby cooed in her arms.

"Where are you going?" James asked.

"I thought I'd go back to bed."

"Why did you come down?"

"The baby woke up. She was hungry and I—I wanted to fix her a bottle."

"When you finished that, you could have returned to bed then."

The mention of the word *bed* from his lips made her cheeks heat. "I wanted to fix you a sandwich. I thought you'd be hungry."

"Somehow I knew I could count on you. Thank you for looking after me and the kid."

She stood rooted, trying to harden her heart against him,

to wipe out the attraction she used to have toward James. Women weren't supposed to chase men.

His lips tugged upward, ever so lightly so that if she didn't know him, she'd barely suspect he was smiling. "I haven't dismissed you yet."

"Yes, sir," she said, returning the humor.

The awkward air between them shifted slightly, onto another footing. A friendlier one.

"Thank you for letting us stay tonight. I'll be out before you open your store in the morning."

"There's no rush for you to leave."

He sucked in his breath.

She groaned softly. Did she sound desperate for his company?

"Thanks, but I need to contact a few people about the kid."

"Of course."

"I know you're busy with your store, so I'll take the baby with me back to the fort—"

"No, please, I'd like to help. There's no one at the fort but a bunch of men and I'm sure they'd prefer the baby stay here. I can manage the store and the baby. I've got family and neighbors to help. And customers will certainly love to see this pretty little face behind the counter."

She rocked the baby, but when she looked up again at James, he was staring at her. "It *is* a pretty face."

Self-conscious of his stare, Maggie listened to the fire crackling. "Where do you think her parents are and what are we going to do with her?"

Maggie moved toward the commercial part of the room, to the racks of Christmas items on display. She felt the weight of her curly hair shift along her robe.

James followed her to the shelves. "I don't know. I'm going to ask around in the morning and see if anyone's heard."

What came easily to him came with so much difficulty to her. This baby had lost her home and her family, and Maggie could barely think about it without crying. James was a policeman who saw the worst crimes, the worst accidents and the worst in people. He was a walking contradiction, so controlled on the outside, yet he plowed forward and simply did what needed to be done in the most emotional of circumstances. He gave of himself and tried to restore things to their normal balance.

Maggie always sought the light and hated looking at that part of humanity. The part that hurt innocents. This little child had been left behind. Maggie prayed her parents hadn't died in the fire, that they were safe somewhere with a logical explanation, but terror rippled to the surface.

James picked up a white candle that had been dipped with grains of glass, so it twinkled like a magical ball in the firelight. "You've done well for yourself, Maggie."

"I like what I'm doing." She adjusted the baby to her shoulder, not quite ready to bring her back upstairs to the makeshift cradle she'd fashioned out of an empty drawer and a soft blanket. The baby felt too precious in her arms, and needed love and attention after all she'd been through.

James watched the candle glimmer. "I'm glad that Sheldon…had a chance to see your store open before he passed on. He worked hard to make your dream happen."

She murmured softly in agreement.

"Do you ever see his folks?"

"They've been overseas for years. But we write to each other."

"What about?"

She gave him a startled look.

Setting down the candle, he picked up a Christmas stocking Maggie was in the middle of cross-stitching. "Sorry, it's none of my business."

"No, I just…no one ever asks me that. Maybe they assume they know what we write about. They assume we write continuously of Sheldon. But we don't. Not any-more." She smiled, curiously free to speak about her late husband, realizing that her grief for Sheldon had finally been replaced by a lasting memory of his kindness. "We talk about their missionary work. Where they've been in Asia. We talk about the people in Britain—the contacts they've given me—who help me import spices from the Orient."

James fingered the evergreen bows on the kissing ball. The intimacy of the gesture made Maggie swallow. "It's been a long time, hasn't it, since we've been alone to talk? Anything on your mind?"

He was joking with her again, but honesty seeped into his every word.

Yes, there was something on her mind. Like why had he kissed her five years ago and had then pretended nothing had happened? Since James *had* kissed her and she *had* been engaged, why hadn't he pushed the point further?

She would have stayed with Sheldon, her soon-to-be-husband, anyway, because she'd loved him, but why on earth stir things up only to walk away?

Maybe the kiss had caught James by surprise, too.

She repeated to herself as she watched him move between the racks—she would have stayed with Sheldon. She would have.

Shaking her head softly, she realized she couldn't ask why he'd kissed her. The man was no longer interested in her. If he had been interested, if anything had changed in his opinion, he would have approached her soon after her proper mourning period had ended. And that was aeons ago.

He looped his long fingers through the red satin ribbon on the till. "You always pull me in a thousand different directions."

He'd said that five years ago on the hill, and it hadn't sat any easier with her then than now. But it was too intimate of a statement to pursue.

"Why don't you enjoy the holidays, James? Don't you ever get the Christmas spirit?"

Pausing, he inspected the satin bow. "Maybe I prefer to celebrate the goodness of mankind throughout the year." His voice was gruff. "Maybe I don't need one specific day or week to tell me that's necessary."

She set the sleeping baby, wrapped in blankets, on the warm pine countertop.

James walked around the counter to her side. "In my estimation, folks use Christmas as an excuse to overeat and drink."

His comment made her angry. "That sounds like something Scrooge would say in a book my sisters read the children yesterday."

"I don't know it."

"Charles Dickens. *A Christmas Carol.* And if you really believe that folks use Christmas as an excuse to overindulge, then you're insulting me and this store, and the very place that took you in and fed you."

"That's not what this store's about, Maggie. That's not what I'm implying. I just don't understand it, that's all. What all the fuss is about."

Adjusting the baby's cloth diaper, Maggie tried to soften her voice. "It's the neighborly aspect. Spreading good cheer and celebrating the birth of baby Jesus."

"You can celebrate those things, and should in my opinion, on the other days of the year, too."

Now he was mixing her up. She wondered if his line of work, in seeing the negativity that man and fate produced, made him turn away from the beauty. "And do you?" Maggie knew she was getting dangerously close to a personal conversation that perhaps she should withdraw from, but she wanted to know more about James. "Do you ever celebrate the goodness of mankind?"

"Sometimes." He heaved in a breath. "Sometimes when I'm alone behind my dogsled and the huskies are barking at a deer they spotted in the woods, and I look back on the town and see smoke billowing from tiny chimneys and children hollering on their skates, sometimes I celebrate."

"That's a beautiful image."

Taking a moment to picture James like that, Maggie ran a hand along her robe. She twisted the lapel, tucking it over her chest. His eyes followed her movements.

He crossed his arms and leaned back. "How about you, Maggie? When do you celebrate?"

"On evenings like this." The baby spurted softly, so Maggie lifted her again and clarified her thoughts. "On evenings like this when I've got a small baby in my arms and she's well fed and safe, I celebrate."

James's intensity still had the ability to nearly knock her off her feet. She felt the satiny smoothness of her gown pressing against her bare breasts. The night was doing strange things to her. It enveloped her in a hazy feeling of safety, as if she could ask him anything and he'd tell her. She probed further. "And so when do you lose heart?"

"What do you mean?"

"We're all human. When do you feel…the opposite of celebrating? When do you feel saddest in spirit?"

He shrugged, but his lips were trembling. The rich outline of his muscles tensed beneath his shirt. "At that same moment, Maggie. When I'm looking back at the deer and the town and the children skating, sometimes I'm hit with a long hollow ping of loneliness. Like there's no one on the planet but me."

She wavered on her feet. He'd drawn such a vivid picture.

"What about you?" he asked. "I know you went through a difficult time when Sheldon passed. Does a woman like you, who's got the world at her fingertips, surrounded by a hundred clamoring beaus and dozens of family members, ever get lonely?"

Right now, as I feel the weight of the baby in my arms and realize I might never have one of my own, and then when I look up to your eyes and wonder what might have been.

"Sometimes." She slipped away to shield her pain, to shield her response. He'd described his feelings with such depth that he'd unmasked her own depth of isolation, despite the crowds around her. "But I try not to dwell on the sadness."

Chapter Four

The gentle fall of ice pellets on the windowpanes interrupted their conversation. James listened to the soft pinging, even as he stood distracted by the beauty beside him, disheveled in her night robe and rumpled from sleep but making him imagine what Maggie looked like in bed. He stepped up beside her and the baby, then looked out over the drifts. The full moon had disappeared behind the clouds again, but light, from candles scattered in neighbors' windows, reflected off the sheets of white snow and thus illuminated the landscape.

"It's an ice storm," he said. "Everything will be covered in the morning."

"I hope it doesn't stop the plows, otherwise no one will be able to move."

"That's why you need to invest in a pair of snowshoes."

James turned, his long arm and sleeve brushing the neck of Maggie's robe. It connected them in an inappropriate way, and he felt suddenly awkward being alone with her. Even the steady drone of Mr. Billings snoring in the next room unsettled James, making him feel guilty that the old man might awaken and find the two "adolescents" alone behind the grown-up's back.

"Snowshoes?" She stepped away from James just as awkwardly. Her movements loosened the opening of her robe and he caught a glimpse of long, straight legs silhouetted beneath a white cotton gown. The bows hanging off the curtains hit her head. She ducked, twirled and shooed them away as if they were troublesome moths. "For a grown woman?"

"Why not? If I recall, you used to love outdoor sports."

"Well, there's no need. I can get around fine with my boots and my horse."

She didn't appear to know it, but one of the bows remained stuck to the top of her pretty head. Her curly hair trailed like ivy down her shoulders and tangled everything in its path. It tumbled over the outline of her supple breasts.

Oh, to be covered by a field of ivy.

He cleared his throat. "Not in the morning, you can't. And what's wrong with a grown woman enjoying herself in the snow?"

"Well," she said as he watched the play of lights at the hollow of her throat, "I'm not going to traipse around in snowshoes with no place to go. At least when *you* wear them, you've got a purpose. Wearing them just for fun, well, that's what children do. And now I really am going to bed."

She ducked past him but before she could escape, the ribbon tightened and pulled her back by the hair. "Ow," she said with a flustered laugh, unaware of the seductive nature of her angled hips.

His hands shot out to steady her. "Here, let me get that. Your ivy—" James cleared his throat again "—your hair's caught."

She gripped the sleeping baby, then stood as still as a quiet lake while he raised his arms to untangle the bow. With their huge contrast in body size, he became aware of his coarse masculinity to her elegance.

"Are you catching a cold?" she asked. "Your throat seems to be bothering you."

He made the mistake of looking down into her face. Inches away from her mouth, he pressed his closed and tried not to breathe in the fresh scent of her hair.

"No cold here." But at her proximity, he felt a slow burn crawl up his body.

She parted her lips. "That's good."

"The ribbon seems to be…oh, there we go." The bow released. Strands of her hair flew up out of place, so he patted them down. Her hair was remarkably soft for being such a flop of curls. Snake that he was, he let his hands drift down her hair along her shoulders for seconds longer than necessary before tucking them securely into his pockets and stepping away.

"My lady," he said, sweeping the air toward the staircase. "Your chamber awaits."

He heard her giggling as she passed.

He watched her walk up the stairs, the entire fifteen steps, her hips swaying beneath her cinched robe, her golden tresses trailing down her arms in mass confusion. When she got to the top of the landing, she timidly looked back as if aware he might be watching her, but he spun on his boots to tend to the fire. He was unsure why, but didn't want her knowing she had his full attention.

"I'll bet ya a peppermint stick he's up in ten minutes."

"Nah, I think he's really tired after yesterday. I'll bet ya two toffees he's gonna sleep for another hour."

"Children, children, come here and let the poor man rest." A woman clapped in the distance.

The clapping jarred James awake. My God, he thought, rolling stiffly on the sofa, he was in a nightmare. Had to be. The sun was streaming in through Maggie's windows, the stove spitting heat beside his head, Maggie's family was working the till, and five children were standing here gawking at him.

"Hi, mister."

James muttered beneath his breath. He blinked but when he opened his eyes again, the elves were still here. He felt like a fool sleeping in when the womenfolk were up and working the store.

Customers walked by. "Is that him?" sniffed one elderly woman into her handkerchief. "Is he the one who found the baby?"

"Yes." Maggie appeared suddenly and placed her hands on the woman's shoulders. "This way to the almonds, ma'am."

Maggie smiled at James, rolling her eyes in exaggerated humor, mouthing, "Sorry."

He swung his legs to the floor, his feet still in cowboy boots, and whispered over the sofa as she passed, "Why did you let me sleep here for so long?"

"I couldn't carry you up the stairs, now, could I? Neither could Mr. Billings." With her blouse tucked into her skirt, the fabric accentuated her shape.

"You could have woken me."

"Well, you looked too sweet on the sofa with your eyes closed. And I figured you could use the sleep."

He groaned with embarrassment. Running a hand through his untidy dark hair, and bending his neck to get the cramp out, he growled at the staring children. Screeching with laughter, they fled.

Ducking into the hallway, James found the spring room with its clean supply of water and towels. As he brushed his teeth, he overheard Maggie's sisters in the room next door, making up the bed that Mr. Billings had slept in overnight.

"Why do you suppose he's not married?"

"Maybe he's not the marrying type."

"That's what Cliff said just two months before he proposed. They all say that at first. It's in their blood."

The younger sister laughed. "Maybe he's afraid of women."

"Afraid? A big strapping lad like James Fielder? The only thing he's got to be afraid of is No-settling Maggie. She's too picky even to go out with him."

"She's the one who's afraid. What do you figure she's so afraid of?"

"With all the men who've asked for her hand, land sakes, I wish I knew."

"Maybe she's afraid they'll take all her money."

Tamara sighed. "Poor Maggie, I wish life were easier for her. I wish she'd let us take care of her the way she takes care of us. It's as if when Pa died, he left her to watch over us. Let's see if we can surprise her this year with something special on Christmas Eve."

The younger sister yelped. "What a wonderful idea."

The women finished making the bed then left the room as James rinsed his mouth and stared into the wall mirror at his reflection. His black hair needed a good comb, and a shadow of a beard was already visible beneath his jaw.

What was he doing here? Last night, why had he entertained thoughts of pretty Maggie Greerson?

Business was good for Maggie, and she had a lot of money. He had little. He wished her well, but money had never meant much to him.

Money ruined relationships. It had ruined the loving relationship between his parents, and it had ruined his relationship with them.

Christmas often did the same thing. People struggled to prove they could feed their families extra, that they could outdo their neighbors with their generosity on extravagant foods, that they could buy fancy clothing they could ill afford.

His parents had felt like failures that they couldn't produce surprises, not even an extra bowl of fruit, on Christmas morning for their children. As a young man of thirteen, James had felt that same abysmal failure when his hopes of working alongside his father had been permanently shattered. James had signed up to work the mines and help provide for his three younger brothers, but a week into it, he'd caught bronchitis, then pneumonia so bad that he'd taken to bed for ten months of recovery. Instead of being a help, he'd been a weight around their necks.

The medicine had cost more than his parents could afford, so much that they had to take in boarders for a year, begging strangers on the trail to stay with them in their home, and the "sickly" child, as he'd been labeled. The arguments between his folks had increased and had never stopped.

Now James was old enough to support himself, trapping and living the solitary life of a Mountie. He was in great physical health and could outrace and outmaneuver any man. The poster he'd seen for enlistment was what drew him into it: *Looking for single men who seek adventure and honor in their lives.*

Single men. The federal government didn't want married men and did everything they could to discourage men from marrying. With permission, officers were allowed, but for enlisted men who'd started out as James had at the fort in Edmonton, traveling for days into the countryside to track thieves or murderers, a wife and family were considered liabilities. They couldn't live at the fort, so would have to live in their own home. Much of the Mountie's time would therefore be spent chopping firewood and hunting for food, providing safety for his own family when he should be dedicated to law and order for the community.

But James was now a sergeant and things were different. His commanding officer would likely give him permission to marry and to settle into easier duties around any fort in the territory, but James had grown accustomed to the travel and he liked his nomad life. He went where he pleased and wasn't responsible for any family but himself. And most of all, money didn't matter.

James washed his face in the basin of cool water.

But every year at Christmas, he still sent money home to his mother, hoping to make up for his failure in the mines to someone, even though his parents now lived apart and his brothers had long ago moved to the West Coast.

It seemed strange to James to be caught up in Maggie's world, a stranger looking in at a household full of the things he'd never been good at—sharing in an overabundance of food and gifts, when for the true meaning of Christmas, all you had to do was look in your heart. That didn't cost a penny.

James strode out of the room to the back door and grabbed his Mountie-issue buffalo coat. He glanced over the crowd, over the heads of the children who'd spotted him and were rushing his way, then to the women weighing sacks of spice. His gaze settled on the baby lying on the counter. She was awake and being entertained by Maggie, who held a rattle above her head.

"Where are you going?" asked young Rebecca by his side.

"To check if anyone in town knows anything about the baby. Has anyone here mentioned they know her?"

"Aunt Maggie's been askin', but no one knows a thing."

"I'll start at Gilbert's Restaurant. Please tell Maggie I'll be back in a few hours to check in with her."

James slid into his big fur boots, then walked out into the glorious outdoors. He took it all in—the busy horse plows, men with shovels, crunching snow, icicles dangling from every treetop and a brilliant blue sky. He heard his dogs barking and playing in the penned area across the street at the Billings household, and knew they'd be fine there for as long as he needed them to stay.

The ice storm had covered everything it'd touched and the town looked mystical, as if James was looking at it through a snowy crystal ball. The wind, warm and gentle, soothed his face. Normally, a day like this would thrill him, but today he wished he had someone to share it with.

He sighed. Sooner or later, money always came between people. He knew that. And the fact was, he and Maggie didn't have a lot in common.

Maggie wondered where he was. James was taking his time in town and she was beginning to wonder if Rebecca had gotten the message straight. It was already one-thirty, everyone had eaten lunch, and yet James was nowhere to be seen. She wondered if he'd gotten word about the baby's family and was perhaps heading off in that direction.

In the small kitchen nestled behind the spare bedroom on the first floor, Maggie cleared the lunch dishes off the table.

"Here," said Tamara, lifting the homeless baby from the cradle that Cliff had brought in from their home an hour earlier, "let me care for the child for a bit. Stretch your legs while I feed her."

Maggie would have gladly held on to the sweet girl forever, but allowed her sister the pleasure of tending to the little one while she tended to the dishes.

And thought of James.

Whenever there were crowds of people around, James disappeared like a caged animal seeking refuge in the woods. What on earth made him so wary? She realized he was simply doing his job today, but she knew darned well if he didn't *need* to return to the store for the sake of the lost child, he wouldn't be returning.

She scrubbed a plate ferociously.

She was so different from James. She loved families and people and little children's voices, and sharing large dinners and planning for social events. James had never shown up at a dance for as long as she'd known him. He never spoke about his family, he didn't drink, he never went to the saloon, he turned down invitations for wedding receptions and dinner parties. It was always just him and his darn work.

He likely preferred the company of his dogs than the company of a woman. Sure, Maggie had occasionally heard of him escorting a woman out, to an officers' dinner at the fort, but his courtships never materialized into anything permanent.

The more Maggie thought about it, the more irritated she grew. There weren't many men in this town who could carry a conversation with her like James could, who could hold her imagination with their words. Why did that ability have to be wasted on a man she'd never be interested in? And how could he be so knowledgeable about the world when he never seemed to be in the center of social activities, where people talked about these things?

Most of the men she met didn't spark much feeling in her other than friendship. It irked her that James seemed to spark life into her just with a mere glance. Last night, she'd felt her cheeks heat the whole way up the stairs when she thought he was watching her, only to be severely disappointed when she turned around and realized he hadn't been looking at her at all.

Some of the men who'd proposed to her were downright rude on how lovely it would be to have a wife who had a small fortune of her own.

But she was worth more to a man than just the sum total of her assets, wasn't she?

Picky? Yes. So what was wrong with that?

She dreamed of a man who could sweep her off her feet and arrange romantic outings with family and friends, who loved to dance and listen to music, who loved everything about Christmas, and most of all, one who loved to *socialize*.

In short, she dreamed of a man the opposite of James.

Maggie dried off the last of the dishes, helped by Rebecca and the other children, when she heard the back door open and close.

"Maggie!"

It was James.

She raced out into the store. "Where've you been? Have you located the baby's parents?"

"Unfortunately, not yet. I've spoken to just about everyone in town." A shaft of sun from the window struck his hair, intensifying its deep rich color. He'd somehow managed to change out of his bulky furs into a tanned sheepskin coat. James held up two pairs of snowshoes.

"What's this?"

"The true meaning of Christmas."

The children giggled.

Maggie dried her hands on her apron, fidgeting with the waistband. "What do you mean?"

A smile softened his sculpted jaw. "I thought I'd give you a destination for the snowshoes, so you've got a purpose and won't feel like a child. Although personally, I don't see a problem with that." James tapped Rebecca's head lightly with a snowshoe and she laughed in return. "I'm headed to the fort to speak to the commander, Maggie, and the others about the baby. The roads haven't been plowed there yet, but we can get through on snowshoes. Maybe someone there knows something we don't. Would you like to come with me?"

Chapter Five

"Go ahead, Maggie." Her older sister nudged her.

With her skirts brushing the floor, Maggie took a step closer to James and his snowshoes. He blocked the entire doorway with his size, but his charming smile did nothing to ease the nervousness she had about leaving her store for hours.

Maggie objected, "But the baby needs—"

"We'll take good care of her," Tamara insisted. "When's the last time you went outdoors? You've been cooped up in the store for the last month, preparing your wares for Christmas. It's a gorgeous day. Go on."

James held out a pair of webbed shoes. The ones he offered her were three feet long, but his were a massive four.

She took one by its leather thong strapping. "But I don't know how to snowshoe."

James rubbed his hand across the back of his neck. She found herself extremely conscious of his capability and appeal.

"If you know how to walk, you'll know how to snowshoe. Just think of these as extra-big feet that'll keep you from sinking into the snow."

"But the snow's got an icy crust to it. It'll be too slippery to use them."

"Not with your weight bearing down on them. These are ideal conditions. It's much harder to snowshoe in powdery snow, where you tend to sink in."

"You see?" said Tamara, untying Maggie's apron.

Her younger sister came up from behind and grabbed the apron, as if she was in cahoots to get Maggie out the door. "It's not too far, so you won't be gone forever. A mile there and a mile back. Wouldn't you like to speak to some of the policemen in person? You were saying that maybe some of the miners up in the area where the baby was found might know something."

She did have a point, thought Maggie. And there weren't many customers in the store today, what with the storm and the blocked roads tying most folks to their homes.

James spoke matter-of-factly, but he didn't look at Maggie when he added a comment about her underclothes. "You'd best put on two pairs of long johns beneath that skirt. And double wool socks. You can use the extra pair of moccasins I brought in my bag."

She pushed back a wayward strand of blond hair. "Where did you get all these things?"

"My shoes and moccasins came from my pack at Mr. Billings'. I exchanged my big fur coat for this thinner sheepskin because it's fairly warm outside. For you, I borrowed the smaller snowshoes and moccasins he had stored away for his grandson."

"What about your huskies? Don't you want to take them with you?"

"They'll have to stay put for now. I'm not sure how much ice is out there, and I don't have snowshoes that fit their paws." James winked at the children and they laughed at the image.

Even as Maggie wondered why James wanted her to go with him, a whirl of excitement started up inside her. The vibrant blue sky and the clear icicles dangling off the rooftops and every pine tree visible gave her an urge to explore the wonderland. And spending time alone with James, well, seemed exciting.

Minutes later in her long johns and wool socks, Maggie held the tiny girl in her arms to say goodbye. The baby's wide blue eyes were a mirror of Maggie's own growing enchantment. "I'm doing this for you." She stroked a soft cheek. Maggie looked to the others in the room. "You know, we really should name her."

Standing at the door tying up his knee-high moccasins, James straightened to full height. He pushed his wide shoulders back and studied her. "I don't know about that. You—*we*—shouldn't get too attached."

Maggie wondered how he could be so aloof with the infant. "We can't keep calling her 'the baby.' We don't know how long it's going to take to find her folks. Certainly not until the roads are cleared. I was thinking something along the lines of Christmas. Something like Holly."

"Baby Holly," said Tamara, waddling closer, rubbing her huge belly. "I'm sure her parents wouldn't mind a temporary nickname. If she were mine, I'd be so grateful she was warm and safe, I wouldn't know how to repay you."

Yet, James peered at Maggie so intently that her breathing grew uneven. He shook his head softly. "I'm not so sure about naming her."

Maggie was already out the door ahead of him when James heard her sisters whispering about this giving them time to work on their Christmas surprise for her. With all the pleasant chirping between the women, James was hit with a sharp pang of regret about his own family. He missed them.

His family had never enjoyed the tight bonds of kinship that wrapped these sisters together. James regretted that, but there was no use dwelling on things past.

"Hold on there, Maggie. Let that second horse pass with its plow, then I'll show you how to lace the snowshoes to your moccasins and how best to move."

"All right." Maggie walked along the boardwalk, her moccasins barely a whisper over the shoveled path that the other storekeepers had already cleared. The roof of the boardwalk cut the high afternoon sun in half, casting crisp shadow lines on her swirling skirt. She'd hiked her skirt high on her waist, which gave her a foot of clearance from the ground, but also exposed her slender legs.

"Here, sit on the steps and I'll help you lace up."

Maggie sat and James kneeled at her feet.

Dressed in a red wool coat that came to her knees, and a red wool hat that she'd pulled over her braided hair, Maggie raised her face to the sun. He watched her close her eyes and bask in its warmth. "You were right, I won't need my fur coat."

"With the exercise, we'd be sweating in no time." He marveled at the change in the weather that a melting chinook wind could bring.

James lifted her left foot and placed it on his lap. Suddenly, sitting at Maggie's feet made James feel odd. He'd never laced up a woman's shoes, nor gotten this close to a hiked-up skirt. In public.

Maybe she suddenly realized the forthright nature of the gesture, for she coughed, looked around to see if anyone was watching, then grew quiet.

Removing his fur mitts, James reached for a snowshoe. "These are good and strong. They're made from tough, seasoned ash. The webbing's made of caribou. If you tuck your toe into the loop at the front, like so—" James took her small foot into his large hand and helped her "—it'll keep your foot in place, but you can get out of it in a hurry if you tumble, so you won't wrench your ankle. And then we just have to tie it loosely."

He worked quickly, but her skirt and petticoat flopped about his face. "Do you mind…lifting your skirt a bit so I can…ah…see?"

Maggie colored to her ears. "Sure."

It was entirely inappropriate to have his hands where they were. On the sly, he turned his head to look down the street. No one seemed to be watching what foolishness he'd gotten himself into, although the tinsmith and his young son passed on the boardwalk behind Maggie.

"Howdy," said James, nodding and feeling as though he should give the man an explanation of what he was doing with his hands up Maggie's skirts.

"Lovely afternoon for…for a walk," replied the tinsmith.

Maggie nodded but didn't look at the passersby, nor could she bring her heated gaze to James's. Biting the side of her lip, she lifted her gray skirt to reveal a glimpse of white long johns stretched over curved, womanly legs.

With his pulse kicking, James quickly laced her up. She insisted on doing the other foot herself to get the hang of it, and he was grateful to be relieved of the delicate matter.

Her conversation came in nervous fire. "How long do you think it'll take us to get there? Do you think we'll have any luck getting new information at the fort?"

"It should take us less than an hour." He tied up his own snow-shoes then stood up tall beside her. "I hope we do have more luck at the fort, and I discovered a few little things about the situation at High River Landing that may pertain to the baby."

"Please, tell me what."

"Let's get going and we'll talk as we hike. Move up here beside me. That's it. Now, ordinary walking and snowshoeing are almost the same. You'll catch on quick. The difference is you have to raise your heel higher. Don't plant your feet too far apart or you'll get tired very quickly, and not too close together or you'll knock your shins. Ready? Let's go."

After staggering with a few strides, Maggie tried moving with a broader sweep, watching and imitating him. He found it personally satisfying when she seemed to get her snow legs.

"Why did you ask me to come with you?" She asked the question several minutes later, after they'd cleared the stores and were heading over a field of snow. Squinting from the blasting whiteness, they could see the fort in the distance, shadowed by the Rocky Mountains. James's eyes watered from the strain.

"Stop for a minute." He reached into his pocket and removed two pairs of wooden-type spectacles he used as snow goggles. He'd carved them from light wood and always carried them in winter months. Instead of glass, they had tiny slits. "Put these on."

"I've seen you wear these to protect your eyes."

"We don't want snow blindness. It comes on quickly if you're not careful."

Before she put them on, Maggie asked again. "You're not avoiding my question, are you? Is the answer complicated? Why did you ask me along?"

His stomach muscles tightened. He sensed a thrill in being alone with Maggie, where he could watch her healthy body moving in the snow, where he might show her the splendor of a beautiful, solitary day in the wilderness.

"You don't have to think too long. The answer's always quite simple with me."

She furrowed her forehead. "Why then?"

"Because sometimes, I just enjoy your company."

Chapter Six

Maggie couldn't see James, but she could hear him. The whoosh of his heavy breathing as they plodded through the snow mingled with her panting. Slightly ahead of him, she enjoyed the heat of the glistening sun, and warmth of the wind as it whisked the hairs at her neck.

If it weren't for snowshoes, the trek would be impossible.

James caught up to her. "Watch out for the fallen branches to your left. Sometimes they're just beneath the surface, ready to snag your foot."

Maggie stopped, then walked around the cluster of fallen birch, leaving webbed footprints in the crusty virgin snow. "The storm must have knocked them down."

The two of them stood along a forest's edge embraced by snow-covered trees—trembling aspens and black cottonwoods.

She turned around for a moment to peer at the gentle slope below. The town of Goldstrike looked like a little village molded from clay, sitting in a wide river valley and cupped in the shadow of great mountains. Smoke rose from faraway chimneys. In the sky, a red-tailed hawk patrolled the ground for signs of field mice, and the caw of other birds beyond the treed slopes aroused Maggie to the beauty of nature. "No wonder you love it out here."

James, brawny beneath his tan jacket and having to duck beneath the branches of a tall pine, gave her a curious look. "I like things peaceful."

"Then why on earth would you choose to work as a Mountie?" She had difficulty understanding him. "I can't think of anything less peaceful than having to break up family disturbances or chase a horse thief or haul off people in handcuffs. I've seen you do that once, you know. Apply handcuffs. It was earlier this year when Rufus Harper's house burned down."

"He committed arson by burning down his neighbor's house, but it caught his as well. He deserved more than handcuffs."

"Wouldn't it be easier to continue working as a trapper, as you did when I first knew you?"

"The Mounties needed men." His voice grew tender, emphasizing his point, and doing odd things to her heart. "I went because they needed me."

"You're right," she said gently, admiring him for his decency. "You do have simple reasons for doing things."

"The more straightforward the better, wouldn't you say?"

He turned in front of her. The expanse of his shoulders blocked the afternoon sun. "You're more complicated. You need...you *like* a lot of people around you."

"Is that how it looks to you?"

His dark hair rippled in a wave of warm wind. "That's how it is."

"And you don't need anyone. Is that what makes you more straightforward?"

He frowned. "We're different, that's all. I was just noticing."

She lifted her chin. "What else did you notice?"

James removed his snow glasses. Sunlight played in his dark eyes. He looked down at her lips, and she swore he was thinking about kissing her.

Blood rushed to her face. Her heart thundered in her ears. Taking a step sideways, she grabbed for a branch and tried to dispel the anxious moment. Staring down at Goldstrike, she ordered herself to stop daydreaming about his kisses.

When he spoke again, she couldn't bring herself to look his way.

"I noticed that we see things differently when it comes to Christmas. You've got a store filled with every imaginable drawing of Saint Nicholas, globes of all colors to decorate the tree, dozens of samples of shortbread and even, I might add, handpicked elves who do your caroling."

Maggie laughed. "They're not elves, they're children. And you make my store sound like it's the wrong way to celebrate the season."

"It's not wrong. You bring a lot of good cheer to the folks in town. It's only…my family never had much money to spend at Christmas."

Something about the way he said these things made her feel targeted, as if he was judging her and her way of life.

Sheldon had once told her James's history, how he'd grown up in the northern mines and that his family barely kept in contact. She wondered if it was only distance that separated them, or deeper troubles.

But James's mention of the word *money* made her straighten her back. What was it with men and money that they always seemed to point it out about her and her store? She was proud to be a successful shopkeeper, proud that she could support herself and that she had enough left over to help her sisters clothe their children.

If James couldn't get into the lively celebrations of Christmas, and if he looked down his nose at her and the rest of them, then she felt sorry for him. As for judging her, well, it'd been many years since she'd let a man influence the way she thought.

Her cool tone deflected the hurt she felt. "What have you learned about baby Holly?"

James seemed stung by her brisk tone. He donned his snow glasses with a snap, as if communicating his disapproval of her. Stiffly, he looked back over the valley, then stepped away to get his bearings on his snowshoes.

She knew he didn't approve of naming the child, either. It seemed he didn't approve of much of what she did, which only made her more defiant.

"The coal mine twenty miles north of the burned-out cabin has been attracting a lot of new miners. Maybe the baby's family was headed for the mines. And the lumber camp east of there had taken out an ad in eastern newspapers earlier in the fall for more men. It seems unlikely that anyone would be traveling in the dead of winter, for lumber or mining, but it's a possibility. Or it could have been locals who stumbled on the ferry house then got trapped by the storm."

"So you believe we should look for Holly's family either at the lumber camps or the mines?"

James nodded. "That's right."

"That seems a fair deduction. But how do we know…what makes you think Holly's parents are still alive?"

"There's no knowing for sure. It's gruesome to talk about in mixed company, but I checked the charred remains of the cabin."

"And?"

"No bodies. Whoever was in there got out alive. Where they went, I haven't a clue. But why they'd leave a baby behind is beyond reason."

Maggie was still thinking about what James had said twenty minutes later as they entered the fort, but was unable to solve the puzzle. They left their snowshoes at the gatehouse and said howdy to several men in red uniform, then entered the barracks in search of Commander Collins.

"He's in with the cook," said the company clerk.

While they made their way to the kitchen, men's voices carried down the hall. They were coming from the officers' parlor, James told her. The men were singing "We Three Kings."

Walking beside her, James hummed along and sang quietly, as if not fully realizing she was there. She enjoyed the tenor of his voice and strained to hear more. The fact that the quiet man sang was still something of a wonder.

"Why are they singing?" Maggie asked as they neared the door leading to the kitchen.

"They've formed a Christmas choir. Some of the men who can play instruments are creating a band."

He must have seen the question in her eyes, for he added, "To pass away the time. Most of the enlisted men are single and don't have family out West."

The single men were lonely, she thought. "Are you a part of it?"

"No." James laughed gently, pushing open a swinging door with a large, forceful hand. "No."

They entered the massive kitchen.

The old cook looked up from his chopping block, doing some singing of his own as he hailed James. "Sergeant! Great idea of yours to form the choir. I haven't sung this much since my Joy and I danced at our wedding. Of course, it wasn't Christmas carols, but…anyway… Miss Greerson, how do you do today?"

"Fine, Mr. Rumley, thank you. I brought you something."

Walking past the fragrant cauldrons of steaming soup, she reached into the inside of her wool jacket for an extra-large pouch. Untying the ribbon, she passed a bundle to the older gent.

He inhaled. "Ah, allspice."

"I thought you could use more. We were short when you put in your last order but got a new shipment last week. Before the trains stopped running because of the ice, that is."

The trains didn't actually run through Goldstrike, but a lot farther north. Scouts brought provisions back and forth on a regular basis.

"Yes, indeed. Thank you kindly." Mr. Rumley bowed. "Your timing's perfect with the song. You are bearing gifts from Orient are."

Maggie smiled at his twisting of the words. She was still amazed that it was James's idea to form a choir and band, yet he wasn't a participant.

They removed their coats while James asked about the commander. Maggie took a moment to glance around. Cloves of garlic, woven together, meshed with uprooted herbs that hung from the rafters and gave the entire west wall a rich, earthy scent. Although she'd never been inside the fort, Mr. Rumley was a frequent visitor to her store, and tiny reminders of the season found its way into his beloved kitchen. Sprigs of holly, dried peppermint leaves floating in water bowls and ornamental candles stood on the mantel above the wall-to-wall fireplace, where the soup was boiling. An oval mirror with a gold-plated frame of Saint Nicholas sat squeezed between two turnips.

"The commander was called away to practice his tuba." Mr. Rumley watched her looking at the mantel. Returning to his chopping block, he diced an onion. Sadness crept into his face. "My late wife, Joy, used to love that mirror. Our granddaughter bought it when she was five, as a gift for her grandma." He wiped a tear from his eye. "Darn these onions, they make me weep like a child."

Maggie guessed what he was cooking as she breathed in a heavenly aroma. "Oxtail soup cooked in ale."

"Oh, you are good." Standing above one of the stoves, Mr. Rumley slid the chopped onions into four large frying pans. They sizzled in bacon fat. She marveled at the remarkable quantities required to feed a troop of men.

"Would you like to stay for supper? I'm sure the officers would appreciate sitting across from a lovely woman."

"No," said James. "We can't stay."

"You should learn to share," joked Mr. Rumley, but it only caused Maggie and James to grow quiet.

Mr. Rumley looked from one to the other.

The commander burst in. He stood almost eight inches shorter than James, and thumbed his thick gray mustache. "The clerk said you were lookin' for me. I heard there was trouble at High River Landing. What's going on, Sergeant?" He nodded at Maggie. "Good afternoon, Miss Greerson."

James explained where he'd been, how he'd been trapped by the snowstorm, then how he'd seen the fire and taken the baby.

"When I heard about a baby earlier today, I couldn't believe it. I've spoken to everyone in the fort, but no one knows a thing about her." The commander and his wife had four children of their own, ranging in age from two months to seven years. "Were there any clues at the site?"

"Nothing at the fire. The house had burned to the ground. The fortunate thing is there weren't any bodies, so whoever was there had escaped. The storm wiped out all tracks."

"What about signs of horses or sleighs?"

"In the forest about a quarter mile away, there were faint tracks of two horses and a sleigh. The trees protected the tracks from the wind. I can't be sure how old they were, maybe weeks old. The ruts had sunk deep into the ground, so the horses were hauling something heavy."

"You've never mentioned that before," said Maggie.

"Because I'm not sure it's connected to the fire. The forest has been logged, so it could have been someone removing a fallen tree for the lumber." James reached into his pocket, twisting his lean physique. He removed a couple of items that he'd wrapped in brown paper, along with a small burlap sack.

The sack had a thread of red string running along its upper edge, and orange markings along its lower.

"I found a tiny yellow bead, sir, in the snow outside the cabin door. And three long black hairs."

Maggie frowned. "What's their significance?"

"I'm not sure about the bead, but the hairs belong to dogs. I don't have any huskies with partially black coats, so they're not from my team."

Maggie pressed her palms against the beaten-pine counter. "But if the baby's family was traveling by dogsled, then where do the horse and sleigh tracks fit in?"

"That's the puzzle."

The four of them stood staring at the items in James's hand, trying to force logic into their reasoning.

Maggie watched the cook pick up his stained wooden spoon to stir the onions. "May I see the burlap sack?"

James swung it into her hand. She opened the sack and found two spoons, a linen napkin and various spices separated into different envelopes.

She sniffed each envelope. "No allspice."

The men stared at her. "What does that tell us?"

"I use similar burlap sacks in my store. They might have bought these spices from me."

"Every merchant from here to Vancouver uses these sacks."

"But if they did buy from me…there's cinnamon here, nutmeg and baking soda, but there's no allspice. It's a common Christmas baking ingredient. It's made from the berry of a Caribbean tree. If they bought these spices from me, then whoever it was passed through town more than three weeks ago, when I was short of allspice."

The commander ran his fingers through his mustache. "That's a pretty outlandish deduction, miss."

"It's logical," she insisted. "But it's not certain."

"It's a stroke of genius," said James.

"Hmm," said the commander. "Why would someone leave a baby behind? That's what I ask myself."

"Maybe they didn't know they left her behind," Maggie offered.

"How could they not know?"

Maggie shrugged. It did seem ridiculous.

"Maybe they didn't want her," suggested James.

Maggie looked at him, horrified that he'd spoken the words she, too, was wondering.

"That doesn't make sense," said the commander, easing everyone's concerns. "If they didn't want her, there were plenty of other ways... She was well fed and looked after when you found her, which means they wanted her."

Mr. Rumley cracked an egg into a pan. "Maybe the family was attacked in the cabin, by cutthroats or bandits who then set the house on fire."

James shot holes into that idea. "But someone must have carried the baby into the spring house. What happened to that person?"

Maggie thought of something else. "Maybe we're looking for a family when we should be looking for only one adult person."

James shifted his weight from one leg to the other. "A woman with a child would find it almost impossible to travel that terrain alone in this weather, I'm afraid. It's highly unlikely. And a single *man* traveling with a three- or four-month-old infant is also extremely unlikely, simply because most men aren't comfortable alone with babies. And because there were no milk bottles to be found, the baby's probably still being nursed, so a woman is mandatory."

Everyone nodded in agreement.

"So we are looking for a man and a woman." James turned to Maggie. His leg brushed hers, drawing her attention to how close he stood. "Do you remember anyone who might fit that description who passed through town more than three weeks ago, possibly even two or three months ago?"

"I get so many customers two or three months prior to Christmas." Maggie sighed. "So many families with children. But some of them don't shop with their children if they're staying with relatives in town, or at the inn, or passing through. I don't remember anyone with a small baby."

Maggie angled her side against the counter, noting that James followed her movements with his gaze. "The fact that these people brought Christmas spices with them…it's encouraging, isn't it? I mean, it says something about their character. Someone intended to bake something nice for themselves or for their family, not to harm someone."

"I used to cook in a penitentiary," Mr. Rumley blurted above his stew. "Murderers like cake, too."

His blunt comment hushed her to silence.

James lifted her chin with smooth, warm fingers. "That's something only a woman would think of, Maggie, but yes, the baby's folks do seem to be good people."

With James's reassurance, Maggie allowed herself the pleasure of optimistic thoughts regarding Holly's family.

James approached the commander. "Sir, I'd like to send a team of scouts back to that area, if I may. One to the lumber camp and one to the local mines. If they take the route along the river, opposite to High River Landing, they can be there and back in three or four days."

"In this weather?"

"The chinook is starting to melt everything. They could take the dogsleds." James spoke in a commanding tone that Maggie had never heard before. "Maybe there's something else going on that the Mounties should know about. I mean, if there was something foul involved in the fire, maybe it's spread to the camps. Folks could be in trouble. I could head one team—"

"No, you stay here and finish what you started with the baby."

"But I could—"

"No." The commander shook his head. "I've got one almost the same age. I reckon the tyke's grown attached to you, and considering the time of year, everyone needs someone to be attached to. Think of yourself as her guardian angel."

The kindness of the commander's words resonated with Maggie. James did make a wonderful guardian angel. He'd found the baby and brought her to safety.

The commander turned to Maggie. "Thank you, Miss Greerson, for keeping her with you in your home, and please relay my thanks to the other women for their generosity in helping. Now, if you don't mind, I'll direct those scouting teams to leave immediately, and then I'm getting back to my tuba."

Their walk back to town on snowshoes wasn't nearly as difficult as their walk to the fort. Maggie suspected it had something to do with the buoyancy in their hearts, at concluding that Holly's parents were loving folks who only through tragic circumstances had left their baby behind. She prayed for a family reunion, that Holly's parents weren't hurt or in trouble, that there was a reasonable explanation.

Yet doubts nagged at her. Even if Holly's parents were good folks, were they the best people to look after a child? How could they leave their daughter behind? Even to an optimist, it was clear there was trouble here.

Taking a deep breath, Maggie wondered what would happen to Holly if no family was found. Would the child be taken away to an orphanage? There wasn't one in town. There hadn't been a need for it, for most families took care of their own if tragic circumstances befell another relative.

Maggie couldn't seem to shut off her mind, no matter how she tried to convince herself that her runaway thoughts were premature. But who would take in Holly? Could she stay permanently with Maggie?

Her mind raced with wonderful possibilities, but in the end, sorrow rooted in her soul for Holly. The best thing for Holly was her own family.

"Hey, what's on your mind?" James stopped beneath the same forest's edge they had three hours earlier. The sun was setting and would soon sink behind the trees. Maggie stared at the long red streaks it cast over bulging drifts.

"You were looking fairly cheerful at the fort," he told her, "and now you've developed a ridge between those big brown eyes."

"I was thinking, what if Holly's family never came back."

"Don't allow yourself to think that way. Tell your mind to stop."

"And I suppose you do that all the time?"

"If I think of every worst thing that could happen in my duties, I'd never get through one day."

"But in order to prepare ourselves about Holly's future—"

"You can think a little bit about it, but just don't dwell on it."

"How do I turn off my mind?"

"Distract it with a completely different topic."

She laughed. "Like what?"

"Like what are we going to do about these feelings between *us*? Between you and me, Maggie."

Strapped into his long snowshoes, James continued on, his powerful stride emphasizing the handsome proportion of his body, leaving her agape at his staggering question.

Chapter Seven

"How can you say that?" Maggie pursued him down the gentle slope.

James heard her panting behind him. She caught up quickly. Her blond braid trailed beneath her red wool cap and flapped against her coat.

The revealing question had slipped out of his mouth. Now he wondered if he should have gone to the fort himself to speak to the commander, and Maggie should have remained in her store.

"Look, Maggie, we both know what's going on."

"What?"

Was she really too stubborn to admit it?

"Every time you come close, we both start twisting out of our long johns struggling so hard not to look at each other, or say the wrong thing."

"You don't know what I'm thinking."

"Oh, no?" He gazed at the blood infusing her face, the overheated brow, the pumping of her hot breath that created clouds in the cooling air. As soon as the sun started to fade, temperatures dropped.

"What I know is that you're just as drawn to me as I am to you."

She sputtered. Her mouth flapped open, then closed. If the topic weren't so serious, he'd consider her reaction comical.

"*You're* the one who kissed *me* five years ago!"

"I don't remember."

"You do so. I can see it in your expression."

"As I recall, you participated fully."

Her gasp echoed down the valley. "What kind of a gentleman are you?"

"A straightforward one."

"Well, I don't think you're straightforward at all. I think you're overly complicated, forcing yourself to remain aloof and pretending you don't give a hoot about folks or feelings or that little baby down there, when secretly you're concerned about us all!"

Maggie stalked off down the hill, fueling his anger. Was she trying to race? Damn it, he'd give her a run for her money.

But she outmaneuvered him, stomping in and out of protruding branches too thick for his bigger shoes, so he had to go around, which took longer.

"Now just a minute!" he hollered down the snow.

But her braid swung faster and faster against her red coat. What was wrong with this woman? Why did she have to compete?

"Slow down! You'll fall!"

"I will not!" she yelled over her shoulder, leaning into the wind and now practically running.

"Maggie! Slow down and let's talk about this. I won't bite!"

He saw the branch too late. It stuck into his webbing and down he went. He toppled onto his shoulder, twisting his ankle in the process.

It was likely his cursing that stopped Maggie from running.

His feet had slipped out of his snowshoes, but they were still loosely bound by the ties around his moccasins. He flopped into the snow and lay there, looking skyward at the speeding clouds as they whizzed past in the deepening hue of the sky, wondering what to do about Maggie.

Her face came into view as she leaned over him. Her cheeks were tinted rosy from the cool air, her lips rich with color. An apology seeped into her soft expression. "Are you all right?"

"Why, in God's name, were you running?"

"Because you make me mad."

"Give me a hand and I'll try not to make you madder."

With a straining puff, her braid sliding over her shoulder, Maggie braced herself and held out her gloved hand.

He took it, but with great delight, gave a playful tug, which propelled Maggie down on top of him. He saw her snowshoes kick off, as they should in emergencies.

Her weight thudded helplessly against his sheepskin jacket and sank into his muscles for a split second before she tried to bounce out of his arms.

"You tricked me! Let me go! You've no right—"

He rolled her over so that she was lying beneath him. He pinned her arms into the crunchy snow. The thong ties of their snowshoes twisted together, but even entangled they still had enough leeway to move their feet. He braced his on either side of hers, enjoying the way the bottom half of his body sank comfortably into hers.

"You were saying?"

"You're a bully."

"No, I'm not, I'm much too soft for my own good. You said so yourself."

"What do you want?"

"This."

He kissed her. Right there in the white field with a hawk screeching above them, the sun dripping red glaze into the snow, and the cooling wind tugging at their hair.

It was more of a slow burn. A kind of heat that built up from inside his chest and made its way through his limbs, tingling beneath his skin and causing a wonderful friction between his lips and Maggie's.

To his surprise and adding to his surge of pleasure, Maggie returned his kiss. As his bare fingers intertwined with her gloved ones and their palms locked, their mouths slid together.

At first he was more adventurous, moving with tantalizing slowness and trying to capture every heated inch of her smooth lips. She moved her mouth beneath his with an even rhythm, responding slowly then just as ardently as he. With eyes closed, he enjoyed the scent of Maggie, the taste of her, the feel of her soft body lying beneath his hard one.

She turned her head softly in the snow and he followed, then gently slid his right hand to rest his thumb at her throat. His long fingers spanned the entire left side of her face. The soft downy hairs of her cheek felt so feminine, so unlike everything in his life he usually touched and held.

He ached to connect with Maggie, and had been aching to connect with her for years. Why had he never realized it?

Her hands remained half buried in snow, above her head, as if the kiss had caught her so completely off guard that she couldn't move.

But real life set in; the logical, unemotional part of him that kicked up a fuss whenever he suspected he was heading in the wrong direction, or too quickly, or that he was implying things by his actions that he shouldn't be implying.

Kissing Maggie was like being caught in an unexpected ice storm. It felt exhilarating, made his senses come to life to details he normally never dwelled on, and brought awareness that he, too, was a living, breathing part of nature.

But when the storm was over, he'd be drenched, slightly stinging from the encounter, and all alone again, wondering if what he'd seen and felt had ever truly happened.

He raised his head and broke from her lips.

She looked at him directly, her brown eyes shimmering in the last strands of the sun's glorious rays, her swollen lips pressed closed.

When she inhaled, her chest drew up beneath her coat. "That's twice now you've kissed me, and both times outdoors. What is it about you and snow?"

Despite the tension between them, James smiled. "I guess it's the chilly air combined with my hot blood and your temper that does something strange to me."

"You *are* strange. First you tell me you enjoy my company, then you ignore me at the fort, then you argue with me, then you kiss me. What are you trying to tell me?"

"I'm not sure." He rolled off of her and into the snow, so that they both faced the sky. Watercolor streaks of pinks, blues and purples announced the coming of nightfall.

Maggie lay remarkably still.

He listened to her breathing. He wasn't sure if he should allow himself to feel something…and if he did, where it might lead them. He wasn't sure if the desire he felt for Maggie was strong enough to overcome his doubts about the future, about what sort of man he might be if he felt harnessed by a woman. By a wife. He'd never felt good being responsible for anyone, and he might disappoint her the same way he'd disappointed his family when he was thirteen. Sure, he was an adult now, but he'd never been able to patch up his hurt feelings with his folks, even after all these years. He sent a brief note home to his mother once a year at Christmas, accompanied by many dollars, but he never spoke to his father. As a policeman, James found it much easier to help others with their problems, much easier to see clearly and advise.

Was it simply lust he felt for Maggie, or was it growing, looming over his head into something much, much deeper and more permanent? And much more terrifying.

"I'm crazy about you, Maggie."

She didn't answer. He listened for a long time, but she said nothing. Maybe she expected him to say more, or maybe she couldn't respond in kind because she didn't return the feeling, but either way, it left him with a large lump in his throat.

On the sullen walk to town, after James said his ankle felt better, Maggie thought about the mess they were in. She knew that James was the type of man who didn't speak unless he had something important to say, so the weight of his words rang in her ears the entire trudge home.

Being crazy about someone meant you wanted to be with them as much as possible. Being crazy about someone meant you tried to get along with their family. Being crazy about someone meant that you opened up about your own family, that you shared your problems and your joys. James hadn't done any of that, and to Maggie, what people *did* counted for much more than what they *said*.

How many men had whispered similar notions to her over the course of the last three years? Four? Five? It always came with a price. Not at first, not in the courting stages, but later, when they suggested matrimony and how they'd share in her house, or how they'd sell *her* business to put the money in their bank account, or how they'd order her around and how she was supposed to adapt to *their* way of life.

Maybe Maggie was just too set in her ways to make room for a man. Too set in her ways to let a man tell her how to live or run her business.

For all she knew, James would expect her to wait for him at home while he ran off trapping and scouting in the woods for weeks on end, only to come home to tell her how to operate her store.

Her sisters called her extra guarded with men, a no-settling type of woman, but Maggie called it being intelligent.

Wait and see, she told herself, *the fabric James is made of, and make your decision then.*

They reached the edge of town. The main roads had been plowed and the lamplighter was shuffling along the boardwalk using a long pole to light the street lamps. Orange balls of light glowed ten feet in the air as Maggie and James passed in silence.

James tugged off his snowshoes and Maggie did the same.

He took them from her hand. "Mr. Billings invited me to stay at his house as long as I needed, so I'll just come inside your store to check on the baby and any news, then I'll be out of your hair."

But Maggie had a lot more to say. "I'd like you to come inside and stay awhile, if you've got the time." Shaky with emotion, she swiped the fallen hairs from her eyes. "We could talk after the others leave."

"Maggie…James! How did everything go? Have you learned any news about the baby?" Tamara greeted them at the door, shooing them inside, offering warm cider and quickly making James feel welcome. Come to think of it, Maggie's family always made him feel welcome.

"We deduced a few things." Maggie untied her moccasins then slipped into her house shoes, avoiding his gaze. "We'll tell you about it as soon as we warm up."

While James stripped off his sheepskin, Maggie did the same with her coat. He ran a hand along the black V-neck sweater that clung to his chest, and was glad to see that his denim pant legs were dry along the bottom.

He wondered what Maggie wanted to talk to him about. The anticipation made him worry, that she might tell him to permanently leave. And maybe that's what he wanted, what was best between them. But then again, his pulse beat with hope that maybe she had feelings for him, too. Hadn't he seen excitement in her eyes when he'd kissed her? Hadn't he felt it?

And if he truly wanted to be straight with her, shouldn't they clear the air and go from there? *Don't be such a coward,* he told himself. *She deserves to know how you feel.*

Tamara brushed at the snowflakes that encrusted Maggie's red coat, then looked quizzically at his, also covered. "Did you two fall in the snow?"

Flustered, Maggie ignored the question and slid the coat from her sister's fingers to hang it on the peg. "How's Holly?"

"She's a darling."

No sooner had they settled into the warmth of the room than Maggie had the baby in her arms and James was standing above her, close to the stove's roaring fire.

"Here, you hold her while I get her a fresh diaper."

"What? Me? I don't think—"

Maggie plopped the infant into his arms. "You carried her against your chest for six hours in a snowstorm. You certainly know how to handle her."

"But those were different circumstances. It was a matter of life and death and I had no choice—"

"She likely grew accustomed to your touch, just like the commander said."

"Yes, yes," cooed the sisters, smiling brightly.

Maggie beamed at him. "There, see how Holly settles into your arms? She remembers you."

To James, it was clearly a ruse by the women to get a man to hold a baby. Why did women love doing that?

But maybe more to the point, why would he object?

He slid onto the sofa and propped Holly on his lap. She weighed almost nothing, and that made him smile. Looking down into her plump round face, he felt the same sense of awe he had when he'd found her, deserted by the fire. A feeling of the power of mankind, the goodness of spirit, the abiding

Kate Bridges 175

love of humanity that attached one man, a stranger to an even stranger child, to fight together for mutual survival. With Maggie's decorated Christmas tree looming to the baby's right and the scent of pine needles filling the air, James could almost feel a spirit of Christmas invading his heart.

"Remember our trip across the snow?" He twirled his finger above the baby's fist. She reached out and clamped onto it, her blue eyes deepening in the flickering light of an overhead lantern.

Maggie's sisters laughed. Their children came around to his side, some sliding beside him on the sofa.

Maybe Maggie was right. James did like people and children; he just never knew how to be around them or how to be himself. Well, he'd been himself the entire six hours he'd fought for Holly. Holding her again relaxed him. She couldn't speak, so there was no need to think of something to say, and to James, that was the biggest burden lifted.

When he looked up, Tamara and Anna were staring at him from the other sofa, sighing in contentment.

He turned back to Holly and rolled his eyes good-naturedly, as if the baby might understand. "Ah, women."

Nine-year-old Rebecca kneeled beside him on the cushion. For a young girl, she was gifted with her hands. He could see that by the cross-stitching she had been working on that she now put to the side. "Aunt Maggie lets me change her diapers. Mama let me do it once this afternoon."

"Good for you. It's an important skill to have."

"Do you know how?"

"I had to change Holly's twice during our trip. I didn't have the proper cloth, so I tore up two of my cotton undershirts and used them." James recalled his childhood and laughter sprung to his voice. "Once when I was your age, I was stuck in the house alone with my youngest brother, so I had a go at his diapers. It was either change his diaper or listen to him bawl forever."

"Did you do a good job?"

"Yes, I did."

"What's his name?"

"William. And I've got two other brothers. Stewart and Daniel."

They were still smiling and talking when he noticed Maggie standing in the doorway, listening. She sprang forward with the clean diapers and a bottle of heated milk.

Maggie lifted the baby from his arms and placed her on a cushioned chair close enough to the fire to keep her warm but turned away enough to provide privacy for the diaper change.

Questions began pouring out of the sisters, with Maggie eager to answer.

"…and James found some dog hairs at the scene…sleigh tracks in the forest…" Maggie told the story as she bottle-fed the youngster.

James sat back and enjoyed the space, the chatter and watching Rebecca cross-stitch a scene depicting three small mice decorating a Christmas tree. The stitching was done on a child's scale, not very intricate, but Rebecca could easily manage.

"…and so James and the commander arranged for two scouting teams to deliver the news to the lumber camp and mines," Maggie finished, and looked to him for agreement.

The crackling firelight illuminated the soft shape of her eyebrows, the rich detail of her lips. He could watch the golden light dance across her features for hours.

Her younger sister rose. "So you might have word by the twenty-third or -fourth?"

"It's possible."

"That's wonderful. We'll pray for good news." Tamara stood up and urged Rebecca to her feet. "Let's go, children. Time to make supper for your father."

Cliff soon arrived and within ten minutes, the families were gone, leaving James, Maggie and the baby alone.

James wondered what was on her mind. He added two more logs to the fire while she slid the sleeping baby into her cradle. When Maggie turned around, she seemed withdrawn. He thought for certain she was about to tell him goodbye, so he prepared to get his coat.

"Would you like to stay for dinner?" she asked instead, sending a stream of unanticipated delight rolling through him.

Chapter Eight

Lord, the man filled the room wherever he went. Half an hour later while the baby slept in her cradle in the sitting area of the front room, Maggie stood nervously beside James in the tight kitchen. She rinsed two steaks in a bowl of water to thaw them while he peeled potatoes. His shoulders knocked the cupboards twice, and he'd just hit his head on the swinging lantern above him.

"Here, I'm sorry—let me move that for you." Maggie slid a wooden chair beneath the lantern, jumping up to move it out of his way, but James reached up first with a long arm and adjusted the chain.

"It's fine, don't worry."

He turned his head toward her. Already standing on the chair with her arm raised, she was taller than James, but what unsettled her was that he took her arm to help her down.

She couldn't deny her response to his touch forever. Her wrist heated beneath his grip, her breathing came with difficulty as his head brushed her hairline, and she felt the blood well up to her forehead even as she stared at the floor to place her step.

Sooner or later, she had to face him without the baby or a

platter in her hands. She had to tell him how his kiss affected her and whether they stood a chance together. But what should she say?

She fought to compose herself, but was somehow feeling very feminine, very out of sorts with her body and much too warm standing an inch away from James.

"Well, we'll get started with dinner, then," was all that came out.

He hummed an agreement and stepped back to peel his final potato.

Maggie had planned on reheating a bowl of soup for herself, but a strapping man like James couldn't survive on chicken broth. With his black sleeves rolled up past his elbows, she became acutely aware of his muscular forearms. They were lightly matted with fine, sable hairs.

James broke the tension. "I never picture you like this."

"Cooking? Why, I cook all day it seems, trying out new recipes for my customers." She reached for the platter of steaks. "You sprinkle one side with salt and paprika, and the other side with peppercorns—"

"No, I mean...like this...alone."

Totally befuddled, she stared at him. Alone. Yes, she was most certainly alone.

"I always thought you hated solitude. I always picture you surrounded by your sisters, in the midst of kids and customers."

"You picture me?"

"Mmm, hmm."

"When do you picture me?"

He seemed embarrassed by his disclosure, for he hesitated for a second, then turned back to his potato. "Just last night as I was staring at the ceiling, trying to get you out of my mind."

Oh! Now, why had he put that image into her brain? A half-clothed Mountie with a lean, muscled leg splayed out from beneath wrinkled bedsheets.

Feeling unsteady, she spun to the stove and dropped the steaks into the frying pan. Crackling oil seared the meat, just as the image of James, potentially naked, seared her silly head.

"Careful," he urged.

Beyond his view she rolled her eyes, vexed with herself for the confusion in her heart and the uncertainty of knowing what to say.

"Everyone leaves by five," she said softly. "They always do."

"Do you mind?"

"Not as much as I used to," she said, surprised by her own answer. "When Sheldon passed away, the silence at nighttime was the worst to bear. But now…I miss the silence, especially if I've had a busy day and there've been tons of people around me for hours. I do love the children, but the adults are tiring. I've got things to do and it's peaceful if—" She cut short at his quizzical look. "Do I sound terribly self-absorbed?"

He shook his head. "Not at all. I know exactly how you feel."

Of course he did. This was the earth's leading soloist.

But maybe they had more in common than she'd thought. She was much more independent than she used to be as Sheldon's wife. When he was here on earth, they'd enjoyed doing practically everything together—whether it was tending to chores, visiting friends, or setting up the store. She had fond memories of her earlier life, but she enjoyed her new life, too.

She felt a trifle guilty for thinking it.

The baby's cry pulled her into the other room. Maggie changed another diaper, settled Holly into another sleep, then finally sat down at the kitchen table across from James.

Over dinner, they discussed news about town, her new spice shipment and the outdoor activities scheduled for Christmas Eve. They talked about everything except personal affairs.

But as the evening unwound and Maggie carried the dirty dinner plates to the washing bin, James came up from behind.

"How long are we going to continue avoiding the discussion about how we feel?"

Still behind her, James cupped his hands on her shoulders. She swore she could feel the outline of each finger as his hot grip penetrated the shimmering linen fabric of her blouse and then seeped into her flesh. She prayed he couldn't feel her trembling.

He spun her around to face him, looming above her, his eyes demanding some response, his breath quickening in time with her own.

Backing up, she bumped into the counter. Its thick pine slab dug into her behind.

James took the opportunity to take another step forward, his thighs grazing hers. He planted one hand firmly on one side of her, and then the other.

With her neck craned, she struggled for words. "I do believe you've trapped me."

He grunted softly in response, his stormy gaze sweeping over her face. She felt the burn of her own blood as it crept into her cheeks.

James kissed her then, and she wanted him to.

Her arms went up around his neck, his came around to cinch her waist, then slid to her lower back. Possessively, he yanked her closer.

She'd never shared a better kiss. His mouth was sweet and warm and loving, and she ached for him to kiss lower, down her throat, her arms, her breasts.

She'd forgotten how blissful it felt to be encased in strength, to be united as a couple, as nature intended.

With a rougher manner, James uttered husky sounds and swept one hand across her blouse, trailing his fingers over the swell of her breast. Mumbling in pleasure, she allowed herself to feel his need, his urge to push further.

But when he slid his hand to her front buttons, she found

herself pressing her small hand over his fingers, indicating he should stop.

She broke free of his mouth. "Don't, James—it's not right."

Panting, he pressed his forehead against hers. "We can make it right. You'll see how good we can be together—"

"I've no doubt it would feel better with you than I can ever imagine, but I'm unmarried and I don't do that sort of thing with anyone."

Her heart thumped wildly at his nearness, but he was gracious enough to give her a moment to recover. She turned around to the counter and tucked in her blouse. Physically, they responded to each other in the most passionate sense, but sentimentally, and in conversation, they were lacking. Maybe there was something she could do about it, letting him linger here tonight with hopes of getting him to talk.

"I feel like I don't know much about you, personally."

"Ask me whatever you'd like."

To keep her hands busy, she began to wash the dishes. After a moment of watching her and tucking in his own shirt, he lifted the tea towel and helped her dry.

"Why is it, James, that you never speak about your brothers?"

"That's what you'd like to know? Of all the things you could ask, you'd like to know about my brothers?"

"Not so much about them, but why you avoid talking about them. This evening with Rebecca was the first time I've ever heard you mention their names. Did they treat you badly when you were young?"

"No, they treated me well."

"Then it must have been your folks who were unkind."

"It was my father."

"What did he do?"

For the next ten minutes, James explained about his childhood, how difficult it was to make ends meet, how many hours his father put into working the mines, how James himself had tried his hand at the age of thirteen. Listening quietly as she scrubbed pots, she could picture him as a sensitive child.

"They must have been very proud of you for volunteering."

James scoffed. "Not exactly."

"But you added food to the table and you were only thirteen."

"It didn't work out the way I'd hoped. I got extremely ill and didn't recover for almost a year."

"Oh, I'm sorry. Then they must have been devastated at how badly you'd suffered."

He snorted. "Not exactly. My father was angry."

"At you?"

He nodded.

"Why?"

"Because I cost him twice as much on medicine than I did before I'd volunteered."

"And that's why you don't speak to him now?"

"It's not so much that we don't speak, it's that we don't feel the need to interfere in each other's lives."

"Huh," she uttered in disbelief. "You're covering up."

His jaw tensed. Turning away to stack a plate, he spoke with a chill in his tone. "You've no right to give your opinion on people you've never met."

"I've met *you*," she said, hoping to keep their conversation going. "And some of your traits are explained by the situation with your folks, but what I don't understand is why you won't forgive your father."

"What are you talking about? He did nothing but yell and curse at us. He and my mother don't even live in the same house anymore."

"I'm sorry about that, but their marital problems aren't your fault."

"I didn't say they were."

"What is your fault is your situation with your father."

James winced. "You don't know—"

"You won't let him apologize. You feel superior by allowing this chasm to separate you."

With a look of disbelief, James backed away from her.

She continued, unable to stop herself, and wanting to help James through his obvious pain. "He's older than you and you should respect your elders. They're closer to leaving this earth, and they've got a right to clear the air before they die. You've got to give him a chance to apologize to you, now that you're an adult."

"He'd never apologize. Not in the next five decades." James looked at her with a harshness she'd never seen before, as if asking, *What do you know?*

"I know how people behave around money," she said sadly, thinking of her own life.

"Not everyone wants your money, Maggie. Don't blame me for things I've never done to you."

She ignored the comment because the conversation wasn't about her, it was about him.

"Have you ever considered, James, that your father wasn't angry with you for getting sick, but with himself for allowing it to happen? Maybe his pride couldn't take the fact that he had to allow his thirteen-year-old son to descend into mine shafts with him every morning, when you should have been at school or playing in the sunshine with the other boys. Maybe your father couldn't stand *himself* for allowing his misery, his inability to make ends meet and provide for his family, to nearly take the life of his eldest son."

"Have you ever considered, Maggie, that it's none of your business, and that you should worry about your own problems with money?"

Her enthusiasm drained, replaced by a kick of anger. "What do you mean by that?"

"You think every man who steps through your door is here to steal your last dollar. How selfish do you think that is?"

Slapping the towel on the counter, James stalked out of the room. She heard him unlatch the back door, then burst out of her home.

Chapter Nine

The next three days were spent in misery.

"Some things should never be spoken aloud between two people," Maggie whispered to herself as she reviewed what she'd said to James.

It was December twenty-third. Late-afternoon sunshine streamed past the storefront curtains while she scooped fragrant coffee beans for customers and listened to the children practicing "Hark! The Herald Angels Sing."

She still agreed with what she'd said to James about his lack of forgiveness toward his father, but disagreed with what he'd said to her about her distrust of men.

However, as the days wore on, with James dropping in to the store to check on the baby and barely mumbling hello to her, she realized how deeply her harsh words had hurt him. And that maybe what he'd said about her held a morsel of truth. With some embarrassment, she wondered if she was really that transparent about her finances. Or simply transparent to James?

It wasn't her place to point out his shortcomings. It was just that sometimes it was so much easier to see the problems in other people's lives rather than your own.

Maybe she should concentrate on her own unhappiness. At how she claimed to love solitude when for the past thirty-six hours, during every spare minute, she'd walk to her storefront window on the guise of checking the weather when deep in her soul she knew she was really checking and hoping for James.

Holly cried in her cradle. Grateful for the distraction, Maggie lifted her into her arms. She rocked the precious child. "Are you hungry? Yes? Let's go warm up a bottle."

When Maggie returned from the kitchen ten minutes later holding Holly, the babe freshly diapered and sucking on the bottle, James entered the store.

"Sergeant Fielder!" Rebecca shouted.

He smiled at the girl, and after nodding hello to Maggie and the other adults, called to Rebecca, "Brought you something."

When he held up his fist, the children swarmed him.

"What is it?" The girl tugged at his fingers, trying to unclasp the surprise.

Crouched low to the children's level, James opened his palm and revealed a tiny copper bell.

Rebecca opened her eyes wide. "Where did you get it? It's pretty."

"The tinsmith made it. I thought you might like to have it for a Christmas decoration."

Rebecca picked it up and shook. "It's a jingle bell."

The children tore off toward the tree. They raced around it, trying to decide where best to put the bell as James rose slowly, like a giant rising to his feet, and glanced at Maggie.

He considered her for a long moment before quietly nodding again. Neither of them had answers to what they'd argued about days earlier, and that still lingered between them on this windswept day.

Her eyes followed the outline of his forehead, nose and set jaw. She wondered if there was more reason to why he'd come today, but as she watched him swallow, his Adam's apple lifting and then settling back down, he didn't utter a word.

Clutching Holly to her chest while she tilted the bottle, Maggie was grateful that she had this tiny inquisitive face to console her. Maggie would personally see to it that no matter what they discovered, even if Holly was orphaned, she'd be taken care of with love and respect. The babe's weight felt comforting, her miniature fingernails mesmerizing, and the tiny smacking sounds as she fed soothed the spirit. There was something about holding an innocent child in your arms that was calming, that ebbed away at animosity. Children were nature's gift to the world, and Maggie would never leave her side.

But just as Maggie thought it, she caught a movement beyond the window. She peered closer, quivering with unexpected nervousness beneath her blue, polka-dot blouse. Outside in the fading day's light, a team of Mountie scouts, leading two dogsleds, rode over the crest of a distant snowy hill. They brought strangers.

Ten minutes later everyone in the Spice Shop had gathered silently around the windows watching the Mounties draw closer, just as they had that first evening when James had brought Holly.

Now, James slid out of his coat and stepped up beside Maggie and the baby as if somehow trying to protect the two. Her heart beat like a drum.

One dogsled appeared to be carrying a woman wrapped in furs, accompanied by a child half her size. On the other sat an unknown man. Four Mounties led the teams.

After what seemed like an eternity, they finally reached her store. Maggie couldn't seem to move her feet, but James sprang to the door to let them in.

One of the constables stepped in first. He nodded to James, but before he could speak, a bearded man, young woman and their young son rushed in. Engulfed by customers and calls of assistance to sit by the fire to warm up, the man thanked them. He bent lower to speak to his son, but his young wife scanned the group. Her fur hat slid down to reveal a head of matted black hair, clear white skin and weathered eyes moist with exhaustion. When her gaze settled on Maggie, then lowered to Holly nestled in her arms, the woman shrieked with joy.

Maggie felt an aching lurch in her chest. She didn't need an introduction; she knew who this woman was. Holly's mother.

"My daughter," the woman sobbed.

Holly let out a weak cry, her weight shifting in the blanket, her body warmth penetrating Maggie's arms.

The group parted as Maggie stepped forward, a lump in her throat the size of an apple, extending her arms and gently sliding the infant to her mother.

The baby gurgled and her mother cried.

Maggie tried to restrain her own tears, but the touching moment grew overwhelming. Holly's family loved her. The mother quietly cooed, kissed and clung to her baby. The father and dark-haired little boy joined her in praise, unable to stop patting the infant. Their skin seemed to glow orange in the streaks of the sunset. Maggie would have this moment frozen in her mind for years to come.

"Thank you," the mother wept, turning to Maggie. "I don't know by what miracle she was brought to you, but thank you."

Maggie nodded, still unable to speak from the ache in her throat and tremble to her heart. She had many questions to ask these folks, but until everyone had calmed down, words weren't necessary.

Her husband repeated the sentiment. "Ma'am, we're forever grateful."

"It was my pleasure," Maggie finally murmured, her arms feeling cold from the baby's absence.

James stood beside her. Had he been there the entire time?

When told by the other Mounties that James was the one who'd found their daughter and brought her here, they thanked him profusely, too.

His mouth tightened with sentiment, his eyes glistened with deep satisfaction, and he couldn't seem to tear away from the vision of the mother rocking her baby.

Then with a tender unexpected touch, James rubbed the tense spot between Maggie's shoulder blades as if he knew just how much she would miss the child. Physically connecting with him in spite of their argument—or maybe because of it— intensified her reaction. His gaze roused an agony in her, an inexplicable emptiness at how she'd argued with him about his family, in sharp contrast to these strangers before them who felt no shame in pouring out their hearts to each other.

Stepping away from her, James kneeled to help the young boy undo his heavy furs. "You must be tired after such a long journey. Here, come here by the sofa and heat up your hands."

"Yes, please," offered Maggie, coming to her senses. "This way for all of you—please sit down." Abiding her manners would restore calm to her disquiet. Fussing around the family would give her something to do with her trembling fingers.

"Are you all right, Maggie?" her elder sister whispered as they made their way to the sitting area.

Maggie nodded softly. There was no need to be concerned about her.

But her younger sister patted her other shoulder when Maggie sat down on the sofa. "Are you all right?"

"Yes," Maggie murmured politely, tugging at a loose button on her polka-dot blouse. Why wouldn't she be? Holly had found her family. But the empty ache of loneliness still scraped at the pit of Maggie's stomach.

Maggie turned her attention to the family as introductions were made.

"I'm Kyle Lattimer and this is my wife, Lynne. Our son David. And of course, you know Angelina."

"Angelina," Maggie repeated with delight, quivering at the beauty of the word, and thanking God that the mystery of the baby's past had ended so incredibly well. "It's a beautiful name for a little girl."

While folks warmed themselves by the fire, Maggie's sisters insisted she sit while they prepared tea and a spread of food for the guests. Maggie relented, but wished they wouldn't treat her as if she was ill and needed to rest. Losing Holly—*Angelina*—to her folks was a blessing and Maggie's feelings were unimportant and irrelevant.

"What happened?" Maggie asked the Lattimers as soon as she could, when the room had settled and she could breathe again. The other children had taken David out of earshot, to the spare room and were playing games. "The ferry house burned down. How did you escape the fire?"

Mr. Lattimer rubbed his beard and sighed. In the light, he looked a lot younger, likely in his early twenties. "It was awful. Lynne here had taken the baby to the spring house to wash up at the pump and collect some water while David and I were building a fire in the cabin. The chimney must have been plugged with a dead animal. Or maybe an old nest. Anyway, we started the fire but the plugged chimney made the fire sweep into the room, just as fast as you might snap your fingers. Before I knew it, David and I were trapped."

Mrs. Lattimer shook her head. Her messy black hair tumbled down her blouse—the same dark color as Angelina's. "I had taken Angelina outdoors for some fresh air and was filling up the bucket in the pump shack when I smelled it. By the time I raced in with my useless pail of water—"

"—the log frame of the house was as dry as cinders—"

"—all it took was one spark—"

"—I heard David screaming—"

"—Lynne left the baby in the spring house where it was safe so she could rescue us—"

"—by the time the lumberjacks arrived to drag us out, the three of us were unconscious from the smoke."

James stood in the corner with the other Mounties, listening to the Lattimers.

Maggie tried to slow them down so she could grasp everything they were saying. "So the three of you were trapped inside the cabin, Angelina was by herself in the spring house waiting for her mother to come back, and passing lumberjacks pulled you out?"

Nodding, Mr. Lattimer confirmed it. "They'd been logging in the forest, caught in the unexpected snowstorm when they saw the smoke. We were unconscious so couldn't tell him our girl was left behind. They took us back to camp and when we woke up the next day—" He choked on his words. "It was the worst day of our lives. They didn't know there was a fourth member to our family. They didn't know to look for Angelina."

Mrs. Lattimer sobbed again. "We thought we'd lost her."

"By the time the lumberjacks went back, she was gone."

"The worst Christmas of our lives."

Turning his head to the Mounties in the corner, Mr. Lattimer scratched his ear. "But then five days later, four Mounties arrived. Like a miracle."

His wife drew in a rattling big breath, then smiled. "And now…we'll never forget this Christmas as long as we live. It's the best Christmas of our lives."

The words brought a hush to the room.

Maggie fought another round of tears. She listened to the wood crackling in the fire, and the gleeful voices of playful children drifting from the spare room.

She lifted her gaze to James's face, searching for a hint of what was going through his mind, finding only that silent intensity that threatened to undo her. She felt as if they'd accomplished this together—the safety and survival of an infant, providing a temporary loving home for Angelina until she could be reunited with her family.

Maybe when the Lattimers left, perhaps James would stay behind and Maggie would offer amends for her earlier comments. The argument still clung between them—she could feel its chill.

"…so we'd best be going. We'll get a room at the inn."

Alarmed to see the couple rise, Maggie jumped to her feet. "You're leaving? But you haven't told us everything. Why were you traveling in the storm? And the clues James found at the burned cabin—did you buy spices from me recently?"

"We're terribly sorry," said Mr. Lattimer with a shaky hand at his wife's back as they walked to the front door. "We're tired and losing track of what we've said. Initially, the purpose of our journey was traveling to a small town beyond the lumber camp to say goodbye to Lynne's mother. She was gravely ill, but she passed away, at least meeting Angelina and seeing David one last time."

Touched by the sorrowful news, Maggie offered condolences. Mrs. Lattimer looked to the floor, then smiled as David came running up with the other children. David was showing them a handful of yellow beads he was playing with in his pocket, identical to the yellow bead James had found at the fire scene.

While his son donned his coat and mittens, Mr. Lattimer finished the story.

"It wasn't storming when we started more than a month ago from Ram's River, about fifty miles south of here. And as for the spices, yes, we passed through here. I waited at the inn with the children while Lynne came in and bought a few things for her mother. I believe your mother, Miss Greerson, served her."

"I see," said Maggie. It finally made sense.

"These warm chinook winds will make it easy to return home. But we're tired now, and need to get back to that inn."

"Of course. Sleep well."

"I'll escort you," said James. "The constables can return to the barracks."

James was going with them? Maggie's heart began to thump. He wasn't staying with her?

She looked his way, but he was already sliding into his sheepskin coat. Maggie told herself it didn't matter, that she had a lot to do to prepare for tomorrow's big day—her busiest day of the year—and that it was better if she was left alone. But her utter, irrefutable disappointment made her speechless.

"We'll see you in the morning, Miss Greerson," said the Lattimers.

Some of the customers had already left—the others did so now, joining Maggie's sisters and their children, the Mounties and then James himself.

"Good night, Maggie," was all James said to her.

Maggie hoped to hold Angelina one last time to say goodbye. With a warm smile she extended her arms, but Mrs. Lattimer hadn't seen it, spinning quickly while scooping the infant inside her coat to shield her from the pressing wind.

Maggie peered into the cool, dark wind into which James and the rest had escaped. The wind bit into her sleeves but she barely noticed.

Closing the door, Maggie listened to the echo of the fire as it caught another log and the crackle loomed in the heavy silence. Her chest rose and fell with her breathing.

She pressed her forehead to the icy door and stood there for a long time. Everything had turned out so well, she told herself. It was for the best. But the pain seeped into her pores, as well as the heat reaching her from the fire.

They'd taken the dear child, and without so much as a blink, James had slipped away from her, too.

Chapter Ten

Palms braced against his mattress, James arose the next morning to the usual sounds of a bugle playing reveille. Except this morning the jokester at the bugle, a lad of sixteen, quickly followed it with an energetic rendition of "Deck the Halls."

Tonight was Christmas Eve.

Swinging out of bed, James planted his bare feet on the cool floorboards. A lot had come to him last night watching Maggie with the Lattimers. It had been emotional for everyone, and especially difficult for Maggie. On his moonlit hike back to the barracks, he'd thought about what a caring woman she was, and how wrong he'd been in uttering the words *selfish* and *Maggie* in the same sentence.

Wincing with regret, he hoped she would forgive him. He planned on saying just that, and a whole lot more, to her today.

At this moment, maybe it was the lively music or the comforting thought that Angelina had reunited with her family that made him smile. Then again, perhaps it had more to do with the difficult letter James had written yesterday…or simply the happiness he felt in seeing Maggie today. No matter the reasons, he had a tingling of Christmas spirit rising within him, as he hadn't had since he was young.

That's how the Yuletide cheer came upon you, he remembered while shaving at his dresser. It would come and go in tiny moments—flashes of sunlight on a freshly painted toboggan, a pair of new blue socks, his mother absently humming "Deck the Halls" while ironing his father's shirt.

James spent the morning attending to his duties at the fort. He met with the commander to outline the work schedule for the first two weeks of the new year, he stopped to listen to the band practicing for the outdoor festival later that afternoon, and then he dropped in to wish the cook good cheer.

At one o'clock when most men were leaving the fort to prepare the town square for toboggan races, sleigh rides, skating and games, James donned his newest red uniform and navy wool breeches. On top of that, he'd wear his buffalo furs. Now that all the roads were plowed, it would be a short gallop into town. The massive horses penned up in the stables needed exercise every day, no matter the weather, and constables were encouraged to ride them.

Still humming "Deck the Halls," James hastened his bay toward Maggie's store. He couldn't wait to see her.

In the early afternoon, the scent of mulled wine greeted James as he strode through the door of the Spice Shop. Sunshine beat through the windows, into the store where a dozen customers had gathered, alongside Maggie's huge family. Some customers carried packages while they shopped, others held cuts of meat from the butcher shop where they'd picked up a Christmas goose or freshly stuffed sausages or a fine cut of beef.

It always amazed James, as he entered Maggie's realm, how well liked and appreciated she was in Goldstrike.

He tossed his coat into the corner and looked for her. James spied her near the Christmas punch bowl, scooping cups of cheer into decorative china bowls for neighbors' extended hands.

He took a moment to savor how she looked, scanning her high collar, the fashionable white-lace blouse adorning her bosom, and her golden hair swept up beneath a red-velvet Saint Nicholas cap. Her long red skirt, also cut from red velvet, followed the movements of her hips as she twisted and turned. Her pointy cap had a small bell sewn onto its long tip, so when she bent over the punch bowl, it fell across her chest and dinged. His muscles tightened watching her.

"Wassail!" the tinsmith shouted as he drank.

Maggie laughed. "Wassail!" Then she caught James's gaze as he towered above the heads. Her face grew somber for a second, and in that second, time seemed to freeze. She didn't want him here, he feared. She didn't want him interfering.

Then the face brightened, revealing pink lips and pretty teeth, a sparkle to her eyes.

"You've come," she whispered, holding out a china bowl filled with red mulled wine. Its fragrance, laced with cinnamon and lemon rind, was irresistible.

Their fingers met on the dainty bowl, someplace over the painted picture of snowflakes falling on a chapel. Her fingers felt warm.

She removed her hand first. "Wassail, James. Merry Christmas."

There was so much he wanted to say to Maggie, but the crowd pushed closer, reminding him they weren't alone.

"A toast to Maggie Greerson," James said softly. He drank the small amount of wine in one gulp, enjoying the way it warmed his throat.

"Isn't it wonderful, James, what my sisters have done for me?"

"What have they done?"

Maggie ran a hand over her misty eyes. Emotions flared through her words. "They invited everyone in town, it seems, to do something for me today, as a Christmas gift. To show me how much they love me, my sisters say."

"Everyone does love you."

The bootmaker's wife whizzed by, piercing the personal moment. "Your bedspread's been darned and the kitchen pantry's scrubbed clean."

Her husband added, "The wood's all chopped and stacked right beside your back door so you don't have to walk too far."

Mr. Furlow, the schoolteacher, squeezed through the pack. "I cleaned out those two spice bins. My wife scoured them with boiling water so they no longer smell like ginger. Now we've gotta run. We're joining our grandkids at the festival. Bye, Maggie!"

"Thank you," she whispered to each one as James watched with quiet pride.

"Oh, and great job, James," Mr. Furlow added, "on finding the Lattimers!"

Just as he left, the Lattimers entered. James heard Maggie's sharp inhale, then watched her eyes follow Angelina's sleeping face.

"We heard what the town was doing," said Lynne Lattimer, extending her hand to shake Maggie's. The woman looked remarkably well rested. Her black hair was tucked into an impeccable bun and her clothes were freshly pressed. "We came to give our warmest wishes for a merry Christmas to you and Sergeant Fielder."

Maggie's fingers trembled at her collar. "Thank you kindly for your thoughts."

"Would you like to hold her?" asked Mrs. Lattimer.

"Very much."

"I'm sorry we left in such a hurry last night. Truth was, we were exhausted and needed our beds."

James watched the woman remove her baby from a roll of

fox skins. As soon as the cooler air reached the infant, she twisted awake.

Maggie laughed gently and lifted the baby. She kissed a smooth cheek and cupped Angelina's soft head.

The embrace lasted for a long time, in James's opinion. Long enough for him to take in and appreciate the gentle wrinkles at the edge of Maggie's brown eyes, the swell of adoration in her upturned mouth and the unspoken bond between her and Lynne, that each woman valued human life above everything else.

Her husband stepped forward. He'd trimmed his beard overnight, so it lay crisp and flat. "We heard you're stuffin' boxes of food to give away to the poorer folks in the valley. Could my boy and I help you pack 'em?"

"Yes, indeed." Maggie looked to the boy, who stood staring at the other children across the room. They were just starting to sing their carols. "The Twelve Days of Christmas" filled the air. "But why don't you let David go join the other children. Maybe he'd like to sing along. Singing's important work, too."

With his parents' permission, the boy raced away.

Maggie turned back to his folks. "I'll just set down the baby and show you to the—"

"Let me," James insisted. "I'll show Kyle to the charity boxes. You stay here with Lynne and Angelina and enjoy yourself."

The smile Maggie gave James turned his heart to mush.

"But you've never—"

"I can figure it out. Your mother and sisters over there can fill me in on what needs to be done."

"Have my sisters gotten to you, too?" Maggie asked with a hint of mischief. "Is this *your* gift to me? Taking over my duties?"

He watched the sensuous play of her lips. In the background, the children were singing about five gold rings, and he was reminded of his first kiss with Maggie, during this very song. If she didn't watch out, he'd kiss her here on the spot again, proprieties be forgotten. "No, I'm saving my gift till later."

"You don't have to give me a gift, James. I'm teasing."

"I'm not." Pressing his shoulders through the crowd, he winked at her. The Lattimers looked away during the exchange, as if Maggie and James were discussing something very private. Either his wink, or their embarrassment, made Maggie blush.

James and Kyle left their women and stepped over to the counter. After Maggie's sisters showed them how to pack the large crates each with firewood, dried fruit, spices and frozen fowl that the butcher and business folks like Maggie had donated, the men worked hard.

Providing charity boxes filled with food and firewood for the poor the day *after* Christmas had been a tradition rooted in Queen Victoria's time, some of the women explained to passing children. There was also a centuries-old tradition of dispersing money collected in church boxes on the twenty-sixth. That's how the twenty-sixth had become known as Boxing Day in England and Canada and elsewhere, a day also known as the Feast of St. Stephen. And this Feast of St. Stephen—the saint who provided for widows and the poor—they explained, was the reference in the song "Good King Wenceslas."

But here in the town of Goldstrike, James told the children proudly, Maggie and the others insisted on creating boxes on the twenty-fourth. She had her volunteers deliver them that evening so that needy folks might enjoy the food with their families on Christmas Day itself, like everyone else in town.

During the next three hours, James could only catch glimpses of Maggie in the busy store. He waited and watched for an opportunity to have her to himself, but none came.

From across the room, James watched her package some baked goods—shortbread cookies and berry pie—to those who hadn't the time or inclination to bake for themselves.

When a woman screeched softly in laughter, his gaze shot to the punch-bowl area. Beneath the dangling kissing ball, Tamara had been caught by her husband, Cliff, who'd rewarded her with a loud kiss.

Folks chuckled. James caught Maggie's eye. Her velvet cap danced along her shoulders. Her trim waist in that red skirt stood outlined by the sunshine behind her. Maybe she could see the desire in his stare, for she glanced away quickly, rubbing the back of her long neck, which left him to contemplate how she felt about him.

It made him wonder if she needed him. She seemed to have everything she wanted. A loving family of sisters, a town full of people who adored her, her store the way she liked it and her life running smoothly without a man.

He was still thoroughly perplexed by Maggie when the afternoon had turned to early evening and folks began to leave.

"We're going to join the others at the town square," some indicated, while others said they were going home to dinner.

When everyone had left—all but Maggie's youngest sister, Anna, and her children—James stayed behind. He knew Maggie was well aware of him, for as he carried crates to the back room, she flushed when he brushed by her thigh. She did her best to avoid standing close to him, and spent more time directing silly questions at the children than speaking to him. There was a lot James had to say, and this time he'd say it before returning to the barracks for another lonesome night.

"Let me take you to the festival," he said to Maggie.

She adjusted her blouse, the lace peek-through at her throat revealing satiny skin beneath, making temptation race through him. "It's been a long day—"

"When's the last time you went?"

"Likely the last time you were there, too. Years ago."

They shared a smile. That was more like it, he thought. *Give me some hope.*

"You two should get out of here," hollered Anna from behind the counter. "I'll lock up. The children will keep me company till my darling husband swings by. We'll join you at the festivities. They're roasting corn and sausages and we plan on eating dinner there."

James found Maggie's fur coat and held it up for her. "It's up to you. I'd still like to give you my gift, but in order to get to it, we've got to go out there."

And there he stood with arms extended, longing that she'd accept, for he couldn't live with another rebuff from Maggie.

The town square was humming with activity. James felt eyes peering at him and Maggie in the setting sun the moment they'd left her store. Some nudged each other and whispered in their direction, making him wonder if they'd known all along about the feelings he had for Maggie.

He walked tall beside her, thrilled she'd agreed to come. But dozens of people walked beside them, making it impossible to share an intimate conversation. Some stopped to enter the competitions—stilt walking, who could spit prune pits the farthest, or who had made the best-tasting fudge.

The Mounties had placed rows of logs onto the hillside, forming rudimentary bleachers. James and Maggie squeezed between the people to sit on the hill and watch the skaters.

After the winter storms of last week, they'd been lucky to get a burst of warm weather for Christmas Eve.

James bought Maggie and himself a cob of corn and a handful of roasted chestnuts. They sat together surrounded by dozens of others bundled in fox, beaver, buffalo and raccoon furs.

"The key to keeping warm in this weather," he said to Maggie as he cracked a chestnut, "is dressing properly."

She swallowed a mouthful of corn. "And what's the key to you?"

"Dressing me properly."

His answer made them both laugh.

The wind whisked through his hair. He removed his buffalo coat and placed it beside him. He'd be warm enough in his wool uniform. Kerosene lamps, strung on a temporary wire above the crowd cast a rich glow over Maggie's face. Her red-colored wool cap and coat made her skin shine like smooth crystal. And her curly hair, thick as ivy and despite her braid, was beginning to unravel at her neck and temples.

James grew serious. "The key to my heart is very simple."

Growing quiet and reflective, Maggie set down her half-eaten cob of corn onto the cardboard platter in her lap.

His bulging shoulder bumped her slender one. "I like being outside on nights like this. I like honest work. Sincere friendship."

"Is that where I fit in? As your friend?"

It was difficult to get the words out, more so when there were heads turned in their direction, negating privacy. "You're more than that, I hope."

Maggie turned her head away to look at the passing sleigh filled with laughing children. He wasn't sure if he'd sprung something on her she didn't want to talk about, or if she was measuring her words. But either way, he watched a tiny frown build between her eyebrows, and gentle lines of concern pucker on either side of her mouth.

And then the musicians, the Mountie band, struck up, interrupting their conversation. It was a warm enough evening for them to play their instruments outdoors, as well as inside the town hall where quieter events were taking place—board games and the stringing of popcorn into garlands.

The hillside grew silent as folks listened to the Mounties play. The sun faded behind the slopes and lavender shadows colored the snow.

"I thought long and hard about a Christmas gift for you, Maggie. What I'd like to do is show you that I'm not that bad, that I *do* like folks. You were right about me in that regard. Being with them and with you isn't torture."

"You don't need to tell me that. What I said about your family was none of my business. It was inconsiderate and I shouldn't have opened my big mouth."

"I'm glad you said it." Then he added, "I'd like to sing you a Christmas carol."

Her tender brown eyes searched his. She smiled gently. "What a lovely gift."

When he saw the commander pressing his tuba to his lips, James excused himself to join the group. He used to be a good singer in his childhood. And so as the commander began playing "Good King Wenceslas," James sang bass in harmony with the others.

It was warm and comforting to be surrounded by friends on a starry night like this. His deep voice filled the cold night sky. He felt the words coming easily, the tune smooth and jovial. James concentrated on enjoying himself, on his many friends in the crowd, on how beautiful the night was and how extraordinary he felt being here with Maggie.

He saw her sitting forward, cupping her palm beneath her chin, smiling at him in a way that made his hopes soar. It had been a mighty long time since he'd sung a Christmas tune, and never, ever had Maggie stared at him like this.

When he finished, the crowd clapped, Maggie the most enthusiastic. The other Mounties continued with another song, but James slid his way around the people to rejoin Maggie.

She stood up, weaving away, her sensual figure dipping out

of reach, making his heart pound an obscene rhythm and his body tingle with arousal. "I've got to tell you, James," she murmured. "I'm crazy about you, too."

Chapter Eleven

Snowflakes tickled her forehead and the wind sent her scarf rolling along her cheeks as Maggie dodged James. She skipped and hurried on toward her store, pleased to see him following, so very pleased she'd heard him sing.

She scuttled through the folks on the boardwalk. Heading back and forth from the square, people swiveled to watch James chasing her, then stared and chuckled.

"Come back here, Maggie! You can't say something like that to me and then run off!"

"You're a great singer, James Fielder!"

"Shh, you'll wake the sleeping!"

"It's early—no one's sleeping yet!"

"The snow owls haven't awakened. They're just rising for their midnight feast!"

With a throaty laugh, she reached her store. Removing her key from the inside pocket of her coat, she unlocked the door and stepped inside. The room was still warm from the last embers of the fire. She raced to the stove, poked the fire and added two more logs.

"If you don't come here right this minute, I'm going to drag you out into the street."

Maggie spun to face him. With hat in hand, he was gazing at her from the open doorway, seeped in moonlight, his fur collar turned high around his jaw while the wind tousled his thick, black hair. The fire glow illuminated his face and trapped tiny shards of light in his dark, intense eyes.

The light caught his forehead, too, his rough cheeks, his tense jaw, making his features stand out starkly against the night sky behind him and the moonlight tracing his body. He smiled a little bit, and still with eyes upon her, tossed his hat to the sofa. She seemed unable to move as she pounded with emotions, all at odds with each other.

He walked closer as she fought to speak. What had she done, telling him she was mad about him, and then leading him to her home? She trembled as she surmised that he might think it an intimate invitation. A sexual one.

She was reminded how big he was by the force of his stance, the size of his boots and that she had to crane her neck to stare up at him.

"Thank you for the song. How did you know I'd enjoy your gift?"

They were completely alone, things were more serious now than out there at the festival and he was unsmiling. "Because you're sentimental."

With one smooth motion, he pulled off her hat and tossed it to the sofa beside his. Then he yanked open her coat and tugged it off one arm. "Shall I undress you here and now?"

"James, don't..." But it slipped off her shoulders into his hands. He tossed it, as well.

"I shall do as I please."

Sliding from his grasp, she escaped to the other side of the room. "Just because we declared we're...we're crazy about each other doesn't mean..."

"It means everything. That's all there is to life."

"We need to figure out what to do. If you'd like to court me, then—"

"Court you? I want more than that."

His meaning was clear when he lowered his eyes over her breasts and the intake of her waist. She felt a flood of heat start in her chest and move to her thighs. He wanted to bed her? Is that what he wanted?

"If you think that all you have to do is look at me that way…and that—and that I'll melt in your arms…then…"

"I'll look at you any way I please."

He came closer but she stepped away.

He laughed as if it was a game, unbuttoning his big coat, dropping it on a chair and leaning back with a rough hand propped against an archway. He stretched his legs, his back, his neck, as she'd seen him do a dozen times before, and each time she was riveted by the size of him. And how breathtaking he was in his red uniform.

"Tell me why you brought me here."

Lord, he sounded like a gruff commander. "To thank you for tonight," she began clumsily. "To tell you how much I admire you for finding Angelina and bringing her to safety."

He tilted his head and brushed his fingers along his jaw. "You know, when the light shines on you like that, it gives your hair the color of spring honey. From the first moment I laid eyes on you today, I wanted to wrap my arms around your tough, proud shoulders and never let go."

"But I hurt you, James. So terribly when I advised you about your father. I don't know anything about your situation and yet I did what I always do. I stuck my nose into your affairs—"

He swooped to her side and spanned her waist with his massive hands, pulling and tugging and telling her to hush.

She buried her face in his tunic, aware of firm muscles beneath the cloth, loving the way he smelled and felt. Maggie sensed his lips brushing lightly against her hair.

"Two days ago, the Mounties started up the dogsled teams again, carrying mail back and forth along the valley," he said. "I've been dying to tell you all afternoon. I posted a letter yesterday."

She looked up and stared at the serene expression on his handsome face. "Who did you write to?"

"My father." James looped his long arms across her back, encompassing her with a stillness as she listened to his every word. "I got to thinking about what you said. I was a child when I attempted to work in the mines. I didn't understand all the angles and how difficult it is for a man to face the world and have to look after a family."

"What did you say in the letter?"

"It was only a Christmas greeting, really, a wish for a happy new year. He probably won't read more into it. He likely won't write me back."

"He might."

"You don't know how stubborn he is."

"I'm glad you wrote to him. Maybe now you can think about your past with a bit more cheer."

"I consider it your Christmas gift to me. You made me see the light. And no matter what happens with my father, I know I tried my best."

His words filled her with an easy warmth. What else was inside of his character that she never would have guessed? "And you, James, you made me realize that I've been making my life more complicated than need be."

"What do you mean?"

She took another breath of him, enjoying the fresh mint traces of his shaving cream. "It seems that for every year that went by, I'd get more determined that every man who showed an interest in me was after my money."

"Some might have been."

"But not you. There are more facets to you than I ever

would have suspected." She gripped his waist. "I was too harsh on some of the other men, though."

"Can't say I'm sad about that. I'm glad you gave them the boot."

She smiled at his possessive remark. "About Angelina…I must confess that I'd grown terribly selfish about her, too. When we couldn't find her folks, I allowed myself to think that maybe…maybe she could stay here with me. That she was a sort of gift sent by heaven. Wasn't that ridiculous?"

"Ah, Maggie…"

"And then when we found Kyle and Lynne and David, I knew in my heart that the gift I'd been given was the opportunity of giving her back.…" Saying it aloud, Maggie felt a joyous exhilaration that Lynne must have felt when she'd finally seen her baby alive.

They relaxed like that for a moment, James and Maggie, listening to the warm howling wind outside, the fire spewing flames in the stove, the crackle of timber around them as rafters heaved and expanded with the heat.

"You know what, Maggie? You're standing under the kissing ball."

Her gentle laughter was caught short by his kiss. A powerful set of hands slid up her back and coaxed the last vestiges of chill from her bones. She felt so protected, so wanted by this man, and for all the right reasons.

But alone with him tonight, kissing him with every nuance of sexuality in her, hearing him moan and pull her closer, wanting more, warned her to stop before they did something she might regret. As much as she wanted this, too…

She broke free of his mouth and, panting, pressed her forehead into his chest. "James, I—"

"Maggie, I'd like you to be my wife."

It took a moment to comprehend his meaning. Slowly, feeling a burning heat in her neck and a thundering in her pulse, Maggie lifted her lashes to study his face. Tenderness etched the corners of his mouth, and that heartbreaking vulnerability unique only to James, glistened in his eyes.

"I love you, Maggie. Will you marry me?"

How could she not have known he felt this way? Joy filled her heart.

"It would be my honor, James. I think I've been in love with you for years, since the first time you sang me a song and kissed me."

Laughing, he swooped down for another heated kiss, but when his hand reached around to cup her breast, she softly nudged it lower.

"Not until we're married."

He growled with a mix of displeasure and open frustration at being told to stop. "You're an honorable woman, but your honor can drive a man insane. I'll respect your wishes, but let's speak to the minister tonight after Christmas Eve services. Now that I've found you, I'd like our life together to begin as soon as possible."

"Will you always be so eager?"

His murmur was almost a plea as he lowered his mouth to hers. "Always." Then to her utter, blissful delight, he added, "I'd like us to have children, Maggie, as many as you want."

Ten days later on January third of the new year, James opened his eyes and adjusted them to the morning light that poured across Maggie's bedroom. Warm and content, he turned to gaze at the naked woman lying on her side next to him.

Maggie was facing the wall, away from him. James devoured the sight of her smooth back, the bumps of her spine, the way her loose blond hair covered the pillow like flowing ivy. He loved the sound of her deep breathing and the way her lungs worked in and out, gently causing her waist to move up and down. She had one knee pressed to her belly, angling her beautiful hips toward him, exposing a smooth white rump. He sighed, longing to make love to her again. But instead, he tugged the goose-down duvet over her hips, figuring she was cold, also stealing a glance at her finely turned calves and slender ankles.

The rustling of the covers made her stir. Rolling around to face him, she opened an eye.

"Good morning, Mrs. Fielder."

"Huh," she said lightly. "If I had known you loved to hog the covers, I might have reconsidered your proposal."

He grinned at her remark, kissed her forehead, then yanked at the portion of the duvet that was hiding her breasts, thereby releasing them for his viewing pleasure.

"That's more like it. I want to see what I own."

She hit him playfully on the arm, but he grinned at the sight of two rose-tipped breasts jiggling beneath her arm.

His body sprang to life. "You're a beauty."

He traced a kiss along her arm, then lowered his mouth to one of the rose tips. Licking lightly, he enjoyed the smoothness of her nipple and the way his wife stilled beneath his touch. He sucked her other breast as Maggie cupped it toward him. How did he get so lucky to marry a woman so full of sensuality and pleasure? And love.

His heart went wild when she slid her hand along his body, beginning with his waist and moving to his bare hip. When she grasped his thickening shaft and slid her silky fingers along his skin, he moved closer to get more of her.

She tossed a leg across his hip. He angled himself to the moist, dark target and gently pressed himself along her opening. She was slick again, and she thrust herself toward him so he could enter.

He uttered indecipherable sounds of pleasure as they made love, lying side by side, he with his hands on her breasts and back, she tugging him by the waist so that he could push himself deeper.

He tried to hold back so that she would climax first, sucking her breasts and her throat until he felt her tense. Without restraint, his beautiful wife released and contracted in wave after wave of splendor. James knew that as long as he lived, he'd never get enough of seeing her like this. He wanted to please her in every way, in every facet of their lives.

When she relaxed, he grinned and playfully tugged at a nipple. She responded with a laugh and pushed his shoulder so that he was lying on his back with her riding on top.

"Hmm," he growled, watching her breasts bounce. "You do know how to please me."

And then it was his turn. He felt the slow build, the tension rising in every muscle, the contractions about to explode. When he reached the pinnacle, he felt her loving touch in the way her hands slid along his chest, and the tiny kisses she planted along his throat. "Oh, Maggie…"

When the interlude was over, she slid off of him to her back, kicking the covers back on top of them.

"No matter how long I make love to you," he said, watching the sunshine pour over her face, "it's never, ever enough."

"That's how I feel, too."

"What shall we do today, Maggie? You name it and I'll make it happen."

With a boisterous smile, she moved closer so they were resting hip to hip. She curled her feet with his so that their toes wiggled together. He loved the feel of that, too. They'd been married since January first, a new year to start a new beginning, Maggie had said, and so far they'd spent almost two whole days in bed.

The first two weeks of the new year were always quiet for her business, she'd told him, and so she'd closed the store. He had two more days of rest himself, then he'd return to duty.

He hadn't told her yet, but later this year when his enlisted time was over, he was planning on retiring from the force to pursue trapping and hunting for a living. He knew she'd be pleased, for Maggie could continue working in her store and not have to relocate to Alberta district once Fort Steele was closed.

"It's time I get you outdoors so that folks don't think I've kidnapped you," he told her. "Shall we visit your sisters today? Your nieces and nephews can show you how the new coats and boots you bought them fit."

"Yes, I'm in the mood for visiting. Let's do that."

He watched Maggie dress. She slid expertly into her corset but asked him to tighten the laces, which he eagerly did, loving the way it made the top of her breasts nearly spill over. They dressed together, as husbands and wives do.

With the barking of dogs outside, Maggie slid the curtains aside to peer out. The many buttons on her cuffs and high-pinched collar glimmered in the bright sunshine. "Someone's coming in on dogsled. Looks like the Mounties with a mail run."

"Let's see," he said, drawing closer, buttoning his sleeves and patting his collar to sit straight over his tie.

James recognized the constable, but there was a stranger rising from the sled. An old man dressed in a faded brown coat with patches on his elbows—

"Oh," James gasped, recognizing the aged face.

"Do you know him?"

"Yes."

"Who is he?"

"My father," he whispered, an ache rising to his throat.

Maggie looked from James to the old man standing out in the cold, who was looking from store to store and home to home, perhaps wondering where to begin knocking. He looked frail, thought James as his heart sped. His father's hair was totally white beneath his old cap, and he wasn't as heavy as he used to be. Not nearly as formidable as he'd once seemed to James.

"He got your letter." Maggie's eyes filled with tears.

"Must have," James replied, trying to suppress his own.

She pressed her hand into his and gave him time to consider what to do.

James clasped her fingers, ever so grateful that Maggie was by his side. "Let's go out and bid him good welcome."

* * * * *

THE CHRISTMAS CHARM

Mary Burton

Chapter One

Grant's Forge, Virginia
December 25, 1869

Colleen Garland had established a strict routine when her husband suffered a devastating stroke seven years ago. Since that day, she rose before dawn, dressed in a starched calico skirt and white blouse, swept her blond hair back into a stern bun and made a modest breakfast of toast and one boiled egg. The early mornings were spent feeding, shaving and dressing her husband and seeing her younger sister off to school. Save for the day of her husband's funeral eight months ago, she always opened the shades of Garland's Mercantile at precisely eight o'clock.

There were so many days and nights when her life felt as if it was spinning out of control. There was no one to talk to, no one to share her burdens with. It was the routine that gave her a sense of control not only over her business but her personal life, as well. Her husband and sister depended on her to keep their home together and her customers depended on her attention to detail, her organization and her talent for finding just about anything anyone needed.

More than a few folks whispered that she was far too young to be so prickly, but girlish whims were a luxury she couldn't afford. So she held her head high and gave them no mind.

However, this morning was different. Not only did she leave her bed unmade, but she didn't bother with the stiff corset. Uncharacteristic excitement bubbled in her as she moved through the simply furnished parlor, past her sister's closed bedroom door and down the back staircase to the kitchen.

Her sister, Deidre, had arrived home yesterday from Hollins Institute. She'd been gone for five months and this was her first break. Today was just for the two of them.

A large cast-iron stove dominated the kitchen. Across from it was a large wooden table, nicked and scarred by over fifty years of use, four straight-back chairs and a sink and pump. The floor was stone, a remnant of the tavern that had stood in this spot years ago.

She flexed her cold fingertips before she opened the stove's firebox and stoked the dimming embers. She started to feed in aged timbers. Slowly, the fire sparked, hissed and warmed the cold room.

She sat back on her heels and watched the fire dance. During the years Deidre had been growing up, Colleen either worked long hours in the store or she was caring for her ailing husband. There was little time for Deidre and fun. She regretted the time the store and Richard's illness took from her life, but there was no getting around it. She had an obligation to her husband, and the store had to stay open if they all wanted to eat.

Still, she couldn't avoid the stab of guilt. Her little sister had grown up and away from her. They'd lost so much time together.

She lifted her chin, shooing the sadness away. No sense fussing over spilled milk. She rose to her feet and smoothed her hands over her skirt.

This Christmas holiday was going to be extra special. No work. Just the two of them laughing and spending time together as they had so many years ago.

Colleen crossed the room to the small pantry. Lining the walls were shelves filled with the peaches, tomatoes and berries she'd canned in jars at the end of summer. Two large ham legs hung from the ceiling. She chose three of her best apples from a basket in the corner, as well as the crock of sugar and the eggs she'd been hoarding for days.

Returning to the worn kitchen table, she assembled her grater, mixing bowls and spoons. She started to shred the apples over a bowl. Apple bread was Deidre's favorite. So many times her sister had begged her to make this when she was little. So many times circumstances forced her to say, "Tomorrow."

By the time she'd finished mixing the batter, a wall clock chimed seven times. The fire in the stove hissed and popped. She slid the pan into the oven and rose. She wiped her hands on a tea towel and in no time had cleaned her cooking utensils and put them back in their places.

Without thinking she started toward the store, then caught herself. Normally at this time of day she was out front in the store, busy sweeping the floors, straightening a canned-good display or polishing the large front picture window. But today was her day off.

She started to wipe down the already clean kitchen table. Once the table was rewiped, she rinsed out her cloth and laid it neatly over the edge of the sink.

Colleen nervously patted her fingers on the side of her leg

as she glanced around the clean kitchen. She was so used to working—it had become as much a part of her life as breathing. So this break in her routine felt awkward. This morning's stillness gave her far too much time to think.

Just eight months ago, all she'd craved was a moment's peace. There'd never been a moment to think or feel. Now, instead of peace, she felt far older than her twenty-six years. Choices she'd made haunted her.

Hot tears filled her eyes. "You won't do this to yourself," Colleen whispered, surprised by the unwelcome well of emotion. "What's done is done."

She focused on her task. Her first Christmas as a widow wouldn't be sad. It would be happy. The apple bread would make this day special. She and Dee would decorate the table-top tree in the parlor with paper chains, ribbons and dried fruit and then tonight they'd go to church. The day would be perfect. Soon she would feel like her old self.

Footsteps sounded on the back staircase as Colleen crossed the room toward the stove to make coffee. Deidre bounded down the stairs, so full of energy and life, she seemed to attack each day. "Good morning!"

Deidre's blue eyes sparkled as she smiled. She'd brushed her blond ringlets back off her face, leaving a few curling strands to dangle just above her forehead. Her new blue wool dress hugged her young body, accentuating curves that had grown quite womanly this last year. Eighteen and all grown up.

Colleen was so proud of her sister. She was attending college as she'd once dreamed of doing. Her sister would have an education and choices—choices Colleen could have had if she'd not sacrificed her own future for Keith Garrett. The young farmer had stolen her heart the first moment she'd laid eyes on him. When the time had come for her to go to school, she'd said no, believing Keith would marry her. But the war broke out, Keith refused to marry her and he'd left to fight. Her parents had died during the next year and she and Deidre were alone.

Even after eight years, the memories still sliced through her heart.

"You are up earlier than usual," Colleen said, grateful her voice sounded even.

Excitement bubbled from Deidre. "I'm off to see Sally and Anne. We're having breakfast."

Colleen didn't hide her disappointment. If only the apple bread had been ready. "I'd hoped we'd have breakfast this morning."

Deidre's skirts brushed the edge of the kitchen worktable as she held out Colleen's best velvet Sunday hat. "Would you help me pin this on?"

She smelled of rose water—Colleen's rose water. "You've been in my dresser."

Her sister smiled. "The hat goes so well with this dress and your bottle of rose water is over half-full. You never use it anymore. I hate to see it go unused."

There'd been a time when she'd used it quite often. Those were the days she and Keith would steal off and spend lazy afternoons together. She realized now she'd not touched the perfume since Keith had left. "You're right, of course."

Deidre angled the hat on her head in a saucy jaunt and held out a long hat pin for her sister.

Colleen wiped her hands on her apron. "Can't you stay a couple of hours?"

Deidre handed her two hat pins. Her blond ringlets framed her heart-shaped faced that no longer looked girlish but quite womanly. "I'd really love to, but I promised Anne and Sally."

Colleen straightened the hat to a more respectable angle then rammed the pin in place. "When will you be home? I thought we'd decorate the tree."

"I promised Ruth I'd go riding this afternoon."

Colleen looked into Deidre's bright eyes and remembered when she'd been *that* young and reckless. It hadn't been that long ago and the realization tempered her disappointment. "Perhaps we could have dinner."

Deidre nodded. "Yes, I will be home for dinner." Her gaze darted to the oven. Sweet smells of baking apples filled the room. "Apple bread. It's my favorite."

"I wanted to surprise you."

"You really are the best, Colleen. I do love you. And I am so grateful for all that you've done for me."

Her sister's contrition didn't ring true. "What are you up to?"

Deidre's eyes widened just as they had when she was twelve and she'd stolen candy sticks from the jar on the front counter. "Nothing. Can't I thank you for being nice to me?"

"You never have before."

"Well, maybe it's the holiday spirit." She hugged her sister. "Maybe now that I'm older, I see what a sacrifice you've made for me. I know you never would have married Richard if it weren't for me."

Colleen straightened and met Deidre's gaze. "I cared for Richard." There was truth in that. He'd been a good man, solid, caring.

"He was older than Father."

"He was kind." And he'd offered her and Deidre a home when they'd had nothing. Though their marriage had lacked passion, there'd been friendship and mutual affection in the beginning. When he'd suffered the stroke shortly after their wedding, she'd stood by him and honored their wedding vows.

A wrinkle creased Deidre's forehead. "You didn't love him."

Absently, she fingered the buttons at her starched cuff. "There are many kinds of love. It's not all poems, roses and passion, you know."

Sadness flickered across Deidre's blue eyes. "It should be." She straightened her shoulders. "But it isn't."

"You had that kind of love with Keith." She spoke softly as if afraid to mention his name.

Colleen couldn't breathe for a moment.

"You never talk about him," Deidre coaxed.

She'd never discussed Keith with her sister. And she wasn't about to start now.

"No, I do not." She needed to do something. The idleness, combined with the talk, was reawakening emotions she'd worked hard to bury. "I was very young when I was with Keith. And I learned the hard way that's it's foolish to put trust in love."

Deidre crossed the room and lifted her brown coat off the peg. She slid it on. "He loved you."

Sudden, hot unshed tears stung her throat. "Not enough to marry me."

"I know he must have had good reasons."

How many nights had she lain awake trying to make sense of that last conversation they'd shared. They'd stood on the hill overlooking the James River. When she'd told him she wasn't pregnant, he'd looked disappointed and relieved. And then said he had to leave. She'd begged him to stay. He'd backed away from her and left.

Colleen straightened her shoulders and pursed her lips. Anger had long replaced the bitter sadness in her heart. "He never shared them with me."

Deidre ignored the icy tone in Colleen's voice. "Why

haven't you gone to see him? Richard is dead. You are free to marry again," Deidre said.

Tension tightened Colleen's shoulders. Keith had come to see her when he'd first returned home from the war four years ago. She'd been shocked by how different he'd looked. The youthful spark had vanished from his eyes, replaced by a hardness that had frightened her. His body had grown leaner, more muscular. Despite the changes and old wounds of the heart, desire had bubbled inside her as she'd stared at him. Lord, but she'd ached to throw herself into his arms.

Instead, she'd been mindful of the customers staring and whispering as she'd moved stiffly across the mercantile. Her bland smile didn't reflect the long tucked-away emotions roaring to life.

Keith's gaze had trailed over her, settling on her wedding band. "Is it true what they're saying in town? Are you married?"

The happiness had vanished and she was left with the stark reality of her life. She couldn't go to him no matter how much she wanted to. "Yes."

"You didn't wait for me?" The raw pain in his eyes still stuck with her to this day.

She'd been annoyed at his arrogance. He'd had his chance to marry her! The desire vanished and she'd met his steely gaze. "No."

Keith had turned on his heel and left the mercantile without a word. They'd not spoken to each other since.

"He's never married," Deidre prompted.

Colleen knew. Whenever there was the least bit of gossip about Keith she listened, treasuring the snippets of news like gold. She knew his ranch was thriving; that he'd courted the Baxter girl for a brief time and that he'd built a fine new house. She'd caught glimpses of him when he came to town but they never spoke. Whenever his ranch needed supplies, he sent his young foreman.

After Richard's death there'd been whispers in town that he'd start courting her. But he'd not and Colleen had refused to sacrifice her pride and go to him even though there were so many nights that she laid awake aching for him.

She shoved aside the stab of sadness. "Too much time has passed."

Deidre stood right behind her now. "I'll bet he still loves you."

A wave of heat stained her cheeks. "The past is the past and there is no getting it back." She bristled. "I'd like you to carve out some time from your schedule today so that we can visit." She sounded pricklier than she'd intended. "I want to know how school is going for you."

Deidre's smile vanished. "What's there to say? I go to my classes, I do what the teachers say and I make excellent marks. It's all very boring."

"Boring? What I wouldn't give to be in your place now. You are lucky we have the money to send you to school, Deidre. With an education, you can be a teacher. You will have choices in your life."

Deidre frowned in disagreement. "I don't want to be a teacher."

Colleen looked at her as if she'd suddenly grown a third eye. "We've talked about this a thousand times. Every woman should have a profession and be independent. Teaching is your dream."

Deidre sighed and started to fasten the buttons on her coat. "It is your dream."

Colleen's starched collar felt tight. "It's an excellent dream for any woman."

Deidre pulled back her shoulders and drew in a breath. "I want to leave school."

Colleen looked up. "What?"

Deidre dropped her gaze and stared at her thumb as if it suddenly held great interest. "I don't like being so far from home. I miss my friends."

Colleen struggled to keep her voice calm. She remembered how her own mother had ranted when she'd announced she wasn't going to school. The angrier her mother became the more she dug her own heels in. "Where did this come from? Your friends will be here when you come home from school next summer. They will be here when you graduate."

Her bottom lip curled into a pout. "I don't like being away."

Colleen swallowed her rising anger. "We all must do things we don't like. Besides, you're too young to make a decision like this."

Deidre shrugged. "You walked away from school."

Colleen smacked her hand against the kitchen table. "And I was a complete and utter fool. Because of that stupid decision I had to get married so that we could eat." Keith was gone, their parents had died and the war was ravaging the Shenandoah Valley. Richard's proposal had saved them both.

Deidre's hands shook slightly as she tugged on her gloves. "You're shouting."

She inhaled, trying to calm her nerves. "I want you to have more choices than I did."

Deidre's eyes glistened with tears. "I've a right to make my own choices. Right or wrong, I am willing to live with the consequences."

"You don't have the sense to think ahead to your future. That is my job. No matter what you say, leaving school is not an option for you. I won't let you make that mistake!"

"You can't live your life through mine."

Colleen tugged her cuffs in place. "I'm not going to have this conversation."

"You are treating me like a child."

Her face felt flushed. "You are acting like one."

Deidre turned and flounced toward the door. "Fine!"

"Where are you going?"

She snatched her reticule off the peg by the door. "To see Sally and Anne. *They* understand that I hate school. *They* care about me. *They* like having me around."

Colleen stamped her foot. "Don't you dare leave this house! We are not finished with this discussion."

Deidre jerked her scarf from her coat pocket and reached for the door handle that led to the back alley. "You've no right to treat me like a child. You are not my mother."

"I've every right—" Deidre slammed the door before Colleen could finish.

She pressed flushed hands to her face. As much as she wanted to run after Deidre, she knew there'd be no talking to her until she returned this evening. The girl could be quite bullheaded. This evening, they'd talk this whole school situation over and Deidre would see reason.

Woodenly, she moved to the kitchen table and sat down. Her legs felt so heavy. She buried her face in her trembling hands.

Lord, but she felt one hundred years old. She laid her head down on the table. Hot tears stung her eyes and for the first time in years, she let them flow. She cried until she drifted to sleep.

The smell of burning apple bread woke her. Jumping to her feet, she pulled the dried-out, blackened bread from the oven.

More tears stung her eyes. This day had gone from bad to worse.

As she swiped a tear from her face, she saw a folded piece

of white paper on the floor by the back door. It must have fallen out of Deidre's pocket when she'd pulled out her scarf.

Slowly she rose, picked up the paper and opened it. What struck her immediately was the handwriting. The author had borne down hard on the page, taking care to form each letter.

> *Deidre—*
> *I've arranged for the minister to marry us. Meet me out-*
> *side of town on Friday morning. I'll be waiting.*
> *Joshua*

Colleen blinked twice and reread the letter. *I've arranged for the minister to marry us.* Her heart hammered in her chest. Joshua? *Joshua Matthews.*

He was the foreman on Keith Garrett's farm. He was the boy who always came to the store for supplies. He was the boy—no, the man—who used to enjoy talking with Deidre.

Friday. Today was Friday. It all made sense now. The Sunday dress. The rose water. The talk of quitting school.

She was eloping with Joshua Matthews!

Chapter Two

Colleen's heart raced as she shoved the letter in her dress pocket and snatched her coat off the peg by the back door. Without bothering for hat or gloves, she ran out the door and down the street. Most of the stores along the brick sidewalk were closed for the holiday. A few people stood in front of the redbrick Massey Hotel. One man even called out to her. But she didn't bother to look back to acknowledge who it was. She had to get to the livery and stop Deidre before she made the biggest mistake of her life.

Her side ached and her lungs burned as she ran into the large stable. "Deidre!" she shouted. No answer.

The large room was dimly lit and it took a moment for her eyes to adjust as the smell of hay filled her nostrils. There were six stalls on each side and most were filled with horses. No one was traveling today. "Deidre!"

Jake Perry poked his head out of the last stall on the right. Past sixty, Jake wore coveralls and a faded red shirt. He rubbed a gnarled hand under his white mustache, which twitched as he sniffed. "Colleen, is that you?"

Breathless, she ran to him. "Jake, have you seen Deidre?"

He leaned his pitchfork against the wall. "Yep, she rode out of here about a half hour ago."

Tears of frustration stung the back of her eyes. "Do you know where she went?"

His eyes narrowed as if he was trying to figure out what all the fuss was about. "Well, she said she was going for a ride with Sally and Anne."

Jake didn't mention Joshua Matthews. No doubt Deidre had been very careful, knowing full well Jake would have alerted her if he'd known her sister intended to ride with a young man.

"Do you know where she was headed?" Colleen said.

"Didn't say." He wiped his hands on his pants.

Neither had Joshua in his letter. There were a half-dozen towns in the valley where they could find a minister to marry them.

"Why are you so upset? I don't think I've seen you this flustered in a long time. She said she'd be back soon enough."

As soon as she was married. "Jake, would you saddle my horse for me?"

He pulled off his floppy hat and scratched his head. "Your horse?"

She struggled not to shout. "Is that so odd?"

He lifted a brow, hearing her frustration. "Well, it is. You drive the buckboard with supplies regularly but you ain't ridden for years."

She started toward the stall where she kept her horse and saddle. "I am today!"

"Well, you don't have to shout," he said, cutting across her path. "I'm old but I ain't deaf."

She felt as if she was ready to jump out of her skin. "I'm sorry."

He hoisted her saddle off the hook on the wall. "Where you headed?"

"To Keith Garrett's."

Colleen mounted her horse and headed out of town in such a rush she didn't bother to return home for her hat and gloves. Her heart pounded in her chest as if the devil himself were following her. She had to stop Deidre from making a terrible mistake. She only prayed Joshua had confided in Keith about where he was headed. There were other towns within a day's ride and all three had ministers.

She was so focused on saving Deidre that she didn't think too much about where she was going. She'd ridden the rolling landscape so many times when she was much younger that her body knew where to go even if her mind was elsewhere.

It wasn't until she reached the entrance to the Garrett farm that she stopped and drew in a breath. Her face burned from the cold. Her heart galloped in her chest. She stared down the long dirt road that led to Keith's house. She'd not been here since she'd married Richard. Her mouth felt dry, and despite the cold her hands sweated.

The entrance to Keith's property had changed a good bit. A split-rail fence lined the property and the sign that hung above the entrance was freshly engraved and filled with gold paint. This was no longer the property of some upstart from nowhere. This was the place of a prosperous man.

So many times in the last few months, she'd thought about Keith—the feel of his callused hands wrapped around hers, his deep baritone voice, the way his belt hugged his narrow hips.

So many times, she'd wondered how he fared. So many times...yet each time she'd never followed through and ridden out here.

Her pulse thrummed under her lace-trimmed collar. She moistened her dry lips.

She kicked her heels into the horse's side and started down the road that led to Keith's house.

A rush of memories assailed her as she moved down the road over the hill and past the last stand of trees. They'd lain under those trees that last summer together and made love under the stars. Keith had promised to love her forever.

However, if he'd loved her he'd have married her before he'd left for the war. If he'd really loved her... She viciously shook off the old anger and sadness, drawing a deep breath into her tight chest.

She'd heard the old house was gone. But it was still jarring to see the two-story white house with a wide front porch and a sound stone foundation. Floor-to-ceiling windows trimmed with black shutters flanked the front door. Twin oak rockers sat side by side on the porch.

An unexpected smile lifted the edge of her mouth. He'd built the fine home he'd talked about so often. Despite all that had passed between them, pride flickered in her.

Colleen rode closer, forcing herself to refocus on the task at hand. There was no sign of Deidre's horse, but with luck she was still here.

She tied off her horse's reins to a rod-iron hitching post in front of the porch and climbed the five front steps. She pulled her coat cuffs over her chilled hands and stared at the freshly painted black front door. She raised her fist to knock and then hesitated. Knots gathered in her stomach. Ignoring the urge to run, she summoned her courage and knocked. She snatched her hand back as if it had been burned.

Purposeful steps echoed inside the house. Her stomach fluttered and she took a step back from the front door. She'd not seen Keith Garrett this up close in four years. Her stomach flip-flopped.

She fisted her fingers to hide her sudden shaking. How would he react? What was she going to say to him? She'd certainly practiced her share of speeches that she'd wanted to give him. They'd all been so eloquent and high-handed. But just as when she'd seen him in the store four years ago, every rational thought she had vanished.

As the steps grew closer to the door, her bravado waned. If not for Deidre, she'd have run back to her horse and ridden away as fast as she could.

The front door jerked open.

Keith appeared in the doorway. Dressed in black, he stood with his legs braced apart in a brawler's stance. His thick black hair hung past his collar and a faint white scar marred his right eyebrow. The sun had turned his rawboned face a deep rich brown.

He wasn't as gaunt as he'd been four years ago when he had visited her store. But the lines around his eyes remained, as well as the hardness in his eyes. He looked more intimidating than he had four years ago when he'd stood in her store.

For a moment, he stared at her, saying nothing, as if he didn't quite trust himself to speak.

Finally, he recovered. His jaw tightened. "Colleen? What are you doing here?" The rough graveled voice held no hint of a welcome.

Lifting her chin, she stood her ground. If he'd thought she'd come for him, then he could think again. "I came for Deidre."

One dark brow rose. "Why would your sister be here?"

With him so close, she could barely string two words together. From her pocket she pulled out the wadded-up letter that Joshua had written her sister.

"My sister has run away with your foreman. They intend to marry today."

Keith took the letter from her. Though she was careful not to touch him, his fingertips brushed her hand. Shards of energy shot through her body. His eyes darkened. He'd felt the jolt too.

Without reading the letter, he said, "Come inside."

She was already too close to him as it was. "Thank you, but no. Just tell me where they are and I will be on my way."

He gave Colleen a considered, unhurried inspection, taking in her red cheeks and nose, her hands tucked under her sleeves and the strands of hair that had escaped her chignon. "You are freezing. Come inside where it's warm, Colleen."

She hesitated. She'd not heard him speak her name in so long. The rough edge to his voice made her very ordinary name sound sensuous.

This was not good. Not good at all. The less time they spent together the better.

He notched his brow higher. "What's the matter? Afraid, Colleen?"

Lord, but he was tall. She'd forgotten that her head barely reached over his broad shoulder. "Of course I'm not afraid."

She was petrified.

As Keith stepped aside and held out his hand, she moved over the threshold, her spine as stiff as a rod. His scent teased her as she moved past him and her heart tripped. In the old days, he'd not had the money for expensive soaps. His scent then had been all male, raw. Yet, she found this new combination equally as devastating.

"Warm yourself while I read the letter." He stared at her through hooded eyes.

"We really must hurry."

"Five minutes won't make a difference." He sounded so calm and reasonable and her nerves had her ready to jump out of her skin.

A clock ticked through the silence. Glancing around the room she took in the rich Indian carpet dyed burgundy and black. She noted the overstuffed chairs by the fireplace built for comfort not fashion; the open book and half glass of whiskey on the ottoman; the mahogany desk by the tall front window and, to her surprise, an upright piano in the corner. There'd been a time when he'd come to her parents' house and she'd played the piano for him.

She moved to the fire as much for the heat as to put distance between them. She stretched out her hands. Her icy skin prickled as it warmed.

He paced as he read. And she found herself very aware of each purposeful step. He sighed and refolded the letter. "They're not here," he said.

Colleen whirled around. Panic burned. "What do you mean they're not here? They didn't meet up here first?"

"I don't know," he said. His tone was so blasted rational and unconcerned. "Josh rode out a couple of hours ago. He said he'd be back in a couple of days."

"Where did he go?"

His gaze bore into her as if he was trying to read her mind. "I don't know."

"You don't keep up with your employees?" she said louder than she'd intended.

Keith fingered the edge of the letter. "It's Christmas, Colleen. Not everyone works through the holiday like you."

She was amazed that he knew that much about her.

"Besides, it's not my habit to question my men about their holiday plans."

"You know I work at Christmas but you don't know where Josh is. Great."

A faint smile lifted the edge of his mouth as firelight flickered on the hard planes of his face. "Has Deidre really run away or is this some excuse you've cooked up to see me?" The condescension in his voice raked her nerves.

Her spine straightened to the point of snapping. Color flooded her cheeks. There had been times when she'd racked her brains trying to come up with a reason to see him. "I wouldn't make something like this up. This is very real. Deidre and I argued this morning about school. She told me she didn't want to return. She said she missed her friends, but obviously, she missed Joshua."

He handed her the letter. His fingers brushed hers and her skin snapped again with energy. "Joshua is a good man. He's hardworking and honest. He'll make Deidre a good husband."

She swiped a loose strand of hair off her face. "I don't want Deidre marrying now. She's too young."

His gaze drifted down her body and then back up to her face. "As I remember, you were much younger when you and I first stole off to the creek with a blanket."

The memory of that warm summer day was sudden and swift. They'd lain on that blanket kissing, touching each other and making love until the sun was low in the sky.

Her cheeks burned. "I don't want my sister to make the same mistakes I did."

Her words, spoken out loud, sounded harsh, and they carried the full weight of the emotions she'd carried for Keith.

His curt nod was proof enough that her words had hit the mark. She'd hurt him. But the knowledge gave no satisfaction.

There'd been a time when she'd depended on him for everything. In those days, she'd have turned to him in a crisis like this. But the truth was, she didn't have the right to ask anything of him now.

He wasn't just a neighbor or friend, he had been her lover, and there'd been a time when she'd loved him with her whole heart. However, the love they'd shared no longer united them. Instead, the memory of it had created a wedge between them.

All that they shared now was a past.

Colleen moved away from the fireplace. Immediately, she missed the heat of it. "I made a mistake coming here. I thought they might still be here. Sorry to have troubled you."

He stared at her with narrowed eyes.

She moved past Keith toward the door. She wanted nothing more than to forget that she'd come or that they'd spoken.

"Where are you going?" he said. His voice was rough, full of emotion.

"To Dixon's Corner. It's the closest town with a minister. It seems logical that they would go there."

He nodded, considering her logic. "Joshua travels there a good bit. He knows many people in Dixon's Corner, including the minister."

Her head bobbed in a curt nod. He was trying to help and for that she was grateful. Perhaps one day there could be friendship between them. "Thank you for the information."

He frowned. "You're going after them?"

"They've got a three-hour head start on me, but if I hurry I might catch up to them."

He glanced down at her bare hands still red from the cold. "You don't have a hat or gloves."

She pulled up her coat collar and managed a smile. "I will be fine."

He muttered a savage oath under his breath. "Do yourself

a favor and stop by town before you head out. Get a fresh mount and decent clothes."

She bristled at his order. "There's no time."

Keith shook his head. He reached his hand out to grab her arm and then caught himself as if remembering he had no claim on her. "Suit yourself. You were always so damn bull-headed."

Colleen had never felt more alone. She opened the front door and stepped out into the cold.

Chapter Three

Keith didn't hesitate to reach for his coat. He watched Colleen walk down his front steps, her head held high, her chin jutting proudly.

And as he shoved his arms into the sleeves, he cursed Colleen a thousand times. The woman had the sense of a tree stump, riding out here without decent clothes. The skies were plump and the scent of snow hung in the air. She'd hit snow before she reached Dixon's Corner.

He buttoned his coat.

Colleen Temple, or rather Mrs. Richard Garland, wasn't his problem. She'd made her choice years ago when she'd chosen to marry her rich shopkeeper. He flexed his fingers and stared at the sway of her skirts. She loosened her horse's reins from the post and mounted the saddle as well as any cavalry officer. She reined the horse around and kicked her heels into its haunches.

She knew the way to Dixon's Corner and she'd always been one of the best riders in the county. But right now she wasn't thinking because she was hell-bent on finding Deidre. At the rate she was going, she would run her horse to exhaustion or get herself thrown into a ditch.

Damn.

Keith shoved on his gloves. He'd known something was up with Josh. His foreman had bathed regularly and had taken to wearing bay rum. There'd been quite a few extra trips to town for things they *needed*.

Keith wasn't blind. He knew the boy was in love, but he'd never figured it was Deidre Temple.

Double damn.

Colleen's horse whinnied, drawing his attention to the road. He watched as she dug her foot into the stirrup and lowered her head to cut the harsh wind.

Today, when he'd opened the door and seen her standing on his porch, his heart had stopped. She wasn't the prickly Mrs. Garland he'd stolen peeks at over the last four years. No, this woman, with her hair wild and her cheeks flushed from the cold, was *his* Colleen. For a moment, all the anger and hurt had vanished. He'd wanted to take her in his arms and kiss her.

He thought she had finally come to him.

But she'd not come for him.

He closed his eyes, refusing to let the pain steal another minute of his life. He'd spent too much time dreaming of Colleen…wanting Colleen. Hell, if he were smart, he'd find himself a wife and settle down—fill this fancy house with children and get on with his life.

Hooves thundered against the ground. He opened his eyes, watching her ride toward the front gate. Her blond hair streamed behind her as her skirts billowed in the wind.

A savage oath exploded from Keith's lips. He didn't owe Colleen a blessed thing.

Yet, damn his hide, she still had power over him. In the last five minutes she'd stirred more emotion than he'd felt in the last eight years.

He grabbed his Stetson and put it on. He flexed his fingers then snatched up an extra scarf and gloves.

He headed toward the barn, cursing the warm whiskey he'd left behind and the cold wind that now burned his nostrils.

A sane man would be inside enjoying this rare day of solitude.

But not him. No, like it or not, he was going to Dixon's Corner with Colleen.

Colleen heard the thunder of hooves behind her a half a mile down the road. Her skin prickled and her nerves danced. Without looking behind her she knew it was Keith. She sensed him.

His black stallion easily caught her mare and soon he was riding beside her. Fear, longing and relief all surged in her veins as she glanced at his profile.

Keith sat tall in his saddle, staring grimly ahead. "Slow your horse down, Colleen. She'll not make the trip if you don't ease up."

He was right, of course. Yet she bristled at the idea of following orders from him. Who was he to tell her what to do? Still, she slowed her horse.

Keith frowned and reached in the pocket of his jacket and pulled out a scarf and gloves. "Put these on."

"I'm fine." Her fingers were cold but she'd been colder before. She could make it to Dixon's Corner if she kept her hands tucked under her cuffs.

"Put the damn gloves and scarf on or I'll drag you off that horse and put them on you myself."

She shot Keith an irritated glance. "Don't treat me like a child. I'm not the naive young girl you deserted."

The faintest hint of pain darkened his eyes before it vanished. "Then stop acting like one."

His brows snapped together. Challenge sparked in his eyes. She had no doubt he'd do it.

She accepted the gloves and scarf and put them on. She slid her fingers into the gloves lined with fur. A thousand needles stung her fingertips as her fingers warmed. She'd never admit it to him, but she felt a world better.

He glared at the horizon. "Colleen, do you realize we have weather coming in?"

She glanced at the thick, gray clouds. In truth, she'd not thought about the weather. "Of course I do. But if I hurry, I should be able to beat it to Dixon's Corner."

She hoped.

He shook his head. "And if you can't?"

She whirled in her saddle and faced him. "I didn't ask you to come with me. I can make it to Dixon's Corner *alone*. God knows, I've done it enough times over the last few years delivering supplies."

When piqued, her words became clipped like a schoolteacher's. He'd teased her about that once.

"Why would you ever travel there alone?" Accusation rang in his voice.

She'd done a lot of things in the last few years she'd never dreamed of doing. "When Richard became ill, I was forced to take over the business. That meant ordering supplies, balancing the books, waiting on customers and delivering goods." For the first six months she'd been so afraid of making a mistake with the orders or the accounting, she could barely sleep at night. And the first delivery trip she'd made alone had aged her a decade.

But as the days grew into months, she'd learned how to run the business.

His eyes narrowing, Keith stared at her. "With all the fighting that went on in this valley, I can't believe Garland allowed you to drive so far alone."

"There was no other choice. He was too ill to travel and during the war we didn't have the extra money to hire help."

His gray eyes narrowed. "Your husband was a fool to take such a risk."

"I never told Richard I drove alone." Richard's mind was sharp even after the stroke, but he couldn't walk or see well. It would have been torture for her husband to know she'd taken such risks, so she'd lied and told him she'd hired a driver.

Keith's eyes intensified with flashes of pity and then outrage. "That was stupid, Colleen. What if you'd run into trouble?"

Her head was starting to throb. Many times she'd seen soldiers, but she'd always been careful to pull off the road and hide her horses and rig in the woods until they passed. "The last thing I need right now is a lecture from you."

"You're right," he said tightly. "Once I get you to Dixon's Corner, we'll be done with each other."

His words knifed into her heart. She'd thought after seven years that she shouldn't feel anything for Keith Garrett.

But she did.

Through hooded eyes, Keith watched Colleen as she rode. She sat straight, her chin held high. She still possessed that searing pride of hers. When provoked, she had a way of looking through someone that cut to the quick.

She'd been sixteen and he'd been twenty-one when they'd met. He'd won his farm in a card game. No one had expected him to put down roots. They'd all figured he'd sell and move on. But the farm was a dream for him. Luck had given it to him but it would take hard work to keep it.

He'd been working his farm for almost a year when he'd first seen Colleen. By most standards he was just scraping by but he'd seen the great potential in the tiny spread. Its location to water was prime and the wide-open grazing lands left a good bit of room for a large herd. A few years of good weather and he knew he'd have something to be real proud of.

He'd been fencing in the back field and it had been as hot as blazes that first day he'd seen her. Colleen had been out riding. Her hat had blown off her head and hung suspended from its tie, flopping against her back. Blond hair, like a golden carpet, had streamed behind her.

Like a magical creature, she had captured his attention. He'd stopped his digging and leaned forward on his shovel. He'd pushed his hat back so that he didn't miss a bit of her. He'd called out to her. She glanced in his direction, flushed, and then ridden off.

He'd fallen in love with her that day.

And it was that love that had seen him through some of the worst battles in the war. He'd weathered the death and destruction because he'd loved her and wanted to return to her. She'd been the reason he'd fought his way through hell.

And she'd repaid him by marrying another man.

Keith exhaled, refusing to let the old anger overtake him.

When he'd arrived home from the war he'd driven straight to her folks' place. Seeing it boarded up, he'd gone to town. He found out she'd gotten married to the shopkeeper. Furious, he'd not asked for details and had gone straight to see her.

Colleen had been so lovely that day and he'd nearly wept at the sight of her as she'd stood behind the counter. When he'd seen the gold band, he'd been devastated.

Keith shoved aside the pain. Instead, he allowed his gaze to linger on her profile. The last few years had been good to her. The youthful fullness of her face had vanished and in its place were prominent cheekbones and a delicate jawline. Her skin, the color of milk, was as smooth as it had ever been; her lips full and ripe and her breasts rounded and high. Even after eight years, the memory of kissing those breasts lingered. He grew hard.

The first flecks of snow caught his attention, dragging it back to the road ahead. He glanced up at the full, gray sky. Dixon's Corner was still two hours away and they'd have to hustle and pray for luck if they wanted to beat the snow.

Fifteen minutes later, he realized their luck wasn't going to hold.

The snow had started to fall in thick sheets, clinging to the trees and covering the road in a dense haze of white.

"We'd better find shelter," he said.

She blinked snowflakes from her eyelashes. Her teeth were chattering. "We've got to keep pushing forward. Any delay and we could be too late."

Bullheaded woman. If he said a lump of coal was black she'd say it was white just for the sake of argument. "You won't do Deidre any good if you die of cold. The snow is going to get worse. You know that."

She glanced mutinously at the sky. "But we're so close."

They were close now and yet they might as well have been a million miles apart. "Close doesn't count." He nodded ahead. "There is a small cabin just down the road. We can hole up there until the weather passes."

Her fingers clutched the reins. Her shoulders slumped from fatigue. "I don't want to stop." When she spoke, her breath puffed from her mouth in white clouds.

He tightened his hands on the reins. "Soon we won't be

able to see five feet in front of ourselves." In truth, they'd be lucky to reach the cabin.

"I'm pressing ahead." Colleen's voice had lost its bravado. The cold was forcing her to see reason even if he couldn't.

"Suit yourself. I'm bunking in."

Chapter Four

Colleen knew when she was beat. Like it or not, the snow had her licked for now. If she continued, she'd be endangering her life.

Her teeth chattered as she followed Keith down the road. It pained her to admit he was right, but he was.

The snow was falling hard now, blanketing the rolling hills in white. But what troubled her more than frostbite or the plunging temperatures was spending the day, and likely the night, alone with Keith.

Her skin tingled at the thought.

Neither spoke as they continued down the road. When Keith veered off toward a cabin nestled in a stand of trees, he didn't ask her to join him. But she noted his head turned slightly to the right to see if she followed.

Seemingly satisfied that she rode behind him, he kicked his heels into his horse's side and picked up his pace. Soon they'd reached the cabin and small barn. The cabin was one level and by the looks just one room. Two frosted windows faced them and a cold chimney jutted from the freshly shingled roof. The house was by no means fancy but it looked to be in good shape.

The place had once belonged to a farmer named Simms. The old farmer had moved West last spring and headed toward the goldfields of Colorado.

Colleen swung her leg over the side of her horse and dismounted. Her fingertips burned with cold and she could no longer feel her face.

Keith dismounted and moved toward her. His shoulders were wide and straight, and though his cheeks were red he looked as if the cold didn't really bother him.

His gloved fingers brushed hers as he took the reins. "I'll put the horses up. Get inside."

Colleen didn't argue. She wanted nothing more than to be out of the stinging wind. "I'll start a fire."

His gaze lingered on her. She wasn't sure if he pitied or respected her at this moment.

Too cold to care, she turned to the door. Wrestling with the rusted handle, she wrenched open the door and stepped inside the cabin.

The cabin's dark interior was only a little warmer than the outside, but at least the wind wasn't blowing. Rubbing her cold hands together, Colleen's gaze scanned the room in search of a lantern or candle. It was only ten o'clock in the morning, but the snow and thick clouds had blocked out the light. She found a lantern and flint on a small wooden table. Carefully, she lit the lantern and turned up the wick.

She held up the light to survey her haven. Save for the cobwebs and dust, the room looked eerily lived in. Two chairs pushed under a small table, a potbelly stove with a rusted kettle atop it, a row of canned goods on the shelf above a washtub, a rope bed with rumpled sheets and blankets, a sink full of washed dishes. Likely when Simms had made his decision to leave, he'd simply taken only what he needed and left.

Colleen moved to a wooden box next to the hearth. As she opened the lid, the hinges squeaked. To her great relief, the box was full of wood and matches. "Bless you, Mr. Simms."

Without delay, she laid a fire in the hearth and lit a match to the kindling. Rubbing her hands on her arms, she squatted next to the hearth and waited impatiently for the fire to crackle and spit to life.

Outside, the wind howled, blowing swirls of snow on the single glass window. She thought of Keith out there, working with the horses. Guilt stabbed her. Deidre wasn't his problem, yet he'd given up a warm fire to help her. Until that last day they'd fought so many years ago, he'd always been the one person she could count on.

Slowly the firelight grew and cast a warm glow on the room, banishing the shadows from the corners.

She started when the front door opened. Snow swirled in as Keith, head bowed, moved through the doorway and closed it. He pulled off his hat and brushed the white snow from it and the black duster that skimmed the top of his boots.

He yanked off his gloves, shoved them in the pocket of his range coat and crossed the room in four easy strides. He stretched out his fingers in front of the fire. "The horses are in the barn. They should be fine."

She could feel the cold radiating from him. "And the weather?"

He glanced down at her. His gray eyes penetrated. "The snow is a good inch thick already."

She tore her gaze from his and riveted them to the dancing flames. "How could this day have turned into such a disaster? I had such plans."

He snorted. "You're not the only one. This is the first day

I've taken off in six months. All I wanted today was to read my book."

She didn't doubt him. He'd always been a hard worker. And he'd had a thirst for learning. He'd once told her that he'd had to leave school at a young age, but he'd never stopped trying to learn. He was always working on some book.

"You're losing one day," she said, hating the guilt that wouldn't leave her. "Deidre is ruining her life."

He squatted to his knees so that he could be closer to the fire. "Maybe she is. And maybe she isn't. Either way, there's nothing you can do about it now."

His shoulder brushed her skirt. "You don't care about this, do you?"

"I'm here, aren't I?"

He reached past her and tossed logs on the burning kindling. Again, his shoulder brushed her leg. And again, she felt the surge of heat in her body. She ached to run her fingers through his dark hair. He'd loved it when she rubbed his head. Once he'd fallen asleep, his head in her lap, as she smoothed the thick strands away from his face.

Colleen caught herself. Lord, but if she didn't put distance between them, she was going to do something very foolish.

She moved away from the fire to the frosted window. "You gave in to the weather too easily. We could have kept pushing."

"I know when I'm beat." His voice was low, full of emotion.

He wasn't just talking about the weather. There was sadness in his voice that spoke to something deeper.

She couldn't deal with his heartache. Knowing he felt beaten tore at her own heart. She needed to focus on her anger and ignore the fierce emotions chewing at her.

There'd been a time when she could goad the full force of

his temper. She moved back to the fire. "I've never known you to give up on a fight. I never figured you for a coward."

He glanced up at her, his gaze razor sharp. "Well, maybe you really don't know me that well anymore. Of course, it's been eight years since we spent any time together."

His simmering fury gave her comfort. *That* she could handle. "People don't change that much."

He rose. He stood only inches from her. "A smart man knows when to surrender."

The heat of his body felt like a caress. "Are you talking about the war?"

"Sure, why not?"

She'd never discussed the war with Keith. But many a night she'd lain awake wondering if he was alive or dead. "In the store, veterans swapped stories about the battles they'd fought. I heard tales of men charging into battle with bullets buzzing around them like bees." She'd lost friends. Nate Sampson had returned home without a leg. Bill Jenkins had lost his right arm. Seven boys from the church had never returned home.

"It was the stench that stuck with me the most. Sulfur and the odor of the wounded and dead."

The war had ravaged the valley and devastated the lives of so many. Suddenly, arguing with him about snow didn't seem so important. No matter how much she wanted to hold on to her anger, she couldn't.

"Jamie Newton wrote his wife, Sue. He said you were with Lee's army in northern Virginia."

He frowned. "That's right."

"Were you injured?" Despite all their troubles it would have broken her heart to see him injured.

Absently, he rubbed his right thigh. "I was shot in the leg in the wilderness."

She glanced at his long lean legs. "They didn't take the leg, thank God."

He grunted. "They would have if I hadn't threatened to shoot the doctor."

A faint smile touched her lips. "I bet you had those poor doctors in a dither."

Dry humor sparked in his eyes. "You could say that."

"How long were you laid up?"

"Three months."

Three months of pain and anguish. And she'd not been there to see him through it.

"I begged you not to leave." The words were out before she could stop them.

A cloud of sadness passed over his face as he stared down at her. He raised his hand as if to touch her, then thinking better of it, let it drop back to his side. "You know I had no choice. Virginia needed to be defended."

"I needed you." Her voice was a hoarse whisper.

"There was more at stake than you and me."

"You left me." The words scraped her throat.

"And you left me back." The anger had returned.

"I had no choice," she said.

Bitterness radiated from him. "Looks like life got the better of us both."

He walked over to the cabinet above the sink and searched until he found a bottle of whiskey. For the first time she noticed the small limp. He poured himself a glass.

Concern washed over her. "Does your leg hurt you now?"

He drank the whiskey in one gulp. "The cold makes it worse."

"Is there anything I can do to help?"

Keith stared at her a long moment. "No. The pain is a fact of life now."

Her gaze slid down his tall, lean body and then up across his wide shoulders. If it were possible, the years had hardened his body. She imagined his belly was just as tight and flat as it once had been and that the thick mat of hair on his chest tapered below his belt line.

She'd kissed that flat belly and trailed her fingertips down that discrete line of hair.

Her pulse quickened.

Lord, but she wanted to touch him again.

White-hot desire surged in her. The feeling was so startling, she took a step back. After all this time, she still wanted him.

Colleen swallowed a dry lump in her throat. Suddenly, the cabin felt very, very small.

Chapter Five

Firelight danced on Colleen's pale face. Keith had seen that look before. Desire. He also remembered the pride he'd felt that a woman as lovely as Colleen had chosen him.

His mind stumbled back to another time when they were courting and they'd been dancing at the Fourth of July picnic. He'd held her a bit too close, letting his erection brush against her. She'd gazed up into his eyes with the same mixture of longing and wanton desire. He'd sensed then, as he did now, that she wanted him.

With a little coaxing he could have her now.

She was a young desirable woman and she'd been married to an invalid for eight years. It wouldn't take much to have her in his arms.

But the sex had been the easy part for them. From the first the chemistry and heat between them had been explosive.

What had been hard for them was finding the resolve to see them through the hard times. Yes, he'd refused to marry her, but in his eyes he'd done her a favor. That last time together, he'd been ready to marry her and then she'd confided that she wasn't pregnant. He'd abandoned his marriage plans and left her, confident that if he died he'd not leave her with a babe to raise on her own. And if he'd been left maimed, she'd not have been saddled with a cripple. He thought in time she'd see the wisdom of his decision and she'd wait for him.

"How did you know where to find the whiskey?" she said.

Keith knew she was scrambling for something to say. She always did hate the silence. "I keep this cabin stocked for times like this."

"This is your cabin?" she said, surprised.

The whiskey had dulled the pain in his leg, but it had also warmed his blood and stripped away some of his reserve. He set the glass down. "I bought it from Simms when he headed West."

"Why?"

He leaned back against the simple counter and crossed his feet at his ankles. "It's good land. And in truth I like the humble cabin. I've never felt quite at home in the highfalutin new place I built. I feel more like myself here."

"That house of yours was quite the talk when you were building it."

"It's too big." *You're not in it.*

Her gaze caught his. She blushed and looked at the stockpile of cans on the shelves behind him. "Simms's land is a good investment."

A faint smile tugged at the edges of his mouth. "I've always got my eye to the future."

She noticed his smile. "What's so funny?"

"Josh asked me about this cabin the other day. He wanted to buy it from me. He'd always been content in the bunkhouse and it made no sense to me why he'd want the responsibility of a house."

Colleen sighed. She crossed the room and tossed another

log on the fire. She pulled a straight-back chair to the hearth and sat down. "I wonder how long Joshua and Deidre have been seeing each other?"

He crouched beside her and extended his hands. The heat felt good. She smelled good. Not the lavender like she used to wear, but a musky womanly scent. "I honestly don't know. He'd made quite a few trips to town this past summer and he was in a real good mood for most of September. I thought he might have a woman, but I never guessed it was Deidre."

Good thing too. When he'd first met Colleen, Deidre had been a scrawny brat with a big mouth on her. But he'd liked the kid and her independent streak. She was as close as he'd ever get to a kid sister.

"Joshua never said anything to you?"

"No. But then, he knew I thought of Deidre as family. When I ran into her in town, she always had a kind word for me."

Her shoulders tensed and her breathing grew shallow. "She always looked up to you."

He stretched out his long fingers, absorbing the heat. "She also kept me posted on you, as well."

"Like what?"

"Colleen got a big shipment of flour in and unloaded it all by herself. Colleen was looking after the Peterses' baby girl and that baby sure did look good in her arms. Colleen was thinking about expanding the store."

She relaxed. "Oh."

Colleen cried when she thought no one was listening. Colleen still kept the tintype of you in the Bible in her room.

Keith had never acknowledged the girl's information with anything more than a grunt, but he'd never interrupted her, either. In fact, he'd soaked up every bit of information as if he were starving.

Colleen rose, inspecting the cabin with a different eye. "I can't imagine Deidre living here," she said.

"Why?"

"It just seems a little rustic for her. I didn't have much time for her while she was growing up, so I spoiled her with nice things when I could."

"This place *is* nice." He sounded offended.

"If you're a farmer or cowhand."

He arched an eyebrow. "You've gotten a bit high-minded these last few years."

"I've done without and I don't want that for Deidre."

"This cabin is hardly *doing without*. It's a sight better than the cabin I first built on my property, and you didn't have any problems with it."

"I was young. I had no idea what it took to live in a place like this."

"When did you become a snob, Colleen?"

She shoved out a breath. "I'm not a snob. I'm just realistic. Love can only carry you so far."

"Folks do put a lot of stock in love."

"Yes, they do."

He flexed his fingers. "It wasn't enough for us, was it?"

She shook her head. "No."

A silence settled between them. Both stared into the fire. When he spoke, his voice was so thick with emotion, he hardly recognized it. "Did you love your husband?"

The question caught Colleen off guard. Hesitating, she rose and walked to the counter. She picked up a tin mug from the shelf above the sink and inspected it. She replaced it. "I cared for him."

"But not love." She heard the satisfaction in his voice.

She clasped her hands together. "As I've told Deidre, there are many kinds of love."

He expelled a breath and his jaw tensed.

"I know that look."

"Really?" he bit back.

"You are angry with me."

"So what if I am?"

Fire singed her veins. "What arrogance this man has," she said to the rafters.

He shot to his feet. "Come again?"

She marched up to him until they stood toe to toe. "What gives you the right to be angry with me? You're the one who wasn't there when I needed you most. You're the one who refused to marry me."

"I was fighting a war!" His voice ricocheted off the walls.

She held up her index finger. "One letter, Keith, that's all I wanted from you, one letter to keep me going. But you never wrote to me once. I poured out my heart and soul to you in dozens of letters and you never wrote me back once. If it weren't for Jamie Newton writing his wife, I wouldn't have known if you were dead or alive."

He moved to the kitchen table and laid his flat palm against it as if he struggled with his temper. "I wrote to you three times that first year."

His words knocked some of the wind from her sails. "I never got one of them."

"No doubt your father did. He never liked you spending time with me."

"He wouldn't have done that. He knew how I felt about you."

A growl rumbled in his chest. "Like hell he wouldn't. He hated my guts." He shook his head. "I was a no-account drifter who'd won a homestead in a card game. I wasn't good enough for his daughter."

"That's not true. He never said anything like that to me."

Tension radiated from his body. "He sure as hell said it to me."

"He wouldn't have taken the letters. He knew how hard Mama's death had been for me. He knew I needed you."

"I know how your father's mind worked. He was more worried about you leaving him than he was about your happiness."

"That's not true!" Her mind reeled. "And Richard would have said something when I visited the mercantile. He always gave me the mail. Why would he hold back your letters?"

Keith leaned forward. "If your father asked him to, he would have. Plus, old Richard had his own plans for you."

She rocked back on her heels. "He wouldn't lie to me!"

He looked at her as if she was a naive fool. "He had his eye on you long before I left. I saw the way he looked at you. That old buzzard's gaze turned lean and hungry when you were around."

Richard had been so kind to her. "He wouldn't lie."

Keith shrugged. "It looks like he didn't have to try too hard to win you over. When were you married? Nine, ten months after I left?"

Pride had her lifting her chin. She could have told Keith about the spring flood that had wiped out their crops and killed her father. She could have told him about how destitute she and Deidre were. That she'd often skipped meals so Deidre could eat. But she didn't. If he knew her, really knew her, he'd know she'd never have married Richard if she weren't so desperate. "I think we've said all we need to say to one another. There's already too much bad blood between us."

He glared at her and in the next instant crossed the room

in three quick strides. He cupped her face in his hands. Need burned in his eyes. "There's more between us than that."

His rough fingers felt warm against her skin. Desire sparked inside her. "Let go of me."

He leaned closer until his lips were only inches from hers. "It makes you nervous when I touch you."

"Yes."

"Nervous in a good way."

She swallowed. "It makes me want things I don't have a right to."

"So you don't deny the attraction."

"No. But I won't give in to it. It has always been easy for us." Her pulse raced. Despite her prim words, she felt anything but prim. She wanted him.

He tiled her face up so that their gazes met. "You've missed it."

She wouldn't lie. "Yes."

Keith nodded, satisfaction glittering in his eyes. "You liked my hands on you."

Lord help her but she did. So many nights she'd lain awake dreaming of him touching her. "Yes."

"I dreamed about touching you every night I was away from you." He ran his knuckle over her cheek. "Soft as silk. In my dreams, I'd strip you down and kiss every inch of your naked body before I entered you."

She closed her eyes. Her center felt moist and throbbed with her racing heartbeat. "Keith, this isn't right."

He captured a blond curl in his hand and twirled it around his finger. "Why? There's nothing standing between us now." His voice was a hoarse whisper.

"There's too much anger," she whispered.

"That's tomorrow's problem."

She leaned closer to him. She'd spent so many years doing for others and she wanted this moment just for her.

Keith kissed her softly on the lips. The chaste kiss wasn't nearly satisfactory enough. It only whetted her appetite for more. She ran her fingers up and down his arm.

"Again?" he said, already knowing the answer.

"Yes."

He kissed her again, only this kiss wasn't as chaste as the last. He coaxed her lips open with his tongue and explored the soft folds of her mouth.

She savored the kiss. He tasted of the whiskey he'd just drunk. Heat seared her veins.

In that moment all the anger and frustration melted away and there was only need. A raw pulsing need. She wrapped her arms around his neck and pressed her breasts to his chest, deepening the kiss.

He kissed her mouth, the hollow of her neck, and nibbled her earlobe. "Do you want this?"

"Yessss," she hissed.

That was all the answer he needed. He banded his arms around her, pulling her into a kiss. His body had always been lean, but there was a toughness to it she'd not felt before. She liked the difference. She wasn't the same flighty girl she'd been eight years ago and he wasn't the same idealistic young man.

His hands moved to her shoulders and he pushed the edges of her jacket off her shoulders. Her coat fell to the floor, puddling at her feet. Without breaking the kiss, he shrugged off his coat, as well.

She slid her hands into the folds of his vest. He was all sinew and bone.

He wrapped his arms around her waist and picked her up and carried her to the bed in the corner. He laid her on the straw mattress. The support ropes groaned under their weight. Immediately, he straddled her, trapping her narrow hips between his legs. He moved his hands over her breasts, squeezed gently. She arched, pressing her center into his hardness.

Keith reached for the hem of her skirt, pulled it up to her waist and revealed white pantaloons dotted with pink ribbons. He reached for the waistband and pulled them down, exposing her white skin. She felt no shame, only heat as he positioned himself above her and unfastened his belt buckle.

She stared at his erection, understanding this wasn't about love but raw sexual desire. And at this moment, that was just fine with her. It had been so long since she'd known such pleasure.

Keith pressed his fingers against her moist center and she hissed in a breath.

"You like this," he said, his voice as rough as sandpaper.

"Yes."

"You want me inside you."

He needed to hear the word. "Yes."

Without hesitating, he pushed inside her. Her body closed tightly around him. He hesitated a moment, letting her become accustomed to him, and then he began to move inside her. His fingers began to circle her moist center, sending shivers of desire through her body. She moved her hands up and down his back, savoring the feel of his body.

The warmth inside her built so quickly. Every muscle in her body bunched as he continued to stroke her. She wanted to hold off and savor all this, but in a split second the waves washed over her, touching every inch of her body. She clutched Keith close and breathed his name into his ear.

He groaned, and unable to hold back, found his release, buried himself to the hilt inside of her.

For several seconds, he lay on top of her. She could feel his heart hammering against her skin. For this one perfect moment, she felt at peace, whole.

But as the moments passed and their heartbeats slowed, words like *foolhardy* and *reckless* came to mind. Dear Lord, what had she done?

Chapter Six

Minutes passed as Colleen lay under Keith. His breathing was ragged, as if he'd just run a mile. And he seemed totally relaxed. He was in no rush to go anywhere.

But Colleen was. She needed to put distance between them so she could think. She started to move under Keith. "I need to get up."

Sensing her discomfort, Keith rolled off. He glanced down at her face, and seeing her frown, realized she didn't share the same kind of contentment he did.

He fastened his pants and rose.

Without his body covering hers, the cold air brushed her skin, making her very aware of her nakedness. She pulled up her pantaloons and pushed her skirts down and covered her legs. "I'm sorry."

He looked down at her, annoyance sparking in his eyes. "Sorry for what?"

"I shouldn't have lost control like that."

"You weren't the only one."

"I should have known better." She and Keith had been together a half-dozen times before he'd left for the war. Each time, she'd feared she carried his baby in her belly. There'd been no child then, but there certainly could be now. The timing was right.

"This was wrong."

Keith's confusion gave way to more aggravation. "You make it sound like what happened was a terrible mistake."

She brushed the curtain of blond hair back off her face. "It was."

His body went rigid. "I've no regrets."

Neither spoke for the next hour. The snow came down harder, blanketing the landscape in white. Frost coated the windows.

Colleen felt as if she was going to go insane with worry. Oddly, she wasn't as worried about Deidre now. Her sister was no doubt married, and if the marriage soured then Colleen would deal with the troubles when they came.

It was her future that was so up in the air now. Her hands slid to her belly. She could be carrying his baby.

A baby. Despite all the reasons why she shouldn't be pleased about a child, she was. She'd longed to hold her own child in her arms for years. So many times her empty womb constricted when she heard a baby's cry or saw a mother cradling her child.

Once Richard had had his stroke, there'd been no more intimacy. She'd moved down the hallway to another bedroom so that he could sleep more comfortably. Silently, she'd grieved for the children she would never have.

And now there could be a babe in her belly.

The dream was tempered by reality. If Keith ever found out she was carrying his child, he'd insist on marriage. He'd told her about his tough upbringing. His father had died when he was six. He'd gone to work in the tobacco fields soon after and his mother took in laundry. They'd barely scraped by and often there wasn't enough food to eat. Then his mother had died when he was twelve and he'd been on his own. He'd always sworn a child of his would never struggle.

She thought back to that last day they'd spent together before he left for the war. He'd asked her three times if she was pregnant. She'd assured him she wasn't. He'd not been worried about leaving her but he had been about leaving a child behind.

Oh, yes, Keith would insist on marriage if she was pregnant.

And marriage between them would be the worst thing. The anger and the hurt between them would doom a union from the start.

She'd grown up in a house where there'd been constant fighting and turmoil. How many times had she taken her baby sister and gone outside to sit under the oak tree so she'd be away from her parents' shouting?

She'd never do that to her child.

Once this mess with Deidre was over, she'd return to her store. And if she was pregnant, she'd find a way to keep it hidden from Keith. Perhaps she'd move to Staunton until the baby was born, or Charlottesville.

Yet, the more she thought about putting distance between her and Keith, the stronger his presence seemed to envelop her. He dominated the cabin.

He had invaded her life.

Keith too was restless. He'd stoked the fire and tossed fresh logs onto it. When the fire blazed he wasn't content, so he put on his coat and hat and went outside to check on the horses.

To keep her hands busy, she decided to cook lunch. She

wasn't hungry, but doing anything was better than sitting here letting the hours tick away. She moved to the small bank of shelves stocked with tins of beans and sacks of flour. She found a pan and went outside and scooped up as much pure snow as it could hold. She set the pan of snow on the stove and knelt in front of the firebox.

The door opened and Keith came back inside with a rush of cold air on his heels. He stamped the snow from his boots and brushed the flakes from his coat before hanging it up.

"Let me do that," Keith said.

She heard him move toward her. "That's okay. I can do it."

He stood behind her. The cold radiated around him. "The stove is old and unpredictable. Let me. I've lit it before."

She moved away from him, fearing if they touched they'd end up in bed again. Despite the satisfaction she'd felt just an hour ago, she realized she wanted more of him.

Standing at the counter, she grabbed a cupful of flour and dumped it into a wooden bowl.

Keith shoved kindling into the firebox and struck a match to it. Soon it crackled and blazed. He closed the metal door and rose. "The stove should be hot in about a half hour."

"Good."

She dumped a spoonful of lard and salt into the flour. With a fork, she started to cut the ingredients together.

He leaned against the counter beside her and folded his arms over his chest. "You look like you know what you are doing."

She felt clumsy and foolish with him so close. Why did he have to stare? "I've gotten pretty good at cooking."

"Last I remember, you couldn't heat beans without burning them."

And he'd bravely tried to eat the charred beans and biscuits just to please her. It took effort to keep her voice even. "I had to learn after I married."

He tensed. "No matter which way we turn, obstacles rise up between us."

"You're right."

She'd expected Keith to get angry, as he'd done each time Richard's name came up. But this time he didn't. "What happened with Richard? He was a strapping man the last I saw him."

She had to struggle to remember what Richard had been like before the stroke. He had been a force of nature; a man who knew what he wanted. "He was working in the store, balancing the accounts. He started moaning in pain. I rushed to his side. He was holding his head. He was in terrible pain." Colleen's heart tightened at the memory. "I got him to bed and called the doctor. By the time the doctor came, Richard was unconscious. He lingered for days and the doctor was convinced he'd die. But he was strong and he woke up. When he did, he couldn't sit up or walk without help."

He stared at her. His gaze took in everything from the flour on her skirt to the way she attacked the dough. "I heard his mind was sharp."

"Yes. He could remember the price he'd paid for flour in '59, but he couldn't do anything physically. It was very frustrating. The last years were very hard for him."

Thinking back to the man Richard had been, she realized he was capable of holding back Keith's letters. When Richard wanted something, he went after it. But if Richard had lied to her about Keith's letters, she couldn't be angry with him. He'd suffered so.

"And what about you?" he said softly.

An incredible sadness washed over her. If Richard had

lied, he'd stolen so much time from her and Keith. Unshed tears tightened her throat. "What do you mean?"

"It had to be hard for you."

The tenderness in his voice was nearly her undoing, but she refused to cry. "I survived."

He tucked one of her stray curls behind her ear. "There's too much life in you, Colleen. You deserve more than just surviving."

She moved way. Her heart slammed against her ribs. "Don't do that."

"Do what?"

"Be nice to me. I like it better when we are angry. I can manage the anger."

He expelled a breath. "Maybe I'm tired of being angry."

Chapter Seven

An hour later they sat down to a quiet meal as the snow howled outside. Neither spoke, but the air was charged with energy. Colleen stole glances at Keith, and several times realized he'd been staring at her.

"Why did they have to marry today?" She spoke more to herself than to him as she swirled her nearly untouched food with her fork. "Why couldn't Deidre wait two more years and finish her education? Why couldn't she figure out what she really wants and then marry?"

He leaned forward. "You're eight years older than Dee. Do you know what you want?"

"Of course I do. I want to build that addition onto the store. I want to be important to my community. I want to help the church build a new sanctuary."

"That's not living. It's busywork."

"It's very fulfilling. It makes me happy." Even to her own ears, she sounded defensive.

He pushed his plate away. "Does it?"

"Of course!"

His gaze was calm, direct. "You were living more when
ou didn't have two nickels to rub together."

His words struck a nerve. She thought about the thousand
ings she did in a day, yet none brought her any joy. And
tely the days had started to stretch into endless activities.

He set his fork down. He'd barely eaten, as well. "Why did
ou marry Garland?"

She sighed. "I discovered Father had taken out another mort-
age on the land. He'd overextended himself on cattle. He ex-
ected his investment to pay off big. That was the worst winter
e ever had. Most of the men had gone to war, and when Father
as killed in the flood, Dee and I couldn't keep up with the ranch.
he cattle died in a late snowstorm. And the bank foreclosed."

He frowned. "I'm sorry."

"I wasn't. The place had become my prison that last year.
watched my parents die there. That ranch was draining the
fe out of Dee and me. I was glad to see it go."

"Enter Richard." He didn't hide the bitterness.

"Richard came by the day the bank auctioned off the place.
e was wearing his Sunday best. He asked me to marry him.
e said he'd send Dee to school. He was kind and loving. And
had no other family to take us in. So I said yes."

Keith's gut was in a knot. Hearing Colleen talk about those
ard times tore at him. It killed him that he'd not been there
or her. "You married in the spring, I heard."

"We married that very day of the auction. Dee and I packed
p what little was left and we got into Richard's carriage and
rove off with him. The minister had us married by supper."

Keith tried not to think about what came next, but he
ouldn't help but wonder if Colleen had enjoyed Richard's
ovemaking as much as his. When his friend Jamie had heard
rumour from his wife, Sue, that Colleen had married, he'd

nearly gone insane. He'd seen countless men desert and he never understood their weakness. But that day he had. He gotten blind drunk and nearly gone as far as to saddle a hors But in the end, he couldn't leave his men. He and Collee might have been over, but the war wasn't. So he stayed.

But that didn't mean he forgot Colleen. Every night he la in bed wondering about Colleen and Richard lying in bed to gether. It had driven a stake through his heart. Jamie was kille two months later at Gettysburg. So there'd been no more le ters from Sue. No more rumours from home. He was alon Maybe for good.

The loneliness had stalked him for years. Only in tho: brief moments while they'd made love today had he felt tru alive for the first time in years. And God, but he wanted feel alive again.

He reached for her hand. "I want to make love to you."

She pulled it away as if she'd been burned. "We shouldn have done it the first time."

"You didn't like it?" he challenged.

Her breathing grew shallow. "What I like or don't lil isn't the point."

"Did you like it?" he persisted.

Her mouth opened, but she didn't seem to know what say. She snapped it closed.

Keith already knew the answer. He'd heard the moan in h throat, and felt her fingers dig into his back as she'd presse her hips to him. He rose, moved behind her and leaned fo ward until his lips were close to her ear. "A simple yes or r is all I'm looking for."

"Yes."

He took satisfaction in that. "What's wrong with givir

ourselves pleasure?" He traced the top of her shoulder with his fingertip.

She closed her eyes and swallowed. "We both know there is too much anger for us to have a future."

Keith trapped a loose strand of hair between his fingers. "I'm not thinking to the future right now. Wouldn't you like to feel something other than loneliness?"

She lifted her chin. Tears glistened in her eyes. "I feel other things."

He laid his hand on her shoulder. This time she didn't pull away. "Obligation, guilt, sadness?"

A tear trickled down her face. She swiped it away. "I am content with my life."

He knelt down and cupped her face in his hands. "Sounds like warm milk. It works in a pinch but no one really likes it."

A smile tipped the edges of her full lips. It had been so long since he'd seen her smile. "I've learned that there's more to life than what goes on between the sheets."

"There is. But let's face it, darlin', good sex does make the long days more tolerable." He traced her lips with his fingertip. She closed her eyes, clearly savoring the touch.

Keith knew when to shut up. And this was one of those times. He rose and, taking her hands in his, pulled her to her feet. He lifted her fingers to his lips and kissed them. He could taste the hint of salt and flour from the biscuits she'd made earlier. She hissed in a small breath.

No matter what misunderstandings and pain they'd had, when they were in bed, nothing else mattered. Her pulse thrummed in her wrist under his fingertips. "Lord, but I want to lose myself in you."

Color warmed her cheeks. She rubbed her thumb over the top of his hand. He saw the desire in her eyes.

Still, he needed to hear her say she wanted this. There'd be no misunderstandings between them in the future. "Is that what you want?"

She moistened her lips. "Yes."

He cupped her face in her hands and kissed her. Just touching her made him rock hard. He guided her toward the bed. "This time, darlin', we're going to enjoy every inch of each other."

Chapter Eight

What little reason Colleen had left in her brain screamed at her to stop this now. Before, when she'd been with Keith, it had been about pure animal need. However, now they were going to make love. She knew how Keith could take his time, stimulating her body until she screamed for release.

Making love to Keith was dangerous. It took her down the slippery path. He'd leave her wanting for more when she knew there would be no more. Once the snows ended they'd go back to their old lives. And she'd be left only with memories.

Yet, despite all the sane reasons why she shouldn't make love to him, she knew she would. She wanted this moment more than she could say. Her body hungered for his touch.

She would savor the memories of this night for the rest of her life.

He kissed her softly on the lips. A shudder passed through her. She'd anticipated a passionate kiss. Tender affection was the last thing she expected.

She slid her hands up his muscled chest and rising on tiptoe, wrapped her hands around his neck.

Keith's hands moved to her breasts, cupping them gently,

thumbs circling her nipples, which hardened into hard peaks. He kissed her again and this time she opened her mouth to him and let him explore the interior.

When he broke the kiss, she could barely breathe. Her heart raced. He reached for the buttons at the top of her bodice. The slight tremble in his hands gave her comfort. They were both nervous. Slowly he worked his way down the tiny rows of buttons that ran between her breasts. When he reached her waist, he pushed the jacket off her shoulders. Underneath, she wore only a thin camisole. She'd forgotten her corset this morning.

Keith sucked in a breath as he drank in the sight of her full breasts pressed against the white sheer fabric. "You're beautiful."

He cupped her breast in his hand, coaxing the nipple to a hard peak again. This time through the fabric, he kissed the pink mound and began to suckle until she closed her eyes and moaned.

Wild sensations exploded in her as she ran her fingers though his hair. If it were possible, the desire thrumming in her veins was more intense than it had been earlier.

She grabbed his shirttail and pulled it over his head. A thick mat of hair covered his chest, tapering down over his belly button to his waistband.

He unfastened the tiny row of white buttons trailing between her breasts. He pushed back the gauzy fabric, exposing her naked breasts. He kissed the valley between her breasts and slowly trailed kisses to her flat belly. The rough skin of his jaw scratched her skin and sent jolts of desire shooting through her body.

She arched against him. "I've never wanted this so much."

He kissed her navel. "I won't rush things this time. I want

to taste every inch of you." He spoke as if repeating a promise he made over and over to himself.

Keith unfastened her waistband and slid her skirt over her narrow hips. She wriggled out of the fabric and her pantaloons, anxious to have him touch her.

His eyes darkened at the sight of her as he picked her up and carried her to the bed. He laid her on her back and covered her body instantly. Again he kissed her belly. She moaned.

And then he moved lower. Colleen's eyes flew open as she hissed in a breath. She clutched a fistful of sheets in each hand, arching her pelvis toward him.

Over the years Keith had tried to hold on to the memories of their lovemaking. Through the long nights on the battlefield, he'd dreamed of her. When fever had ravaged his body after he'd been shot, images of Colleen had seen him through. During the long trail home, he'd stopped often to look at the picture he'd carried of her.

But he realized now how much he'd forgotten. His memories paled in the face of Colleen's passion.

His arousal was so hard he feared he'd explode from wanting her. Unable to keep up this tortuously slow pace he backed away from her long enough to strip off the remainder of his clothes.

Light from the fireplace illuminated her pale, damp skin. As smooth as porcelain, her skin, her body, were so stunning it could still take his breath away.

He lay on top of her, nestling his erection against her center. She arched and pressed her body against his as she opened her legs.

As much as he wanted to take his time, he could wait no more. When he slid into her, the moan that rumbled in her throat was primal. The sound nearly drove him over the edge. But he willed himself to hold back as he moved slowly back and forth inside her. She cupped his buttocks, arching her back.

He opened his eyes and savored the play of desire on her face. At this moment, she was so wonderfully expressive, so open.

This was his Colleen.

The muscles in her body tightened as she whispered his name. As she climaxed, the pure, raw pleasure on her face was his undoing. He let himself go, pumping faster until he too found his release.

They'd made love a third time. And it was well past two in the afternoon when they'd both crawled under the covers of the bed and fallen asleep. She'd curled beside him and he'd draped his hand over her waist.

Colleen wasn't sure how long she slept. She felt so warm and cozy, so at peace. She could have cheerfully stayed in this cabin with Keith forever.

She raised her hand and let it fall to his side of the bed. The sheets were still warm, but he was gone. She opened her eyes and let her gaze drift in his direction. He wasn't there.

The fire in the hearth had died down and there was a chill in the room.

The dewy, boneless feeling vanished. She sat up, suddenly fighting a wave of panic. Her gaze scanned the cabin. He wasn't there. Clutching the sheet to her chest, she hurried across the room to the window. The snow had stopped and the sky had cleared. The sun hung low on the horizon but there was at least two hours of daylight left. Enough time to get to Dixon's Corner.

Colleen had been in such a rush this morning to get to Dixon's Corner and to stop Deidre's wedding. Now she questioned her reasoning. Her sister was young but she wasn't one to give her heart easily. Several men in town had tried to court her last summer. She'd not given her heart to anyone. But she'd chosen Josh.

Colleen understood the power of such a love. Because the love she had for Keith was just as strong today as it had been eight years ago.

She didn't regret any of the decisions she'd made in her life. Each and every one had been necessary. But how she wished life had gone differently.

She refused to dwell on the past. Especially since the future looked so bright. She and Keith hadn't spoken of tomorrows, but their lovemaking had spoken to her better than words.

"I need to get dressed." She looked at her skirt, which sat in a puddle on the floor by the bed. Her shirt and chemise were tossed recklessly over a chair. She swallowed a grin when she ducked her head under the bed and retrieved her shoe. Lord, but she was wanton.

She quickly wriggled into her skirt and buttoned her shirt. She wanted to find Keith. Anxious to see him, she wanted to tell him her truest feelings.

Colleen loved him.

She'd always loved him and would love him forever. During her years with Richard, she'd done her best to shut out her feelings for Keith for fear that she'd go mad from the loneliness. But now that they'd shared these last few incredible hours, there was no hiding her heart.

Their past had been riddled with heartache, separation and loss. But the future would be so different. There would be love, laughter and children.

The whinny of horses drifted inside. She grabbed her coat and rushed to the door.

Keith stood in the front yard. The ankle-deep snow accentuated his black coat and pants. His Stetson shadowed his gray eyes.

"Hey there," she said, her voice warm and inviting.

"Hey," he said softly.

"I was wondering where you were."

"The snow has cleared. We can travel." There was no missing the disappointment in his voice.

"Deidre and Josh are likely married by now."

"Likely."

She moved toward him. The cold from the outside clung to his range coat. "We could leave at daybreak."

He smiled, rubbing his gloved hand over her arm. "Very tempting. But we better get going while the getting is good. The snows could return."

Regret slashed at her. He was right, of course. "I'll get my coat."

He frowned. "Colleen, about what happened today…"

"I don't have any regrets."

A faint smile tugged his lips as he moved quickly toward her. "Neither do I. But what about tomorrow? Is this it?"

She tensed, fearing she'd say the wrong thing and ruin what they had. "I was hoping it wasn't."

He cupped her elbow. "Marry me."

She jumped into his arms and gave him a hug. "What took you so long to ask?"

He sighed his relief and banded his arms around her.

He kissed her on the lips, savoring the sweet taste of her. His body hardened and he was so very tempted to take her back to bed. With an effort he broke the kiss. "We better get moving."

"Okay." She picked up her coat and the hat and gloves he'd

given her earlier. "It's going to be different this time, Keith. The troubles are behind us."

He kissed her lightly on the lips. "Good."

Outside, afternoon sunlight glistened on the snow blanketing the countryside. The land had been transformed into a mythic place. Everything at this moment was perfect.

They rode in companionable silence for fifteen minutes, but Colleen could barely contain her excitement. "The town is only a two-hour ride to your ranch. It will be easy to move back and forth between the two."

"It will?" He sounded confused.

"I should only need to be in the store a couple of days a week. I will hire a clerk to oversee the days I'm at the ranch."

He paused, his jaw hardening. "You're not going to sell the store?"

"Sell the store? It's a good source of income. It could be quite useful for us."

He frowned. "I don't want you to keep the store. Your place is at the ranch at my side, not running a business owned by a man who plotted against us."

The anger surprised her. "I will be at your side most of the time. I'll just be in town a couple of days a week."

His jaw tightened and then released. "And when the children come?"

Children. The idea softened her heart. "I'll take them with me, I suppose."

"No."

"What do you mean, no?"

"I mean, I don't want you to keep the store. You need to sell it."

"It's a thriving business. It's seen me through some tough times."

"You don't need to worry about money anymore. I will take care of it."

A bitter smile lifted the corner of her lip. "My father said the same thing and his ranch failed. Richard said the same thing and then he got sick. If not for the store, I'd have been lost."

Arrogant, he lifted his chin. "I've done well—you don't need to worry."

"I will never forget the days I went hungry. I won't go back to that."

"So you don't trust me to take care of you?"

"It's not a matter of trust. I'm being practical. The store can protect us both."

"I won't have it. *Richard Garland* won't be supplementing my income."

"Richard may have lied to me, but the store has been mine for many years. *My* sweat and *my* worry kept it going these last eight years."

He shook his head. "It's either the store or me. You can't keep your hand in two worlds, Colleen."

"You're being stubborn."

"You're being selfish."

"You didn't want to marry eight years ago, so we didn't. You don't want the store, so I must sell it. Why is everything always so black and white for you? Can't you see the gray?"

"No."

"I thought after today things had changed between us."

His eyes were as dull as his voice. "I did too, but I guess it didn't."

She spoke carefully as she tried to quell the bubble of fear growing inside her. "But what we shared was special."

"It was great. I won't deny it. But I won't do this marriage halfway. You're either in all the way or you're not."

He was slipping away from her. "I want us."

His jaw tightened. "Then sell the store."

"I won't do that."

"Then there's nothing more to say." He shook his head. "I think we set a record."

Hot tears stung her eyes. "What do you mean?"

"We have a talent for bumping into insurmountable obstacles. We reached this one in record time."

Bitter tears spilled down her face. "That's not funny."

"I'm not laughing."

Colleen had her pride. Losing Keith would dig a hole in her heart that would likely never heal. But she would not beg him. She would not. If he was going to be so bullheaded, then the devil take him.

Still, the pain was unbelievable. She swiped away a tear. "So this is it? We just pretend today never happened."

"Yes."

"You're doing this to punish me."

Shards of anger shot from his eyes. "This isn't about hurting you. It's about saving my sanity."

Chapter Nine

The ride to Dixon's Corner was a blur to Colleen. She rode beside Keith but neither of them spoke. The clouds had parted and turned a crystal blue. The setting sun bounced off the clouds, splashing oranges and reds on the white landscape. It was a stunning evening. And she couldn't have cared less.

When they arrived in town the sun had sunk below the horizon. They moved down the single main street past the wood-framed buildings with the false fronts. Lights sparkled through windows decorated with sprigs of greenery onto the snowy walkways. The church at the edge of town was dark. If there had been a wedding, it was long over. Keith led Colleen to the town's only hotel.

"I'll take care of the horses," he said.

She nodded, unable to trust her voice. How could something so beautiful and special have withered away so quickly?

Colleen went into the hotel. Bells on the jamb above jingled. To her right was a simple front desk and to her left a small carpeted staircase that led to the second floor. Lantern light flickered in the room, casting long shadows.

The lobby was empty, but from the back room behind the

counter she heard laughter. She walked up to the front desk and ran the small handbell.

"Hello?"

No answer. She rang again.

She peered behind the front desk, trying to see beyond the curtained door. The smell of roasted vegetables and meats permeated the lobby.

"Hello?" she said louder.

This time, the laughter stopped and she heard someone stand and walk toward the hotel lobby. A man poked his head out from a side door. His thinning hair was slicked back. He wore a white shirt and black pants. Tucked in his starched collar was a large red-and-white-checkered napkin stained with gravy.

"How do you do? My name is Mr. McGraw. Will you be needing a room this evening?" He pulled the napkin from his collar and tucked it in his pocket.

Colleen felt as if she'd changed so much today. "I am looking for my sister. She might have come here this morning. Her name is Deidre Temple."

He nodded slowly. "Oh, yeah. She's in room number six. The honeymoon suite. She's been up there since noontime. Won't come out."

Deidre was with her new husband. Deidre was married. Colleen shook her head. So hard to believe that the little girl who had depended on her was all grown up.

Like it or not, Josh Matthews was a part of her family now. Keith had said he was a good man and she'd hold on to that. She'd find a way to like the boy and accept this marriage.

"Perhaps I'll see her in the morning at breakfast," Colleen said.

The hotel manager's eyes narrowed. "Don't you want to see her?"

"It's not appropriate that I knock now. I don't want to disturb her."

The manager shrugged. "I guess you'll be wanting a room."

There'd be no getting back home this night. Like it or not, she'd be spending Christmas Eve in Dixon's Corner. Alone. "Yes."

"I'll put you in room number eight. It's small but it's clean."

"Any room is fine."

"Want me to take your bags up?"

"That's not necessary."

She ignored his surprised look and headed for the stairs. Outside, the sun was setting. The day was over. And she felt so bone weary she suspected she could sleep for a month.

As she moved down the upstairs hallway, the sound of weeping caught her attention. Someone was crying. She slowed her pace, listening at each room as she passed. And then she realized that the crying was coming from room number six—the honeymoon suite.

Colleen's fatigue vanished. A mother's protective urge welled inside her. She marched up to the door. If Josh Matthews had hurt her baby sister, there would be hell to pay. She pounded on the door.

The weeping stopped. She heard footsteps and then the door inched open. Deidre's tear-streaked face peered back at her.

The instant Deidre saw her, she flew into her sister's arms. "Oh, Colleen, I have made the worst mistake of my life!"

Keith pulled the horses into the livery. He was exhausted and mad as a wet hornet. This had to have been one of the longest days of his life. When he'd woken this morning he'd expected calm and quiet, not the firestorm Colleen blazing through his life.

The livery was dark. Likely the liveryman had gone home early to spend the evening with his family for the holiday. Keith led the horses toward the back of the barn toward several empty stalls.

This morning he'd almost convinced himself that life without Colleen was possible. Each day since her husband died, he'd prayed she come over the ridge and ride back into his life. But as the days turned into months, he'd begun to accept the fact that she wasn't coming. Any possibility of loving her had died long ago.

And then today, there she was looking so beautiful that it nearly knocked his breath away.

Their lovemaking had rocked him to his soul, igniting the love that had once burned so fierce in him.

It had scared him to death.

Colleen had the power to crush the life from his heart. No one else had the ability to bring him to his knees, but she did.

She'd crushed him twice before, but never again.

Never again.

If she couldn't commit to this marriage one hundred percent and trust him to care for her then she didn't belong in his life.

He guided the horses to a stall and started to unsaddle them. He hung her saddle next to his on the sawhorse outside the stall and then stripped the bridles and sweat-dampened blankets off each horse. He filled each of their feed bins with sweet hay.

The memory of her eyes filled with tears gnawed at his gut.

The rustle of straw caught his attention. He whirled around, half expecting to see Colleen.

To his surprise, Josh stood there. The young man stood, his shirttail out, straw in his hair and a bottle of whiskey in his hand.

"What the hell are you doing in the barn?"

Josh moved toward him, swaying as he moved. "Getting drunk. What are you doing here?"

"Looking for you." The kid smelled of rotgut whiskey. "Not a good start for a marriage if you ask me."

Josh took a sip from the bottle. "I didn't get married today." He raised the bottle to his lips again, but Keith swiped it from his hands.

"What do you mean you didn't get married today? Where's Deidre?"

"Up in the honeymoon suite of the hotel, I reckon." He shook his head. "That room cost me a week's pay."

"What the devil is going on?"

Josh drew in a shuddered breath. "She got cold feet."

"What?"

"We was standing in front of the preacher. And when the preacher asked her if she would stay with me until death do you part she started to bawl."

"Why?"

"Said it weren't right to marry without her sister there. They'd had some terrible fight this morning and Deidre was feeling awful about it. Deidre said getting married without Colleen present was a bad-luck kind of beginning."

The Temple women were trouble all around. "Maybe it's best you didn't get married. Maybe she is too young."

"She loves me," he said, thumping his hand on his chest. "I know it. She needs her sister's blessing and then she'll be glad to exchange *I do*s."

"If she wanted you, none of that would matter."

He sighed. "She ain't like you or me. We know what it's like to live without family. We don't answer to no one. But Deidre loves her sister. She kept talking about how hard Colleen worked to keep them fed when their daddy's ranch was failing. She said Colleen skipped a good many meals so she could eat. Colleen worked in that store until she was so tired she'd fall asleep standing up. Colleen is everything to Dee."

Keith's throat tightened. Each time he was reminded of the struggles she'd faced alone, it gnawed at his gut. "Let's get you inside and get some coffee into you."

"I don't want coffee. I want Deidre." He staggered a few steps alongside Keith before he stopped. "Maybe I could ride to Grant's Forge and talk to Colleen. Dee is right. I should have looked her in the eye and asked for her sister's hand."

"She'd likely have run you off with a shotgun."

He nodded. "That's what I figured." The boy staggered out the livery into the night. He stared up at the clear sky and the thousand stars winking down on them. "Boss, what am I going to do? I love her with everything in me. Do you know what that feels like?"

"Yeah." That kind of love was pain and pleasure all rolled into one.

"Do you think if we went back to Grant's Forge you could put in a good word for me?"

"I would, boy, but I'm afraid that Colleen would run me off with a shotgun now."

"Dee said you two had a history. But I figured it was over and done with."

"Not so long ago." He could still smell her scent on his skin.

"Dang." The boy sounded miserable.

God help him, but he wanted Colleen. Hell, he'd had her and tossed her away over a damn store. What the hell kind of fool was he? He needed to make things right between them. "Let's head to the hotel."

"What for? Dee won't see me."

"As it happens, Colleen is there now, too."

His eyes brightened. "She is? Do you think she'd listen to me?"

"Won't hurt to ask." He watched the boy stagger his next step. "But before we do anything, we best get some coffee into you. You're going to need your wits about you because I think all hell's about to break loose."

Deidre melted into Colleen's arms. "Oh, Colleen, I've made the worst mistake."

"What did he do?" Ice coated her words.

"He didn't make any effort to understand what I was feeling."

Colleen guided her sister into the room and shut the door. She glanced to the bed, surprised to see that it was made, not slept in. "Maybe you'd better tell me what happened today."

Deidre sat on the edge of the bed. Colleen pulled a handkerchief from her pocket and wiped the tears from her sister's face.

Her sister drew in a shuddering breath. "We were standing in front of the minister. Everything was perfect and then I realized it wasn't."

"What do you mean?"

"You weren't there. I realized I couldn't marry without you there."

Colleen's heart twisted with love. She tucked a stray curl behind her sister's ear. "I always dreamed of giving you a perfect wedding."

"I remember how we used to talk about it when times were so tough with Father. We talked about silk dresses, flowers and a fancy cake." She sniffed. "But it wasn't any of that I missed. It was you. You should have been standing next to me and been my matron of honor."

"So what happened?"

"I told Josh I couldn't marry him without your blessing.

He got upset. He didn't see any point in waiting. He said we would make things right with you after we were married. But I didn't want to wait until after. I wanted you at my side."

"Where is Josh now?"

"I don't know." Her shoulders slumped. "He looked so sad and miserable. I think I broke his heart."

Colleen remembered the look in Keith's eyes. She'd not forget it if she lived to be one hundred. "Do you love Josh?"

"With all my heart. I know you think I am young and I don't know what I want, but I know. I love Josh."

She'd loved Keith with the same kind of fierceness when she'd been younger than Dee. She understood the power of that kind of love.

And she'd let it go. Lord, but she'd been a fool. The store had kept her safe these last eight years, but it was time to let go. It was time to give Keith her love and her trust.

She only prayed it wasn't too late.

"Let's wash your face and brush your hair."

"Why?"

"Because we are going to look for Josh. You two are going to get married and I will be there to witness it."

Thirty minutes later, Keith led a steady, if a bit blurry-eyed, Josh into the hotel. He marched to the front desk and rang the bell. The manager pushed through the curtain. He had a cup of coffee in his hand. Chokeberry pie stained his shirt. "Can I help you?"

"Deidre Temple's room," Keith said.

The manager sighed as his gaze drifted between the two men. "She's a popular lady this evening. Room number six."

Josh held his hat in his long slim hands. "Her sister was asking for her?"

The manager nodded. "I'm assuming."

"Are they both still upstairs?" Keith said.

"Yes."

That was all Keith needed to hear. "Let's go, Josh."

The two men headed toward the stairs.

"Now wait just a minute," the manager said. "If you two men think you can visit unmarried ladies in my hotel then you are wrong. I run a reputable house."

Keith was in no mood for this. "We'll be quick about it."

The manager reached under the front-desk counter and pulled out a shotgun. "You'll stay right the hell where you are or I'll shoot you to high heaven."

Colleen had dried Deidre's tears. She'd left her sister in her room and gone downstairs to fetch tea and something to eat. She was headed downstairs when she heard the shouting.

"Now look here, mister," Keith said. Anger coated each word. "We aim to see those women."

"Unless they are your lawfully wedded wives, then you got a snowball's chance, buddy." The manager's Adam's apple bobbed in his thin neck but the firm set of his jaw and the shotgun showed he meant business.

"Get a minister," Keith said.

The hotel manager's eyes narrowed. "What?"

"Get a minister," Keith said. "We'll marry those women right here and now if that's what it takes."

Colleen's heart caught in her throat as she moved down the carpeted steps. "Don't you think we deserve to be asked?"

Keith turned around. "I have." His eyes softened when he looked at her face. "You turned me down."

Her knees felt weak and the world, save for him, vanished. He was her life. "Maybe you should ask again."

He moved to the bottom step and took her hand in his. "I should have married you eight years ago. But I thought I was protecting you."

"I don't need protecting. I need you."

"You can keep the damn store. I don't care about it."

"Is that a proposal?"

A grin tugged at the edge of his lips. "It's feeble, I know." He straightened his shoulders. "Colleen Temple Garland, will you marry me?"

She kissed him. When she broke the kiss she was breathless. "I don't need the store. I just need you."

"Is that a yes?"

She laughed. "Yes, it's a yes." She kissed him again. "I love you so much."

"I love you."

They'd have stood there forever if they hadn't heard Joshua clear his throat. "Pardon me. But you two mind if I see Deidre?"

Colleen smiled. "She's upstairs."

Joshua's hands twisted around the brim of his hat. "Mrs. Garland, I should have spoken properly to you before all this."

Colleen pulled out of Keith's embrace but he took her hand in his. She stared at the boy but said nothing. She wouldn't make this so easy. If he loved Dee he'd have to work for it.

Her icy glare had the intended effect. He started to squirm. "Well, what I mean to say is I'd like to ask for her hand in marriage."

Colleen hesitated a beat. "If you ever hurt my sister, I will hunt you down like a dog, Mr. Matthews."

He paled. "I won't ever hurt her."

She relented. "You have my blessing."

Joshua let out a whoop. "Thank you, Mrs. Garland. I will take care of her for as long as I live."

Keith grinned. "Best go get your bride to be, boy."

Joshua started for the stairs.

Mr. McGraw cleared his throat. "Where are you going, kid?"

"I'll be downstairs in two shakes."

The manager nodded. "You'd better. The minister is here having supper with my family this evening and I intend to see all y'all married proper before my pie goes cold."

Keith hugged Colleen to him as Joshua bounded up the stairs. "This will be a Christmas to remember."

Colleen nuzzled her face against his. "It surely will be."

Epilogue

Nine months later

The baby was a week late.

Virginia's Shenandoah Valley was unseasonably warm that September and Colleen was none too pleased about it. Her belly was huge and the babe inside her kicked constantly. Her ankles had swollen and her back ached something terrible as she climbed the front steps of the home she shared with Keith. Dr. Dobbs, a former physician for the army, had just come to Grant's Forge to set up a medical practice. Today, he'd come to check on Colleen.

While Dr. Dobbs visited with Keith, she started back toward the house. "If you gentlemen will excuse me, I think I'll sit down."

"You all right?" Keith said, coming up behind her. "You look like you can barely walk."

The concern in his eyes touched her heart. "I'm fine—it's your son that won't settle down. My stomach feels like he's tightening into a ball. I just need to sit down. You go and have your visit with Dr. Dobbs."

The doctor was a young man, not older than his midthirties, but he possessed a steadiness that wasn't easily rattled. Keith didn't leave her side. "Let me help you to the rocker on the porch."

Dr. Dobbs nodded. "Is your back hurting?"

"Like a fiend."

The doctor smiled. "Today just might be the day."

"Really, I'm—" Before she could finish her sentence, her water broke.

She was mortified.

Keith panicked. "Dr. Dobbs!"

Dr. Dobbs, with his black doctor's bag in his hand, opened the front door. "Let's get her to bed."

Keith scooped up Colleen, took her into the house and straight up the stairs to the room they'd shared since their Christmas day marriage.

As he laid her on the bed, a contraction ripped through her body. Everything in her told her to push. "He's coming now."

The doctor frowned. "That's fast." He examined her. "Looks like it's time."

Keith got behind Colleen and cradled her in his arms. The doctor barely had time to help get situated, when another contraction came. She pushed hard and in the next instant her baby's head appeared. Before she had time to look, another contraction came. She pushed again, and this time the baby slid out of her body.

Dr. Dobbs picked up the babe and rubbed its back until it cried.

Keith kissed Colleen on the temple. "It's a boy."

Colleen savored the sound of her son's cry. "Michael

David." She glanced at the baby's face for only an instant. Another contraction hit her. "I think there is another one."

The doctor glanced up at her, saw the strain in her face and set the squawking baby on the bed beside her. Five minutes later, Michael David's brother, Jackson Andrew, was born.

Later, when the excitement had died down and the doctor had left, Keith sat beside Colleen's bed rocking Michael while she fed Jackson.

Keith kissed his wife on the forehead. "I love you."

Her smile was tired yet satisfied. "And I love you and these two charms you gave me last Christmas."

* * * * *

If you enjoyed what you just read,
then we've got an offer you can't resist!

Take 2 bestselling
love stories FREE!

Plus get a FREE surprise gift!

A BRAND-NEW BOOK IN
THE DE WARENNE DYNASTY SERIES
BY *NEW YORK TIMES* BESTSELLING AUTHOR

BRENDA JOYCE

On the evening of her first masquerade, shy Elizabeth Anne
Fitzgerald is stunned by Tyrell de Warenne's whispered suggestion
of a midnight rendezvous in the gardens. Lizzie has secretly
worshiped the unattainable lord for years. When fortune
takes a maddening turn, she is prevented from meeting Tyrell.
But Lizzie has not seen the last of him....

Tyrell de Warenne is shocked when, two years later, Lizzie
arrives on his doorstep with a child she claims is his. He
remembers her well—and knows that he could not possibly
be the father. Is Elizabeth Anne Fitzgerald a woman of
experience, or the gentle innocent she seems?

THE MASQUERADE

"A powerhouse of emotion and sensuality."—*Romantic Times*

Available the first week of September 2005
wherever paperbacks are sold!